SOLDIER OF FORTUNE 6

THE KHMER HIT

SOLDIER OF FORTUNE 6

THE KHMER HIT

Doug Armstrong

First published in Great Britain 1994
22 Books, Invicta House, Sir Thomas Longley Road,
Rochester, Kent

Copyright © 1994 by 22 Books

The moral right of the author has been asserted

A CIP catalogue record for this book is available from the
British Library

ISBN 1 898125 29 5

10 9 8 7 6 5 4 3 2 1

Typeset by Hewer Text Composition Services, Edinburgh
Printed in Great Britain by Cox and Wyman Limited, Reading

1

The air was thick with the smell of sweat and tobacco. Blue tendrils of smoke curled lazily above the ring, working slowly up into the high rafters, where some of the children had climbed, eager for a view of the coming fight on which the adults were furiously laying their bets. Whole fistfuls of banknotes waved in the air as men screamed to be heard above the uproar. Out in the night, the River Chaophraya swirled darkly past, on through the floating market towards the filth and the jostling crowds of Bangkok's night-time streets beyond.

Crammed into the warehouse that served as the Black Lotus Boxing Stadium, several hundred men were nearing hysteria. Any moment now, Than Promarik would appear, the Thai boxer whose name was on all their lips. In previous bouts that week he had already killed two of his opponents, but in the murky world of the illegal gambling dens, that was all part of the excitement. With General Sarit Chamonon in charge of the evening's entertainment, another kill was to be expected. As owner of the Black Lotus and a chain of other gambling dens, he had carved out the biggest underground empire in the whole city. At his own expense he kept a stable of the very best Thai boxers, and none was as vicious or experienced as Than.

On a raised dais at the edge of the maelstrom, General Sarit Chamonon sat at his ease behind a table of intricately carved Burmese teak. Inlaid with mother-of-pearl, it had been a gift from one of the drug barons with whom he frequently had cause to do business. He ran his hand unthinkingly over the smooth teak as if it was the skin of one of the Burmese village girls who had accompanied it on its journey from the opium fields of the Golden Triangle. The drug baron had sent a dozen of the girls with false promises of employment as maids in the wealthy suburbs of Bangkok, the only way that any of them could ever hope to escape from the grinding poverty of their hill villages. But as soon as they had arrived in the capital, they had been redirected into slavery and prostitution in the General's brothels. Those who resisted were savagely beaten, and the rest quickly submitted, adding through their pain and suffering to the General's ample fortune.

Watching the clamour through the haze of smoke, the General drew on his long green Burmese cheroot, pulling the smoke deep into his lungs. He would normally have preferred to smoke opium but tonight he had to keep a clear head. Sadly he would be unable to enjoy the purity of a good kill for there was business to be transacted and however much of a hedonist he might be, the General never failed to put his business interests first. It was a discipline that had turned him into one of the most powerful men in Thailand. He had nothing but contempt for the bungling civilian democrats who had held sway in his country ever since the army had lost power after firing on student demonstrators in 1992. Since then he had been obliged to keep a low profile. No one would have dared bring him to trial, but it was best to wait for a change in the balance of power and the return of the army to government before coming out into the open again.

For now he would play the role of dutiful commander of the crack Roaring Tiger Division based on the Thai–Cambodian border, for there he was his own boss and no one could challenge him. In the heart of his own realm he was a virtual warlord, surrounded by loyal troops, ruler of the towns and villages within his domain. It was a fortunate consequence of his official position as a divisional commander in the Thai army that he had legitimate reasons for frequent visits to Bangkok, for when he had finished briefing the High Command on the Cambodian border situation, he could spend time managing his boxing dens, casinos and brothels, before returning to the relative discomfort of his jungle divisional headquarters.

He looked up as a huge roar rose from the crowd. Than Promarik was being led towards the ring. Deceptively small and wiry, the Thai boxer pranced like a gazelle, casting his eyes arrogantly over the crowd of worshippers without bothering to conceal his contempt. He accepted adulation as his right and he was fully confident that within half an hour he would have added to his reputation as the top kick-boxer in the Far East.

Waiting in a corner of the ring his challenger was limbering up, shaking his arms and legs to loosen the joints and muscles. In shorts and boxing gloves they would fight barefoot, the combat a mixture of conventional boxing, karate kicking techniques and, in the clinches, anything they cared to use from biting to head-butting.

Than glared at the man. He looked like a northerner,

tall and thickset, but Than was too experienced to be deceived. Anyone that the General had decided to allow into one of his rings would be a good opponent. Than knew that the General's reputation depended upon providing good, hard fights on which men could gamble. Without the element of chance, the General's boxing dens would lose custom and if that were to happen, the stable would be closed and he, Than Promarik, would be out of the best job he had ever had.

As Than strutted down the path that his minders had cleared through the crowd, he petulantly shrugged off the many hands that reached to slap him on the back and wish him well. What need had he of luck? He was the General's own man, the best and the fastest in all the boxing stables of Bangkok. Having reached the foot of the steps he jogged nimbly to the top and ducked through the ropes. The crowd roared its appreciation as he danced around the ring, his arms above his head as if already proclaimed the champion. Dancing close to his waiting opponent, he smiled mockingly at him and flashed his gold tooth at the man's trainer, who looked on with resignation.

'Better get yourself a new dummy,' Than said, skipping ever closer to his opponent's corner.

The trainer spat over the ropes. 'Let's see if the General still fancies you when your face has been rearranged.'

In a flash Than was lunging towards him, but the wary ringmaster quickly pushed in between them.

'Save it for the fight. You're not being paid for this.'

Reluctantly Than pulled away. 'Get your body bag ready. This lump of mutton'll be going home in it tonight.'

Prancing back to his own corner, Than stripped off his bright red gown and prepared himself for combat. His muscles were as lean as a whippet's, his stomach flat and solid, his arms almost thin and puny, but to everyone who had seen him fight he was a ruthless killing machine. He could move his hands and feet as fast as a whip and then dart away out of reach, leaving his opponent reeling and bloody.

Seated behind his table on the dais, the General smiled at the spectacle. Than's antics before a fight never failed to amuse him, but when the opening bell sounded the opponent would see a change indeed. From a pouting slip of a figure, Than would turn into a whirling devil, his fists and feet seeking ways through the very best of guards, demolishing the most accomplished defence and dismantling, piece by piece, his bewildered opponent to the point of death, and, on occasion, beyond.

With a barely perceptible movement of the head, the General ordered a refill of whisky and soda. A bar had been set up on the far side of the warehouse and a moment later a waitress hurried over. Admiring her trim waist and well-defined breasts, the General reached out to trail a caressing hand across her hips. She smiled openly and paused to see if she was required to stay, but the General's attention had already wandered back to the ring where the fighters were being brought into the centre of the canvas before the start of the bout.

Throughout the audience the excitement heightened until the ringmaster could hardly hear himself speak. But it didn't matter: the bets had been laid and it was now up to the two fighters to do what they did best. With a cursory wave of the hand, he moved quickly aside and darted over the ropes to the safety of the sidelines. The referee pushed the boxers apart, there was a moment's pause during which even the crowd quietened, and then, to renewed screams of encouragement, the fight was unleashed.

Than Promarik didn't wait to size up his opponent. Like a chess player he had a well-tried set of opening gambits that he could produce in a variety of combinations. Covering the intervening canvas in three brisk strides, he spun into a turning back kick then jumped to deliver a roundhouse kick directed at his opponent's jaw. Pressing home his attack, he immediately hurled in a series of lightning punches, shortening the distance to close quarters and bringing his left knee up and into his opponent's flank. The crowd went wild as they saw the tell-tale trickle of blood from the man's nose, betraying a hit whose pain he was trying to ignore.

Countering with a flurry of well-placed blows, Than's opponent drove him back to the centre of the ring. One of his front kicks found its way under Than's guard, but with a rapid body shift Than turned aside just in time to avoid a broken rib. Pivoting on his right leg, Than effortlessly flicked up his left foot and caught his opponent on the cheek, sending him reeling backwards across the canvas. The crowd roared, but instead of following up the success Than danced round the ring, acknowledging the cheers and praise, purposely giving the other fighter time to recover.

Behind his table the General smiled, not taken in for a moment. Than's gesture had nothing to do with mercy. He had the measure of his opponent and was now fully confident that it was only a matter of time before the destruction. But to do so early would rob the crowd of the spectacle for which they had paid good money. No, the kill could wait. In the meantime Than relaxed and started to enjoy the bout. He had smelt blood and was already on the high from which he would only descend later in the dressing room. Then the General would come to congratulate him, perhaps even bringing a gift. Than already had several gold watches, bracelets and rings, but he was happy to receive more; he came from a large family and there were always relatives to whom he could pass the General's tokens of gratitude.

Biding his time until his opponent had recovered himself, Than darted back towards him, revelling in the new glint of fear in the man's eyes. This would be the best part of the fight, the stage where Than could demonstrate his prowess to the audience. From now on he could show why he was the highest-paid fighter in the business.

Whenever he came to Bangkok, Lon San went to do business with the General. He had made numerous visits over the past few years, ever since the hated Vietnamese had ousted the Khmer Rouge government from office in Cambodia. As far as he was concerned the Khmer Rouge party of Pol Pot had been the rightful rulers of the country and Lon San had initially been surprised to discover that the outside world was incapable of understanding their revolutionary policies of reform. Only by starting again from the grass roots could they hope to build a new society devoid of the corruption of capitalism. It was vital that the family unit should be broken down so that everyone could take their place in the Communist order as individuals answerable only to the Party.

Likewise, intellectuals had to be purged because they were the very harbour and bastion of revisionism. Thus, tens of thousands of teachers, doctors, engineers and so-called professionals had been eradicated. It was inevitable and, indeed, desirable. If the outside world couldn't comprehend this they must be truly mad. Lon San had been driven out of Cambodia a confused man.

Now, however, he no longer cared what anyone else thought. How could they be expected to understand? He himself had been fighting in the jungle for as long as he could remember. He had been so young when he had had his first experience of carrying a real gun that he couldn't even remember it, but he did remember staring in complete bafflement one day at a doll. They had entered a village and the males, men and boys alike, were being taught a lesson by Lon San's elder comrades; there had been rumours of collaboration with the forces of the capitalist government. Lon San had drifted away, bored with the public beatings and executions and had discovered an empty hut. Inside on the floor he had been startled to see a doll and, wondering at its function, had asked one of the female comrades. She had explained that it was a capitalist tool for propagating policies of hereditary enslavement to the village women. Lon San had been congratulated for drawing the offending article to her attention, the parents of the family concerned were singled out, humiliated in front of their newly liberated children, and then shot.

The recollection of that incident still brought a smile to the stone of Lon San's usually expressionless face. Of course he had progressed beyond the simplicity of those early days of revolutionary fervour. He had long ago seen through the subterfuge of Communist jargon and claptrap. Nevertheless, faced with the same situation now, he would still have had the parents executed, the only difference being that he would have had the children shot as well.

Sitting upright in the canoe he listened to the hum of the little motor and the sounds from the busy streets bordering the river. The wash from the boat swept across the dark surface and lapped against the wooden stilts on which the neighbouring shacks were propped, sticking out of the water like squat tree-houses in a flood. Behind him the boatman cleared his throat noisily and spat into the white foam.

'You're late if you were wanting to see the fight.'

Lon San, who had been trailing his fingers in the water, gently removed them as he imagined what else might be floating in the river apart from the boatman's spittle.

'That's of no interest to me. It's all rigged anyway.'

The boatman pounced like a shot. 'Ah, but you can never be sure. Than Promarik's good enough I'll grant you, but everyone's got to have a bad day.'

'You're an expert, I suppose?'

Too stupid to catch the sarcasm, the boatman swelled with pride. 'I've had my successes. I won over five hundred baht last month.' He shrugged. 'Admittedly that was with a bet on Promarik, but I reckon his run's almost at an end.'

'And who's going to end it? You?'

The boatman chuckled. 'Chance would be a fine thing. No, one of these days someone'll get the better of him.'

Lon San dried his fingers on his shirt. 'Well, when

you find such a man I am sure the General would welcome prior notice.'

Although a dedicated Communist, Lon San had long ago reached the stage in his career when he refrained from associating with individuals of lesser rank. He preferred to limit communication with such people to the giving of orders and the receiving of reports. The cheery camaraderie of the boatman had irritated him. It would never have happened at Pailin or Anlong Veng, where he was known, respected and feared by everyone. However, since the Khmer Rouge had been driven out of their traditional Cambodian strongholds they had been obliged to take refuge deep in the jungle, even in their reserve camps in Thailand. Since then the leaders' standing had suffered to the point where some of the junior commanders even dared to mutter openly about a leadership reshuffle.

Lon San spat into the water. That would never happen so long as he had breath in his body. He had worked hard to get to his present position as the most ruthless field commander in the organization. His sights were set on the top and a place at the side of Pol Pot. Then, with a return to power in Cambodia, he would get even with all those underlings who had dared to speak against him. More to the point, he would be able to pursue the Khmer Rouge policies of reform even more vigorously than before. But for that he would need the help of General Sarit Chamonon.

By the time the boat drew alongside the pier that serviced the Black Lotus, Lon San had focused his mind on the coming meeting. He reluctantly paid the boatman and strode away down the uneven planks, his leather shoes pinching; the sandals that he wore in the jungle had been left at his hotel along with his loose-fitting clothes. He knew that the General was a man who respected fine things, and on a previous visit to Bangkok Lon San had purposely equipped himself with several western outfits. Having chosen a high-class tailor in one of the big hotel's shopping arcades, he had selected the materials that the man had recommended. After that he had bought shirts, ties and shoes, completing his new wardrobe with a genuine gold Rolex bought from a man in the street. Later he had admired himself in the mirror of his hotel bedroom, thinking how closely he resembled one of those smooth characters in the big cigarette adverts adorning the sides of the local buses. Instantly recoiling from the thought, he had marvelled at the seductive power of capitalism and ever since had felt physically uncomfortable in anything but his jungle clothes and sandals.

The entrance to the Black Lotus was guarded by a clutch of burly henchmen. With cigarettes dangling from thin lips and eyes half closed against the smoke, they aped the postures gleaned from a diet of cheap Kung Fu movies. When Lon San approached, one of them rose threateningly from the rattan chair where he had been slouching and looked the newcomer slowly up and down.

'You're late for the fight. Time you bought a watch, arsehole.'

Lon San stared evenly back at him, his heart filled with loathing. For centuries both Thais and Vietnamese had been the traditional enemies of the Khmer peoples, carving up the Cambodian land that lay between them and over which they still exerted a powerful influence.

'Tell General Chamonon that Lon San is here.'

He spoke casually, forcing a smile. Unbalanced by his calm attitude and suspecting that his own manner might just have been out of place, the henchman shouldered his way back into the club.

'Wait here.'

'My pleasure.'

Lon San moved to one side, turning his back on the Thai guards. When the henchman returned his face was pale.

'This way, sir. How are you enjoying your stay in Bangkok? We are always glad to entertain comrades such as yourself here at the Black Lotus. It's a pity you missed the start of the fight, but Promarik's still showing that northern fucker how to box. Have you seen Promarik fight before? Wow, that man's an artist! You should have seen him last month . . .'

As they entered the main hall the guard's nervous chatter was drowned out by a roaring cheer as the northern boxer tumbled back across the ring with Than Promarik in hot pursuit, blows raining down from his huge gloves and tiny feet.

'The General's waiting for you, sir,' the guard shouted above the noise, indicating the dais and the carved table on the other side of the hall.

'Enjoy the rest of the fight.'

Lon San looked pleasantly at the grinning face of the guard, noting the sweat beading his forehead and the man's ingratiating manner.

'Thank you. You've been most helpful.'

Ecstatic with relief, the guard disappeared quickly from the room, leaving Lon San to make his way through the crowd towards the welcoming smile of General Sarit Chamonon.

Rising from his table the General opened his

arms in a generous show of friendship at his ally's approach.

'Comrade! Welcome back to the Black Lotus. We haven't seen you here for too long. Sit, sit, sit.'

Waving him into the only other chair at the table the General beamed merrily at Lon San.

'What can I get you? Singha beer?'

Lon San nodded but no further signal was required from the General as a waitress was already on hand with a laden tray. As well as drinks she deposited a selection of food. There was a bowl of rice birds, each sparrow-like creature marinaded in spices and then deep fried; a plate of *khanom*, sweet rice wrapped in strips of banana leaf; charcoal-baked crab with the rich orange egg roe in a side dish; and *khao-pad*, fried rice with chicken and pork.

The General gestured effusively and said: 'Eat, eat.'

Lon San selected a tiny rice bird and popped it into his mouth whole. The marination process had softened the beak, claws and bones and as he munched he could taste only the delicate blend of spices flowing over his tongue. He looked up as a roar from the crowd announced another flurry of attacking moves from Than Promarik in the ring.

After waiting until sufficient pleasantries had been exchanged with the General, Lon San spoke of the reason for their meeting. The General smiled warmly in response.

'Of course, my friend. I will arrange everything as usual.'

He sipped his Mekong whisky, the fiery rice-based spirit diluted with liberal amounts of soda.

'We have come a long way, you and I. Old

comrades-in-arms should always remain true to one another.'

He raised his glass in salute and chinked it against Lon San's beer. Lon San smiled back, not fooled for a moment that, should expediency dictate, the General would desert him at the drop of a hat, stabbing him in the back for good measure.

'On behalf of the subject Cambodian peoples I thank you,' Lon San said pleasantly. 'Through your good offices we will liberate our comrades and drive the foreign-inspired government from Phnom Penh.'

They both tipped back their drinks, whereupon two girls instantly appeared to refill them. Trying to ignore the noise, Lon San leaned forward across the table.

'Do you foresee any problem with the quantity of arms that I require? I know it's considerably more than usual but if we're to stop the desertions from our ranks we must launch our offensives soon and in great strength. Once we are re-equipped we will hit them right across the country, severing every major road, attacking isolated army outposts, ambushing rivers and lines of communication, driving them back from all they've gained over the last disastrous months.'

The General nodded sagely. 'They have indeed been bad days for your organization. The UN pulled off a rare success. Too bad it couldn't have been another fuck-up like Bosnia or Somalia.'

Pivoting back in his chair, he concentrated once again on the fight, which had entered a new phase of savagery. Than Promarik had demolished the last of his opponent's defences and was now celebrating his coming victory with a relentless barrage of kicks and punches to appreciative roars from the crowd.

'But, no, I don't foresee any problems with the

delivery. However, it might take just a little longer than usual. The supply dumps that were set up on our side of the border during the Vietnamese occupation of your country have been all but exhausted. If you want new weapons and ammunition they're going to have to come from China.'

Lon San stared at the General in consternation. 'But the Chinese won't give them to us. They're not the friends they used to be. These days they're too busy licking the arse of the Americans to further their precious trade deals.'

The General reached across and patted Lon San soothingly on the arm. 'I know, I know. No one has any principles left nowadays. All they want is money.' He shrugged. 'However, being realistic, it is going to cost you. I still have contacts in China who are less ready to desert an old ally like the Khmer Rouge, but with the changes that have taken place there, they have to bribe officials and pay off the middlemen like the rest of us.'

Lon San felt his blood begin to boil. So this is what the revolution had come to. He had always known that Sarit Chamonon was little better than an opportunist, but that the Chinese should falter was unthinkable. Once, they had been the main source of supply for weapons and finance for the Khmer Rouge, but the march of time had brought about the Vietnamese withdrawal from Cambodia, the UN-organized elections and China's desire for continued free trade with the West. Suddenly the Khmer Rouge were being shunned by their erstwhile allies, obliged to deal with corrupt Chinese arms suppliers operating through this unpleasant Thai general who was like some regional warlord.

Lon San forced himself to smile. 'We are in your hands, General. As usual you alone have proved to be our friend when all others have deserted us.' He had been about to call them 'cynical capitalist swine' but stopped himself just in time, remembering Sarit Chamonon's own rapacious greed. A moment later, with a light cough, the General broached the question of payment for his services.

'It's not simply the fee, you understand,' he announced apologetically. 'Heaven forbid. I'll be the first to admit that I have gained immeasurably from our border trade over the years. No, this time my Chinese contact will require a handsome reward for his services, and then there'll be the usual palms to cross with silver.' He smiled thinly. 'We've got to cope with a democratic government ourselves, you know. It's always more expensive to buy a democrat than a tyrant. No doubt if you have any friends still in Phnom Penh they're finding the same.'

'Oh, I've got plenty of friends there,' Lon San said meaningfully. 'Waiting for the word.'

'Yes, I don't doubt. Anyway, there'll be government officials and border-control officers to pay off, and then the officers of my own division. They are my very power base and I have to keep them sweet. The last thing I need is a squealer and a government inspection team from Bangkok looking into my finances.'

Lon San took a drink of his beer. The chill had left it and the warm liquid frothed unpleasantly in his mouth. He felt suddenly depressed. He longed to be back in the jungle. It was the only place he felt in control these days, even with the troops of the government army snapping at his heels. He found a purity in combat that he had first discovered as a boy.

Realizing there was no alternative to the General's shady scheming, Lon San sat back and looked at the plump, sweating face before him. He would have liked nothing more than to twist his bayonet into it and then pull the trigger until all sign of the self-satisfied Thai border commander had been eliminated. But this was the new way of waging revolutionary war. With a slow smile he lowered his wet glass to the table. A thrill of pleasure shot through Lon San as he noticed the flicker of distaste on the General's face as the condensation and spilt beer pooled on to the ornate mother-of-pearl, staining the fine teak. You need me too, you oily bastard, he thought. As much as I need you. Your insatiable appetite will always put you in my power. So long as I can pay you, you'll be there like the whore you are.

'So how would you like payment?' he asked, noting the General's ugly leer that came with the allusion to money.

'Timber and gems, fifty-fifty.'

Lon San whistled. 'Timber's not as easy as it was. We're on the run in a lot of our old forested areas. Gems would be easier.'

'A pity. Our own forests have been all but depleted. You know how these foreigners love their Thai furniture.'

The General reflected a moment, twirling his glass in his hands. 'OK then, payment in gems.'

'We can pay part of it in heroin if you like?'

'I've got more than I know what to do with,' the General replied, shaking his head. 'I can't shift the stuff. I've got a new contact in the Golden Triangle. He channels it down through Chiang Mai.'

'OK, gems it is. What about the timing?'

The General was starting to get bored. He always did once the matter of finance had been cleared up. Detail was a vulgar subject to be left to subordinates.

'I can arrange for the arms to be flown in to my airstrip at Paksaket. From there we'll bus them out to you.'

Lon San had had enough of the General's company, but this one final thing could be crucial to success. 'Can you make it Rurseng?'

The General stared at him in amazement. 'Are you mad? Fly them into Cambodia itself?'

'General, time is of the essence. If they have to be transported through the jungle they may arrive too late. I need them at Rurseng. It's safely in our hands.'

'For how long?' the General scoffed.

'Long enough,' Lon San said levelly. 'Well?'

The General tapped irritably on the table with his manicured nails. Mistaking it for a signal for another refill, the waitress approached him with a smile.

'Fuck off, whore!'

The girl almost dropped her tray, bowing and backing quickly away.

'All right. But don't ask any more favours.'

'Oh, I'm not asking for favours at all, General. You'll be well paid for the extra inconvenience.'

Recovering his temper, General Chamonon smiled awkwardly at the Khmer Rouge commander. 'Of course. I never meant to imply that you were short of funds.'

Lon San got up and shook hands with the General, drawing the meeting to a close. Stating that another meeting would be needed to confirm the details of the shipment, the General suggested that his Chinese contact might also attend.

'That's fine by me,' Lon San said pleasantly. 'I'm always ready to meet another Party member.'

As Lon San made his way to the door to be met by the same ingratiating guard, the General glared after him with contempt. It was obscene that he should have to treat with such a person, but business was business, and after all, the Khmer Rouge had been good trading partners. Sitting again, he ordered another whisky and smiled warmly at the waitress, who, for some reason he couldn't fathom, seemed to be afraid of him. What an absurd creature that nasty little Khmer was, he reflected. Like all of his race. It was too bad that Thailand had never been able to seize complete control of that unfortunate country. He remembered Lon San's absurd clothes and grinned. He must have bought them from a blind man, he thought with amusement. A dark purple jacket, unmatching trousers halfway up his ankles, plastic shoes and the crudest fake watch the General had ever seen. Still, he didn't doubt that in his own Stone Age jungle environment Lon San would be an adversary to avoid.

The thought of battle and renewed shouts from the crowd brought him sharply back to the present. Looking back at the ring, the General was sorry to see that he had missed the best part of the fight. The northerner's face was unrecognizable and he staggered round the ring like a drunkard. Any semblance of a defence had ceased and his arms hung useless at his sides, crippled by devastating kicks to the nerve centres. By contrast, Than Promarik danced lightly to the applause of the crowd, who threw fistfuls of banknotes into the canvas ring.

The referee looked worried and seemed about to stop the fight but, being on his feet, technically the northerner was still a contender. Glancing at the General, the referee sought his employer's guidance. Bathing in the applause and cheering of the paying audience, General Sarit Chamonon sipped his whisky and savoured the taste of power. With the slightest shake of the head he signalled the referee to step aside, away from the reeling northern boxer, leaving the ring to Than Promarik.

For a moment Than was still, bowing to his master, who had presented him with another opportunity to practice a blow that he rarely used. With a series of hops, each of which gave him greater height, he whiplashed into the air above his staggering, dazed and blinded opponent. As he drove his heel into the base of the man's skull, Than Promarik felt the spinal cord sever, and in that moment knew that he had boosted his renown as the most deadly weapon in General Sarit Chamonon's impressive arsenal.

2

Whenever Yon Rin came out of an audience with Prince Sihanouk he always felt encouraged in the true sense of the word. He thought about it as he walked down the long palace corridors. The Prince literally put courage into whoever came before him. After all he had been through it was really quite remarkable.

Clutching a sheaf of papers under his arm, Yon Rin shuffled along, trying to straighten his back into a posture befitting a senior security minister in the new Funcinpec government of the liberated Cambodia. But it wasn't easy. His years of imprisonment and torture at the hands of the Khmer Rouge had broken his body even if his will had remained resilient. The combination of forced labour and malnutrition had aged him far beyond his years. Nevertheless, at least he was alive. Two million of his fellow-countrymen had perished in the 'Killing Fields' into which the Khmer Rouge had driven the entire city-dwelling population after their victory in 1975, marking the start of their rule of terror by declaring the new date Year Zero. There had then followed nearly four years of murder until the Vietnamese had invaded and halted the genocide in 1979. Despite his country's historical antagonism towards their expansionist Vietnamese neighbours, Yon Rin would never forget his joy at their arrival.

Sadly it had not come in time to save the rest of his family. His wife had died soon after they had been driven out into the countryside after the fall of Phnom Penh; a simple cut had gone septic and blood poisoning had carried her beyond his pleas. Then, one by one each of his children, his parents, his uncles, aunts and cousins, nieces and nephews, had all perished in one way or another. Starved, murdered, diseased, executed, all had gone. But perhaps he had been most affected by the suicide of his youngest daughter.

From the beginning of the terror all family ties had been forcibly severed, but although it would have meant instant execution to be caught speaking, they had managed to keep in touch with a passing smile, the touch of a hand, a silent look loaded with compassion. But one day, with all the rest of the family dead, Yon Rin's daughter had learned that she was to be moved to work on a new labour project for a dam on the other side of the country. Yon himself was to stay behind. Passing him in the fields one day shortly before the departure date, she had walked close by and dropped a small wood carving at his feet. It was a carving of a bird, not very proficient, but a work of love. After stuffing it hastily in his jacket, Yon Rin had stared after his daughter, who that evening wrestled the gun from one of the female guards and shot herself.

Yon Rin cursed himself for weeks afterwards for not having had the courage to speak to her. He only survived himself by disguising his identity, pretending to be a car mechanic; if the Khmer Rouge had discovered that he was a fast-rising government clerk he would have been shot without question. But as he laboured on in the fields after his daughter's suicide, he wondered what point there was in his own survival. With everyone dead whom he had ever loved, and with his country in the hands of genocidal maniacs, what point was there in trying to hang on to his own life?

He was on the point of giving up when the Vietnamese arrived. Stunned by his sudden and unexpected liberty, Yon Rin drifted across the countryside for weeks. Everywhere he found people wandering like ghosts. It was as if the doors of hell had been opened, the devils driven away, and the lost souls left to emerge in bewilderment to reclaim their inheritance. And it was in the process of reclamation that Yon Rin found new meaning for his life.

The years under Vietnamese rule had been hard, but after the Killing Fields he found himself able to endure absolutely anything. Then, following the Vietnamese withdrawal and the return of Prince Sihanouk from exile in Peking, the unbelievable happened. The United Nations brokered a deal, elections were held and, for the first time in decades, the people of Cambodia had a real say in the governing of their country. The Khmer Rouge boycotted the elections and the Royalist Funcinpec Party was democratically elected to a majority in the new National Assembly. Yon Rin was hardly able to believe it.

But then the old demons returned. Secure in their jungle bases in the far north-west, the Khmer Rouge restarted their campaign of terror in the remote countryside, murdering peasants and attempting to regain by force what they had lost by democratic process. In response, the government army performed miracles, every man desperate to hold the demons at bay. But, with poor training, insufficient equipment and indifferent leadership, they reached the limits of their endurance and the Khmer Rouge campaign continued unabated.

Despite protestations of innocence, the Thai government was hardly enthusiastic about assisting in cross-border security with its new Cambodian neighbours, and one or two Thai border generals were openly in league with the Khmer Rouge. Yon Rin knew that democracy in Thailand was itself far from secure so there was little the ministers in Bangkok could do. General Sarit Chamonon in particular was well known to Yon as a leading border warlord who blatantly carried on a vigorous trade with the Khmer Rouge. He had profited handsomely during the years of war and could hardly be expected to desert his greatest source of revenue overnight.

But what troubled Yon Rin even more were the reports he had recently received from his agents in the border region. Intelligence was particularly difficult to come by in the impenetrable jungle areas, but peasant farmers, remembering the years of terror, were usually willing to part with valuable information at a price. The talk now was of a major new offensive being planned by the Khmer Rouge and to be led by Lon San. He was well known to Yon. In the early days of the Killing Fields, Lon San had commanded the irrigation project on which Yon had been sent to work. As a commander he had proved to be ruthlessly efficient, but his outstanding achievement had been to drive his workforce to reach record levels of productivity. It had been done with the whip, the bayonet and the gun and Yon Rin well remembered the sound, day and night, of the firing squads.

Emerging from the palace, Yon Rin squinted in the sudden glare of the sunlight. Shading his eyes, he went across to a large banyan tree and sat down heavily on the bench beneath it. The sounds of the busy Phnom Penh streets came to him over the palace walls and closing his eyes, he could almost dream that he was twenty years younger, sitting in the Phnom Penh of his days as a junior clerk. His wife would have been at home preparing lunch and his children would all have been at school. All except for his youngest daughter. Too small to go, she would have been in the kitchen getting under her mother's feet, singing quietly to herself in her dream world far from the everyday cares of her parents.

Yon Rin was startled by a light rain falling on his hands in his lap. Opening his eyes, he looked up and was puzzled to see not a cloud in the sky. It was a beautiful light blue and it was only then that Yon Rin realized that he was crying. Feeling in his pocket, his fingers felt the familiar shape of the rough wood and taking out the little carved bird, he held it on his knee as if by stroking it he could bring it to life.

But there was work to be done. Over the past months of peace he had found himself reflecting uncontrollably on the past and whenever this happened the only escape from the overwhelming flood of sorrow was to bury himself in work. After putting the wooden bird back in his pocket, Yon Rin dried his eyes and sniffed. He opened the sheaf of papers on his lap and surveyed the documents on which he had been briefing other government officials throughout the morning.

It had been surprisingly easy to convince them that his proposed course of action was the right one. To varying degrees they had all suffered at the hands of the Khmer Rouge and no one wanted to see a return to the bad old days. If Pol Pot's men ever retook the country it was unlikely that a single person would be left alive. And who would rescue them next time? Vietnam was floundering under its own economic problems. Foreign aid was slowly pulling them out of it, so they would never risk losing such a priceless lifeline by another intervention mission.

Thailand had shown time and again that it was in sympathy with the Khmer Rouge, and so long as there was no threat to themselves, the Thais could only be expected to remain silent behind their frontiers. As regards the international community, there was really no community at all. The United Nations had been unable to agree over the Bosnian tragedy and the Serbs, playing one state off against another, had been able to rape and murder their way to victory in the very heart of Europe. Hardly evidence of a spirit of community. If the UN was powerless to stop the Serbs in the accessible and high-profile arena of Europe, how could it be expected to send troops to assist a tiny Third World country in the outback of South-east Asia, against a hardened jungle enemy, invisible and ruthless?

No, foreign troops could never again be expected to come to the rescue. Organizing an election was one thing; becoming embroiled in a jungle war was another. With the new government installed, most of the UN personnel had withdrawn, leaving only a handful of observers to monitor the situation. Yon Rin had attended the ceremony at the palace when Prince Sihanouk had thanked the UN mission for their work and it had been there that he had come up with his idea.

He had been talking to one of the foreign military

personnel, a British officer from the Royal Marines, and had been lamenting the latest set-back suffered by the government forces.

'What you need is to take out the leaders,' the British officer said in a rather simplistic way.

Yon Rin shrugged. 'That's easy to say, but not to do.'

'Not as hard as you think. You might not be able to conquer the whole jungle, but a small select force could get in undetected and do the business. Professionals could, at any rate.'

Again Yon Rin objected. 'But we don't have any professionals. Not even a few.'

The British officer became furtive. 'I might be able to put you in touch with some people if you'd like.'

At first Yon Rin had laughed the whole thing off as a poor joke, but later that night he awoke in his bed, perspiration soaking his body, his heart pounding with excitement. Why not? These were desperate times and he was damned if he was going to sit by and watch the nascent democracy perish at the hands of the hated Khmer Rouge. Anything was worth trying.

The very next morning he sought out the British officer and enjoyed a longer conversation in private. The officer suggested an outline plan whereby a small band of native Cambodians could be selected from the best units in the army, and then trained to the required level by foreign mercenaries. If paid enough, such men might even be willing to plan and lead the operation themselves, but Yon Rin would have to take that up with the mercenaries themselves.

Several names were mentioned, addresses supplied, and Yon Rin retired to his bungalow to gather the information he needed. Finally, clasping his sheaf of papers, he went to brief those whose permission he needed to obtain the necessary financial backing and to get the operation under way.

Now, sitting under the banyan tree, Yon Rin looked down at the documents, wondering what kind of man would leave the safety and security of his own home to fight in another man's war. A face stared blankly up at him from the pages, the lines and features blurred by the photocopying process. It was a thoughtful face, not at all the sort that Yon Rin would have expected. But then, after all he had been through, Yon Rin had learned to expect the unexpected. It was the name, however, that puzzled him the most.

'Dojo! Get your arse in gear. If we don't find a b. & b. by four the fucking Germans'll have pigged the lot.'

On the end of the rope Terry 'Dojo' Williams felt for a handhold in the smooth rock. Splayed against the cliff face, his knee started to tremble, poised at the angle of bend where the muscle decided to call it a day.

'Shit.' Struggling to still his shuddering leg, Terry lunged upwards and found the hold he had been seeking.

'Gotcha, you bastard.'

Then, with his fingers secure in the groove, he took the whole weight of his body and pack with the one hand and dangled in mid-air while his other hand reached up for the next hold, easier than the last. Far below him he could see the tiny dots of cars buzzing down the Llanberis Pass. For a second he thought about the kids in the back whining for ice-creams or wanting to stop for a piss, but no sooner had it entered his head than he suppressed the image. His marriage was over and this time there was no going back.

It was a good two months since his last row with Liz had ended with him storming out of the house in the middle of the night, only to realize minutes later that he had left his wallet and credit cards behind. He had spent an uncomfortable night curled up in the back of his Opel Manta, listening to the rain drumming on the roof and watching the outside world slowly disappear as the windows misted with his breath.

The next morning he had tried to make it up, but Liz had rejected him in no uncertain terms. The kids had been packed off to her mother's, Terry had been allowed into the bedroom to pack his clothes and had then driven to the gym, where he set up his old army camp-bed in his office. The sign outside proclaimed to the world: 'Karate Dojo – Terry Williams, 4th Dan. Children's classes every Saturday,' and underneath in bold letters he had added: 'Unarmed Combat for the Disabled on Wednesdays'. He might not have the gift of making the lame walk, but he could sure as hell teach them how to make a mugger's eyes water.

After that he had entered his usual dark night of the soul, questioning the direction in which his life was going and burning out his fury and frustration in devastating training sessions that left his students dazed and wondering what they had done to upset the *sensei*.

The answer to the immediate problem had been the same one as always: a climbing holiday in Snowdonia. He found someone willing and stupid enough to accompany him and together they had spent the past week touring the most severe rock-faces in the region. But Willy Mailer was becoming a pain and Terry was starting to wish he had come on his own. All Willy ever thought about was getting settled into a good bed & breakfast; everything else was subordinated to this pathetic aim. There was no adventure in his life, just an endless comparison of the bacon and sausages in a string of miserable farmhouses and semi-dees. It had become their only topic of conversation.

'You know, I preferred the tea bags in the Glamorgan Arms,' Willy would say. They might be sitting on the top of a sun-drenched peak with the world's splendours laid out below them and a rainbow arching overhead, iced with a sprinkling of silver rain, but for Willy the true splendour would be his recollection of the satellite TV facility: 'And all for only twelve quid a night, mind. Bloody marvellous, I say.'

Terry wasn't sure how much more he could take. Still, it was hardly surprising. Willy had been in the bloody Logistic Corps, whereas Terry was an infantryman through and through. What could you expect from the loggies? If they hadn't come from the same Swansea housing estate they would never have been friends but their relationship went back to schooldays and punch-ups round the back of the Imperial, the local flea-pit. Willy wasn't such a prat then, as they stood back to back, beating the shit out of the skinheads. He was great with his fists until the day the army tried to turn him into a gentleman. Commissioned through the ranks, he ended up counting stockpiles of baked beans in the Rheindahlen NAAFI in Germany. Poor sod. He had even worked at losing his Welsh accent, and ended up with a sort of pompous drawl that sounded neither English nor Welsh.

Nevertheless, he had always kept in touch with his old friends despite the fact that Terry had never got beyond the rank of warrant officer. Whenever their periods of leave coincided and they both found themselves in Swansea they always got in touch for a climbing trip up north.

Hauling himself on to a ledge, Terry slumped down to catch his breath. In his late thirties he was starting to feel the strain of excessive physical exertion. There had been a time when he could have scaled four cliffs like this in a single afternoon, but not any more. He called up to his unseen friend.

'Just taking a breather, mate.'

'Right you are.'

Terry gazed out across the pass to the range of hills on the far side, where he could just make out a string of tiny dots as climbers made their way painfully up the opposite rock-face. He undid the side pouch on his bergen and took out his vacuum flask and poured himself a coffee. Might as well enjoy it here, he thought. If I wait till I get on top I'll have to put up with the story of this morning's breakfast all over again.

It wasn't long before Terry found his mind drifting back to the strange letter that had dropped through his letter-box two days earlier. The English was a bit ropey but a glance at the letterhead and postmark left him stunned. A Royal Palace, no less, and from Cambodia. The information in the letter was sketchy but it seemed that someone had recommended him as a good trainer and he was being offered a contract for a couple of months. The Cambodian army apparently wanted to draw on his expertise to train a small commando force they were forming.

Terry assumed it would be a sort of palace guard. He had done much the same thing before for an Arab sheikh in a minor Gulf state. It would be money for old rope. The troops probably wouldn't be up to much, but what kind of opposition did they expect to have to face? Probably no more than a bunch of thugs with shotguns. Usually people who wanted their own bodyguards were just suffering from an ego problem. The Arab had equipped his men with gold-plated Kalashnikovs, of all things. Every evening the weapons would be taken away and locked up in a strong room, leaving the guards with nothing more than a handful of ceremonial daggers.

Still, if someone was foolhardy enough to foot the bill Terry would oblige. He needed to get away for a bit and think things through, and if he could earn some cash at the same time that was fine by him. He would give them training in close-quarter battle techniques, unarmed combat, anti-sniper procedures, anti-ambush drills – all the usual sort of stuff that any self-respecting bodyguard should know. When that was done he might take a look at the country, have a bit of a holiday and return to Wales refreshed and ready to prepare himself for his trip to Okinawa in the spring, when he would go for his fifth Dan. He had decided to try for it some while ago, and had written for the details and booked himself into the training gym. He hadn't been there for years, not since his second Dan. Master Nishime Higashi would notice the change in him and probably call him a fat toad. That had been his favourite western expression last time.

'Fat toad, likey bullfrog,' and Master Higashi had puffed out his cheeks and swelled himself up until the class collapsed in stitches. But he had followed it with a stunning demonstration of the most intricate and beautiful *kata* sequence that Terry had ever seen, confirming him, at least in Terry's mind, as the greatest living Karate Master in the world.

Terry leaned his head back against the rock. He couldn't wait to get back there. There was a purity in the training and the hardship, as if each person was an uncut diamond of infinite potential, but dirty and lustreless, needing dedicated work and the daily polish of rigorous exercise to produce at least a semblance of worth. But it was not merely the physical exercise and training routines that Terry prized. Master Higashi put equal emphasis on the development of the spirit, incorporating into the programme long sessions of meditation, lectures and discussions. There was no doubt in Terry's mind that he would be taken beyond every limit he had ever attained if he was to achieve the required standard and return from Okinawa with his fifth Dan.

But first of all he would undertake this Cambodian business. With a heavy sigh he shook the last drops of coffee out of his plastic mug and screwed it back on the flask. He didn't have any strong feelings about it either way. He had enjoyed being in the jungle and was one of the best jungle warfare instructors in the army. He had done a two-year tour at the British Jungle Warfare school at Tutong in Brunei, had trained the Paras in Belize, attended familiarization courses at the American schools in Panama and Florida's Everglades, at the Australian school in Queensland, and with the Malaysian Rangers at the ex-British school of Kota Tinggi. All in all there were few people who knew as much about jungle warfare as Terry Williams. It would be no great problem to design a simple training course for the Cambodian army.

'Have you fallen asleep down there, boyo?'

Terry looked up. 'On my way.'

Shouldering his bergen, he stood up on the ledge and scanned the rock-face for the next set of holds as Willy took up the slack in the rope.

'That's me!' Terry shouted as the rope bit. Reaching up, he hauled himself off the ledge and began the last stage of his ascent.

'Climbing!'

'Roger to that.'

Far below, the cars made their lazy progress up and down the pass, the children with their noses pressed against the windows pointing at the spider-like figures spread against the distant mountain wall. As their parents argued over the best place to stop for the next cream tea, Terry pitted himself against the mountain – man versus nature in a contest that was as old as the human race itself.

Tommy Liu had caught the last train out of Central before the MTR had closed for the night, and had arrived in Diamond Hill at a bad time. Carved out of the rock at the northern end of the overcrowded Kowloon peninsula, the Diamond Hill housing estate was one of the oldest and most crowded in the whole of Hong Kong, but to Tommy it was home. A western friend he had once taken there had likened it to a vast chicken battery for humans and had marvelled that the place didn't explode. Built in the fifties and sixties, it was one of the numerous clusters of high-rise flats that had been put up by the colonial British government to accommodate the various influxes of Chinese immigrants from the mainland who had flooded into the tiny colony. Successive waves had fled the Communist victory of 1949, the famines of Mao's Great Leap Forward of the late fifties, and the Cultural Revolution of 1967.

Since then the jam-packed concrete towers had taken in yet more residents, mostly illegal immigrants lured as ever to the great city-state by tales of streets paved with gold. In truth, all they had found was hard labour in a sweatshop with imprisonment and repatriation as the price of capture by the Royal Hong Kong Police. Tommy, on the other hand, had been born there. His parents arrived from China as refugees with little more than a bundle of clothes and his father's scissors and barber's implements. Living for the first few months on the streets, Tommy's father set up shop with an upturned orange crate and a shard of broken mirror. Eventually they were allocated housing in a tiny one-room flat at Diamond Hill and there they had lived ever since. Tommy's mother was carrying him when she and her husband made the tortuous overland journey to Hong Kong, and he was born just weeks after they moved into the new flat. Deciding that the family's new start should be marked in some special way, Mr and Mrs Liu gave their son a western name and so, suitably christened, Tommy began his journey through life.

It was hard from the start. The housing estates were the recruiting ground for the Triads, Hong Kong's own brand of gangster and every bit as ruthless as the Mafia. The particular group that controlled Diamond Hill was the Dragon K gang. Tommy was coerced into their ranks as soon as he entered secondary school and thereafter obliged to take part in protection raids on the local fish-market stalls and restaurants. There were a couple of pitched battles with the Mountain River gang, who ran the neighbouring estate, arising out of a dispute over control of a new shopping precinct built on the waste land separating the two estates. Two youths were stabbed to death, after which the gangs dispersed and lay low until the police investigations cooled down.

But it had been a turning-point for Tommy. One of the dead youths was his friend and hero, Vincent Win. In Tommy's eyes Vincent had the world at his feet. He was the school basketball star and consistently top of his class academically. When Tommy saw him lying in a pool of blood, the promise of his young life seeping out of his crumpled body, he had resolved to break with the Dragon K for good. But few who left a Triad were allowed to forget their treason. There had been induction rituals and oaths had been sworn. Nevertheless, Tommy was determined. In his favour was his skill as a street fighter. He had become a capable boxer and was good with a knife. A couple of times after the break he fought with other gang members and they left him alone only after he seriously hurt one of them with a machete.

Tommy had never looked back since. He had joined the Hong Kong Military Service Corps and received a commendation for outstanding achievement after rescuing some children from a landslip. Then he moved to the police, ending up with a job in Special Branch. But the Triads never forgot and were only biding their time before getting even. A police raid discovered heroin in his flat. He had been set up. Discharged from the force in disgrace, he found himself living again in Diamond Hill, back where he had started, with the Dragon K waiting to settle the score once and for all.

As he came out of the MTR station, Tommy checked his back before crossing the road and starting up the steep hill towards the towering H-block where he shared a single room with his mother, his sister, her husband and their three children. Tommy's father had died shortly after his discharge from the force – of shame, his mother had said accusingly.

He could see the huge, cold building ablaze with light, a naked fluorescent strip light glowing in every dismal flat. Washing hung from every window and balcony, and the chatter of thousands of voices mixed with the noise of TVs, the clash of mah-jong bricks and the whine of Chinese music from a myriad transistor radios. Above, the sky glowed orange with a combination of street lamps and car fumes from the nearby flyover.

But Tommy didn't have time to look at the sky. His eyes were on the street corner where two youths lounged against the wall. His undercover work for Special Branch had filled the few gaps left by his past work as a junior soldier in a Triad, the two experiences combining into a sixth sense when it came to detecting the approach of trouble. Crossing to the other side of the road, Tommy continued until level with the youths. Unperturbed, they ignored him as he walked on to the entrance of his H-block, but he had barely gone fifty yards when another two men, older than the first pair, appeared in the doorway towards which Tommy was headed.

OK, he thought, this is it. Glancing over his shoulder, he saw that the first two youths had

peeled themselves off the wall and were moving up
behind him, cutting his retreat.

Fifteen yards from the doorway Tommy stopped
and called to the men blocking his path.

'Are you going to let me pass or do I have to
fight you?'

The elder of the two men grinned stupidly and drew
on the cigarette stuck to his lower lip.

'You've let us down, Tommy. You broke the oath.
You know the Dragon K can't let that go. Otherwise
every little fucker who gets cold feet would be doing
it. Then what would we do?'

'Grow up?' Tommy offered. The smile died on the
man's face and he squared up to fight.

'You don't learn, do you, Liu?'

'No, I guess I don't.'

From under his jacket the man pulled a meat
cleaver, his partner producing another. Behind him,
Tommy saw the two youths closing fast, each of them
with switch-blades.

'I don't want it like this,' Tommy called out.

'Well, you've got it,' the man replied, starting
towards him.

Tommy sighed. 'No, my friend. You have.'

Reaching to the small of his back under his quilted
Mao jacket, Tommy pulled his Glock 17 from his
belt, dropping to one knee and bringing the pistol
to aim in a combat grip. With no external hammer
or safety-catch, the Austrian-made handgun was the
ideal close-quarter weapon for undercover work,
the usual heavy metallic working parts replaced by
a tough polymer material that made it light and
durable. It was as simple to operate as a revolver:
a single trigger action cocked and fired the first of the

seventeen 9mm Parabellum cartridges waiting snugly in the magazine. For Tommy it had enough stopping power for the toughest shoot-out.

But even as Tommy was preparing to ground the man about to throw the cleaver, behind him he could hear the sound of running feet. Cursing under his breath he went into action, squeezing off a rapid 'double tap' at each of the two men silhouetted in the doorway, then instantly executing a forward roll and turning to engage the two youths at his back. Another double tap crumpled the nearest of the youths at Tommy's feet, the flick-knife sailing harmlessly past Tommy's ear. Seeing his companion lying dead on the floor and the bodies of the two senior Triad soldiers motionless in the H-block entrance, the last youth stopped dead in his tracks, his mouth open.

'Do you want some too?'

Tommy's one open eye stared coldly at him down the barrel of the Glock. The youth backed away, gaping at his friends.

'You . . . you'll pay for this. You don't know what you've done,' he stammered.

As the youth turned and sprinted off down the street, Tommy relaxed his grip on the pistol. Looking at the three bodies, he noted that he still ranked as a competent marksman. Each of the six rounds had found its mark and all the targets were stone-dead. But he did know exactly what he had done. He had just exiled himself from his family and from Hong Kong. Discharged from Special Branch and now wanted by the Dragon K for the killing of three of their soldiers, there would be nowhere for him to hide. Even over the border in mainland China the Triad would be able to hunt him down.

Replacing the pistol in his waistband, Tommy stepped over the bodies in the doorway and made his way up to the flat. The crack of his six shots had been swallowed up by the general cacophony but it wouldn't be long before the bodies were discovered and then a full police cordon-and-search operation could be expected. Hong Kong was one of the most heavily policed cities in the world and one of the safest places to live and work – unless the Triads were after you.

Estimating that he would just have time to pack a bag and tell his mother he was going away for a while, Tommy decided that his best bet would be to hitch a ride on a fishing junk to the neighbouring Portuguese colony of Macau on the other side of the Pearl River estuary. It would be quicker by hydrofoil or ferry but that would be the first place both police and Triads would look for him.

And when he got to Macau? Tommy had several ideas. He always did. Identifying a broad range of options even in the tightest corners had kept him alive in the Hong Kong underworld on both sides of the law. But for now he reckoned that the Cambodian job would be the best.

3

The airstrip at Paksaket, on the border of Thailand and Cambodia, had been carved out of the jungle by the Thai army engineers in the early days of the Vietnamese invasion of Cambodia. It was a time of panic, rife with fears that the domino theory was about to be proved correct. With Vietnam, Cambodia and Laos all in Communist hands, the Thais reckoned that they were about to become the next victim in the unfolding drama of Southeast Asia. With massive foreign aid and military equipment, Thailand prepared itself for the coming onslaught and in capitals all over the free world, Intelligence chiefs waited expectantly for the battle to begin.

But, with the Khmer Rouge driven from power, the Vietnamese stopped well short of the Thai border. They had enough trouble on their plates with an economy in ruins and their country devastated by decades of war. The last thing on their minds was yet another bloody campaign against the Thais, who, unlike themselves, had escaped occupation by the old European colonial powers in the previous century. Any invader would be unlikely to find a sympathetic population waiting gratefully for release from the oppressor's yoke. Nevertheless, in readiness for war the Paksaket airstrip was built in case the Thai border forces needed to fly in reinforcements, ammunition and supplies.

However, when the Vietnamese withdrew, leaving Cambodia in the care of the UN, General Sarit Chamonon was quick to see the value of maintaining the airstrip to further his vibrant border trade that had developed with the Khmer Rouge. Rather than for flying in war supplies, it could be used to fly out his stocks of contraband. Indeed, it was so successful that his military duties were soon superseded by his entrepreneurial business activities.

Sitting in the shade of a gnarled banyan tree, the General lazily peeled a lychee, stripping off the hard, red skin with his long, polished thumbnail. Popping the soft, white flesh of the fruit into his mouth, he worked the stone free and spat it into the dust, relishing with delight the sensual taste of sweetness that flooded his mouth.

'You know, the thing I like about you, Comrade, is that you always know a good deal when you see one.'

Slumped in the chair opposite, Lon San looked up. He felt better than he had for days. He brightened immediately he was out of the traffic and smog of Bangkok and back on the border in his jungle fatigues. He even managed a smile in response to the General's remark. Of course it was complete rubbish, but then the General himself knew that. Lon San had no choice but to deal with Sarit Chamonon and the General always made sure that the Khmer Rouge paid for everything at many times the real value.

Lon San shrugged and said: 'Our business hasn't done you any harm either.'

The General laughed and passed Lon San his bag

of lychees. He was about to reply that he would be sorry if his relationship with the Khmer Rouge were ever terminated, when he heard the sound of an approaching aircraft.

'Ah. This will be the Colonel.'

Stepping into the dazzling sunlight, the General shaded his eyes and squinted towards the north, and a moment later a black speck became visible, growing into the shape of a light passenger plane as the drone of its engines got louder. The General looked at his watch and then at the road winding out of the jungle on the far side of the airstrip.

'Where the devil's Eddy?'

As if in answer to his query, a jeep appeared round the corner in a cloud of dust, followed by a battered Nissan land-cruiser and then a second jeep. In each jeep four heavily armed Thais in jeans and cotton shirts clung to their seats, mirror sunglasses masking eyes that searched the roadside jungle for any sign of trouble. In the passenger seat of the Nissan, one elbow leaning from the open window, Eddy Passenta grinned and waved to the General.

Lon San got warily to his feet. He had met Fat Eddy once before and had taken an instant dislike to the Thai drug baron from the heroin fields of the Golden Triangle beyond Chiang Mai. He looked quickly at the General, wondering what he was up to. The General smiled simply.

'I have more than just one client after my services. Eddy has also requested a meeting with the Chinese Colonel. I think he's looking to expand his business and like all those involved in expansion plans he needs to make a little investment first.'

Lon San could well imagine what kind of investment Fat Eddy had in mind. No doubt a full-scale gang war against his rivals.

After screeching to a halt, the convoy disgorged its load of armed guards, who jogged into fire positions, a little theatrically to Lon San's eye. These drug barons were all the same as far as he was concerned, arseholes who loved a big show of strength. Their credibility relied upon it. Rolling out of his seat, Fat Eddy swaggered across to the General, holding out a pudgy hand.

'Sarit, you miserable fucker.'

Lon San was surprised at the familiarity but the General seemed to take it in good heart and after shaking the offered paw, turned to introduce the new arrival to Lon San. Fat Eddy narrowed his eyes into a half smile.

'So, the Khmer Rouge are still in business, are they? I'd heard you'd all been voted out of office by a pack of UN peaceniks.'

Lon San forced a smile though he would rather have slit the man's throat. Perhaps, he consoled himself, one day he would. Noticing the tension, the General placed himself between the two men, an arm round each.

'The Khmer Rouge is very much in business,' he said accommodatingly. 'In fact, that's why Comrade Lon San is here. If the Colonel can produce the goods you'll increase your share of the drugs business, Lon San here will help the Khmer Rouge back into Phnom Penh, the Chinese Colonel will have done another good deal . . .'

'And you'll be even richer and more self-satisfied than you already are,' Fat Eddy concluded with a huge roar of laughter that sent shock waves shuddering through the rolls of fat coating his frame.

'How well you understand me,' the General replied, leading the two men across the baking sand of the airstrip. 'It's wonderful to be surrounded by such good friends.'

At the far end of the runway the small plane dropped out of the sky, bounced on to the dirt strip and taxied towards them. When it had come to a stop, the pilot hopped out and ran round the tail to open the door, from where a surprisingly tall Chinese man in slacks and matching safari jacket eased himself to the ground. Striding across to them, he introduced himself as Colonel Leonard Kon.

'I find the westerners are happier dealing with a Leonard rather than another Lee or Chee or Wee,' he joked as the four men walked towards the small office building that doubled as a control tower. 'They condescend to treat me almost as one of them.'

The General had arranged for light refreshments and in the office two soldiers passed round iced drinks and some delicately prepared snacks that had been brought from Bangkok especially. The main room was dominated by a long teak table, not as splendid as the one at the Black Lotus, but big enough for the four men each to have ample room to spread out their maps and papers without encroaching on anyone else's territory. The General well knew that each man present was used to giving orders and having others give way. With business in mind he had no intention of upsetting his potential clients.

'Right then, allow me to welcome you all here. I'll keep this brief as we all have other calls on our time. Colonel Kon, thank you for coming all the way from

Yunnan. Mr Passenta and Comrade Lon San here will be your customers and I'll be acting as the simple go-between as usual.'

Gesturing to Fat Eddy, the General withdrew into his iced Mekong whisky. Clearing his throat, Fat Eddy outlined his requirements. Listening intently, Lon San marvelled at the long list of weaponry that the drug baron was ordering. Money seemed to be no object. The demand for heroin was obviously as strong as ever. Lon San had dealt in it himself but since the UN elections the government army had overrun most of the Khmer Rouge's opium fields. That, combined with the loss of their vast timber forests, had forced them to concentrate on the gems trade, although now they were running short of even this precious commodity.

When Fat Eddy had finished and Kon had made careful notes of the substantial order, the Colonel turned to Lon San and smiled.

'So, how are my old friends in the Khmer Rouge, these days? I haven't seen Comrade Pol Pot or Khieu Samphan since they were in Beijing.'

Lon San returned the smile with a little nod of the head. He liked the look of the Chinese Colonel. Perhaps not all the Chinese had deserted the Khmer Rouge after all.

'When I last saw them at Pailin they were well.'

'Ah yes,' the Colonel frowned. 'Pailin. What's the status of that now? You lost it to Sihanouk's troops, didn't you?'

Lon San flushed. 'It was only in their hands for a matter of days before we drove them out again.'

'Of course, of course,' the Colonel reassured him quickly.

Across the table, Fat Eddy sniggered.

'Colonel, we need arms,' Lon San continued. 'Lots of them if we are to retake Phnom Penh.'

'I understand. How do you intend to pay?'

'Gems.'

The Colonel shrugged. 'The market for amethysts and topaz is not what it used to be.'

Lon San smiled. 'I'm talking about rubies, Colonel.' He noticed the instant change in Kon and thought: So you are just another greedy capitalist.

'Or may I call you Leonard?'

'Please, be my guest.'

'We have a large supply of rubies.'

'Synthetic?'

Lon San snorted. 'Leonard, these are as good as anything the Burmese can produce. The colour of pure pigeon blood. And then there's jade. As much as you want.'

A broad grin spread across the Colonel's face. 'General, why didn't you say you had such fine customers for me today? I would have brought a bottle of the finest Maotai brandy.'

'If you want I can also offer you emeralds, sapphires and lapis lazuli,' Lon San continued nonchalantly, noting with pleasure that he had completely upstaged Fat Eddy. 'Of course, if you'd rather have opium for the masses . . .'

'No, no, gems will be fine,' the Colonel cut in rapidly, and taking up his pen he turned to a clean sheet of paper.

'So then, Comrade, what is it you require? Or may I call you San?'

Now it was Fat Eddy's turn to sit back with open mouth, marvelling at the ambitions of the Khmer

Rouge commander, and when Lon San had finished detailing his order, the General drew the meeting to a close with a toast to their mutual good fortune and the success of their various plans.

Out in the sunlight again, Colonel Kon strode back to his plane, Fat Eddy scurrying after him with a last-minute request for explosives.

Watching them go, the General couldn't help laughing. 'They make quite a pair, don't they? Like Laurel and Hardy.' He noticed the blank look on Lon San's face. 'Laurel and Hardy? No? Oh well, never mind.' The only teams that Lon San might have heard of, he reflected, were Heckler & Koch, or Smith & Wesson.

Drawing Lon San aside as the plane taxied away and Fat Eddy shot off back into the jungle with his jeep loaded with bodyguards, the General had one final piece of information to impart.

'Comrade, I have friends in Phnom Penh and they've brought me word of new developments.'

'Oh?'

'Apparently your opposition have decided to hedge their bets and are intending to bring in some outside specialists.'

'Specialists?'

'Mercenaries, to be precise. It seems they've got wind of your intentions and are going to try and forestall your offensive by using foreign know-how to train up their miserable rabble of an army.'

Lon San gazed mysteriously into the distance until the General wondered if he had heard him, but just as he was about to repeat himself, the Khmer Rouge commander spoke.

'Thank you. That is interesting indeed. Fortunately

48

I too have friends in Phnom Penh. Now that you have warned me I will take steps to ensure that these specialists don't live long enough to pass on their so-called expertise.'

He turned to the General and smiled as he added: 'I am in your debt.'

Taking a handkerchief from his pocket, Lon San carefully unrolled it until a large red ruby lay in the palm of his hand, shining brilliantly in the sun.

'Please. Accept this,' he said. 'Never forget that it is the Khmer Rouge who are your true friends, however much noise Mr Passenta might make.'

General Sarit Chamonon was speechless. It was the most beautiful ruby he had ever seen and he was so mesmerized that he missed the tone of warning in Lon San's voice, and the hard glint in the eyes of a man who was thought, even by his own guerrillas, to be hardly human.

Since his posting to Phnom Penh, Captain Manny Tron usually tried to get home early in the evenings after work. He had spent the past two years in the north of the country fighting the Khmer Rouge and had distinguished himself on numerous occasions in combat. Some people said he took unnecessary risks, but then he had good reason to. The Khmer Rouge had murdered his entire family. In the days before Year Zero, his had been one of the largest and most influential families in the country, with connections to the princes of the royal Norodom family itself. But that had all changed with the arrival of Pol Pot's murderers.

Within three years the entire edifice had crumbled and Manny's network of relatives had been eliminated. Of the whole family only two had survived, Manny and his younger sister, Sitha. He never spoke about the third survivor, his brother in Bangkok. As far as Manny was concerned, Sy Tron was as good as dead. If Manny ever came across him again he would probably kill him himself.

As soon as the new government was installed, Manny had been given a commission as a reward for standing by Prince Sihanouk throughout his years in exile in Beijing. But it was no sinecure: he had a mission to fight the Khmer Rouge wherever, whenever and however he could all the while he was strong enough to draw breath. On being appointed he had pushed for a combat command and had soon found himself on the front. Now at last he could start to get even with the men and women who had murdered his family. Once a helpless witness to their genocide, he was now an avenging angel and in his first-ever battle he discovered a sheer joy in the pursuit of his sworn enemies.

He was disconcerted therefore when he was recalled to Phnom Penh and assigned to the command of a minister in the Security Bureau, Yon Rin. He had requested and received an interview and had protested that he was ill suited to the role of bodyguard, even though he did appreciate the honour. But the minister played it vague and gave nothing away, simply reassuring him that he should be patient and not judge things by appearances. Manny would be delighted, the minister said, with his new assignment when it could be revealed in full. And revealed in full it duly was.

Walking back through the busy streets towards the

old family villa, Manny's head was spinning. That afternoon he had been summoned to Minister Yon Rin's office, sworn to secrecy and then briefed on the forthcoming operation. He was clearly being honoured and the only fly in the ointment was the employment of foreign mercenaries. Why couldn't the job be done with Cambodians? Manny himself knew of a dozen top-quality soldiers that he would like to have beside him. Yon Rin noted their names and said that they would be summoned immediately, but regarding the mercenaries he was unmoved.

'These are specialists,' he said. 'You will co-operate with them and give them every assistance, and that is that, Captain Tron.'

By the time Manny reached the villa the bicycles had thinned out as people made their way home. The house stood in a quiet part of Phnom Penh. Like much of the city it had been built by the French colonists. They had arrived in 1864 and stayed for ninety years, leaving reluctantly only after their drubbing at the hands of the Viet Minh at the battle of Dien Bien Phu. But during their tenure they had built beautiful buildings that even Manny had to admire, even if today they were mere shadows of their former selves.

Turning into the gateway, he walked up the driveway towards the majestic front of the splendid villa where he was born and spent his childhood. It was still painful and, he feared, it always would be; wherever he looked he could hear the echoes of a vanished life. Ghosts patrolled every patch of grass and every bush, tree, window and balcony. There was the place where he had fallen as a boy and banged his head on the paving stone; his mother had rushed from the house and had him carried inside. Then there were the many celebrations of New Year when all the family's relatives, friends and neighbours would come; this very driveway would be packed with their cars and Manny and his brothers and sisters would peer from the upstairs windows and joke about the ladies' dresses or laugh at their Uncle Rama's antics. But now weeds protruded from the cracked paving stones. The ornamental pond was dry, and Uncle Rama had been beaten to death at a public execution in the Killing Fields of Choeng Ek. His skull was now just one of the thousands heaped in desolate piles.

Hearing him return, Sitha came out to the ground-floor balcony, smiling warmly. Manny marvelled that she had recovered so well after the years of suffering, although at night when he heard her cry out in her room, whimpering in her sleep, he knew that she was being brave for his sake, helping him cope with the guilt he felt at not having stayed and suffered with the rest of the family. Exile in Beijing had not been easy, but at least he had survived physically and mentally unscathed.

'Home early again.'

When she spoke, it was neither statement nor question, but rather a sigh of relief at seeing her brother, her last remaining relative, before her eyes again. Manny went up the steps and kissed her tenderly on the cheek. He could smell the fragrance of orchid blossoms in her hair that she had always had ever since she was a child.

'What have you been up to today?' he asked, holding his sister by her narrow shoulders.

Sitha led him into the sitting-room, where she had laid the table for supper. Each evening since Manny's return from the front, she had set their places at one end of the large dining table. Manny had noticed how, during the meals, she often seemed to be looking around, deferring to the empty places as if the rest of the family were somehow there, watching them and listening to their chatter.

'I've been trying to get someone to work in the garden,' she answered. 'You know, tidy it up a bit.'

'Any luck?'

'Not really. An old woman was quite eager but she hardly had the strength to walk up the drive. There just aren't any extra hands to spare for non-essential work these days.'

Manny knew the truth of that perfectly well. With the past butcheries and the present war, the country's manpower had been drained to the bottom of the barrel. Most able-bodied men were drafted into the army and despite the need for them on the farms, they went willingly.

Sitha had prepared a meal of spiced chicken and rice. She had been to one of the markets that had reappeared and bought some fresh green vegetables which she had lightly boiled and served as a side dish with chopped almonds and herbs. As he ate, Manny stole a glance at his sister. She was beautiful. Even as a child he had known that one day she would blossom into someone very special. Miraculously the years of hard labour had failed to destroy her looks. The damage had all taken place inside, out of sight, in the fragile arenas of the soul.

When they had eaten they moved on to the veranda to sit in rattan chairs as the light faded and the cicadas stirred to life in the surrounding casuarina trees. Sitha poured two glasses of fresh lime juice and sipping it in the twilight, brother and sister watched the night come on and felt the ghosts of the past move slowly about them in the darkened house.

'You're not going to be here for long, are you?'

Sitha's question caught Manny off balance, but he stopped his reflex answer just in time. She deserved something better than lies.

'Not too long. Another couple of weeks, certainly.'

'Ah.'

They sat in silence until the mosquitoes started to bite, driving them inside behind drawn blinds. Electricity was still a random affair, so Sitha lit an oil-lamp and placed it between them.

'Where will you go? Back to the front?'

'I'm not sure. Probably. Look, Sitha, those murderers have to be stopped. You know that. And if people like me aren't prepared to try to stop them, then who will?'

She held up her hand. 'I know, I know. It's just that we've done our bit, surely.'

Manny looked at her warmly. 'Everyone has. But there's no one else left.'

Sitha got up and walked around the vacuous sitting-room. In the months and years following Year Zero and the evacuation of the city, the house had stood empty. The furniture had mostly been looted and when she and Manny had finally returned to pick up the few remaining pieces of their past lives, they had found the villa a desolate shell. Nevertheless, they had scoured the markets for chairs, tables and beds, and had even come across some items taken from the house. But it would never be a proper home again. It had become a mausoleum and would remain so, Manny felt, until the end of time.

His last words echoed through the room. There's no one else left, he thought. Perhaps Yon Rin was right after all. Perhaps the foreigners were required. He had an instinctive revulsion against mercenaries. How could they ever be trusted? What commitment did they have to the cause apart from money? Who could say that they wouldn't change sides if the Khmer Rouge offered them gems in the same way that they had bought the co-operation of the Thai border commanders? But perhaps there wasn't any choice. If Yon Rin was correct, then the Khmer Rouge were on the verge of a new offensive. Manny had seen the demoralized government army and knew that they were near the end of their tether. A string of Khmer victories might be all it would take for the troops to break and run. If that happened the road to Phnom Penh would lie open.

With one swallow he finished his lime juice and put the glass firmly down on the table. That could never be allowed to happen. He would do everything in his power to make Yon Rin's plan work. Even if it meant working alongside this 'Dojo' Williams and his team. Manny Tron would ally with the devil himself if it meant the defeat of the Khmer Rouge.

In the building occupied by the UN observer team a single light was still on. Behind her desk Miss Suki Yamato was puzzling over a telegram from the Geneva office. It was a request for her reports to be filed using a new format that would enable them to be processed with greater ease by the computers at the Geneva end. She shook her head in exasperation.

Whoever had sent it obviously had no idea of the local conditions in Phnom Penh.

Since the majority of the UN team had pulled out following the hand-over of the country to the newly elected government, the remaining observers had been rushed off their feet trying to keep tabs on all the developments that were under way. The layout of her reports was the very last thing on Suki Yamato's mind.

Doing something that she had never done before, she glanced with disgust at the telegram one more time and then screwed it up and threw it across the room into the bin.

'That's what I think of your formats.'

She got up from her desk, packed her papers in the filing cabinet and locked it, draped her cotton jacket round her shoulders, turned off the light and made her way down the stairs and out into the courtyard. Bidding goodnight to the sentry on the gate, she took a deep breath of the fresh air and set off on foot for her rooms at the Monorom Hotel. Despite all the other privations of the posting, it was wonderful to be able to take in the air without first having to cut it with a knife and fork as in Tokyo. Still, no doubt it would all change eventually. If things worked out, the businessmen would be in here like a shot, selling their Datsuns and Suzukis, filling the streets with thick, blue diesel fumes before you could blink. It seemed to be the way in so many Third World countries. Suki had worked in a number of them for the UN, the Red Cross and other relief agencies. The first thing everyone wanted was a Honda scooter and then a pick-up. Cambodia had been different. People had suffered too much for that, but who could tell how the next generation might feel?

Turning into the grounds of her hotel, she almost jumped out of her skin when a figure emerged from the bushes.

'Hi there.'

'Jesus, Jerry! You almost scared me to death. What the hell do you mean, creeping up on me like that?'

The tall, handsome American bared his teeth in a relaxed smile that he knew the ladies found irresistible.

'I reckoned you wouldn't be much longer, so I decided to wait.'

Regaining her composure, Suki carried on across the lawn.

'Yes, I noticed you never waste any time in getting out of the office.'

'Hell, why shouldn't I? I'm sick of this shit-hole of a country. The goddam Khmers can have it for all I care.'

'You don't seem to care about anything or anyone.'

'I care about you.'

'Sure you do, Jerry. All the way to the bedroom.'

Jerry Mandelson laughed. 'Well, at least I'm honest. Come on, Suki. How about it? One more for the road?'

Turning on him, Suki looked with distaste at her ex-lover, hardly believing that she had ever been taken in by the blue eyes, Californian suntan and protestations of sincerity.

'I've told you it's over, so just go away, grow up, and leave me alone.'

She started to move away but he caught hold of her arm, gripping it tightly in his strong fist.

'Ow, you're hurting me. Let go.'

'Listen, Suki. I meant everything I said. I'm crazy about you. I always have been. Can't we try again?'

'What? Until the next dumb nurse or aid worker comes along and lifts her skirt for you?'

'Barbara meant nothing to me, you know that.'

'Sure I do. The moment she flew out of here you rediscovered your love for me. You fooled me once. Don't expect to do it again.'

Tearing away from his grasp, she went quickly into the hotel lobby, Jerry following behind like a stray dog.

'I need you, Suki.'

'You can get what you need behind the marketplace. Only you'll have to pay for it.'

'You'll be sorry.'

His words followed her as she quickly climbed the stairs to her room. Once inside, she locked the door and slid the bolt. She found that she was trembling and breathing heavily. Jerry Mandelson disturbed her. He was big trouble. At first, soon after her arrival in Phnom Penh, she was flattered by his attentions. He brought her flowers and made a big fuss, and stupidly she believed that he really loved her. One evening they had too much to drink, one thing led to another and he ended up in her bed. In the morning she realized that he had planned the whole thing, even lacing her drinks while diluting his own. But she didn't mind. It had been wonderful and she shrugged it off as just good fun.

But Jerry grew ever more demanding and the tender side of his nature vanished. When she tried to distance herself to give them both time to sort things out he became violent. Eventually she had given in but it had been more like rape than lovemaking.

Finally Suki discovered that Jerry was sleeping with a British nurse, Barbara. It seemed that she didn't have Suki's qualms and so long as she got her fill of enjoyment, Jerry could do what he liked. It had provided Suki with the break she needed. With Jerry occupied with another woman, she had travelled up-country to observe the election process in the outlying towns and villages. By the time she returned Jerry appeared to have accepted the end of their relationship. At least until the departure of Barbara. But now he was back again. Suki had resisted him so far but he frightened her. She knew enough about him to know that he was not a person to be trifled with or taken lightly.

Closing the shutters, she went into the adjoining bathroom. After the feel of Jerry's hand on her arm she felt the need to run a hot bath and scrub herself clean. But she would have to be careful in future. There was no telling what a man like that was capable of.

The hotel grounds were in darkness. It was getting late and the generator had been turned off to conserve fuel. Leaning with his back against a palm tree, Jerry lit a cigarette and looked up at the glow of the oil-lamp from Suki's room. Although the shutters were drawn and he could only catch an occasional glimpse of her silhouette as she busied herself about the room, in his mind he could see every shape and contour of her, feel the smoothness of her skin and smell the scent of her. His imagination was almost driving him mad. She had no right simply to break off their relationship like that. OK, so perhaps he shouldn't have screwed around with Barbara, but she was the one who had seduced him. It wasn't his fault if the Brit had been crying out for it. And now Suki Yamato thought she was rid of him. Well, they'd see about that.

Checking in his pocket, Jerry counted out the loose change, and stubbing out his cigarette in the grass, he sloped away to buy some temporary relief with one of the market whores.

4

As soon as the plane doors were opened a rush of hot, moist air flooded the compartment.

'Welcome to Phnom Penh. Will all passengers please make their way through customs.'

Rising from his seat, Terry Williams stretched his legs and retrieved his hand luggage from the overhead locker. The short flight from Ho Chi Minh City had taken them across the Mekong Delta and Terry had been glad to have a window seat. Looking down at the network of waterways, thick jungle and paddy-fields, it was hard to imagine that it was already twenty years since the peaceful scene below him had been a ferocious battlefield on which the greatest superpower on earth had been humbled by a peasant army in flip-flops. Terry had grown up to news reports on television showing American GIs and bombing runs, and the Vietnam war had often been the main talk in the playground at school in Swansea. Now there was Vietnam below him, calm and peaceful.

Staring at the watery green and brown landscape, Terry shook his head in wonder. 'How are the mighty fallen, and the weapons of war perished.'

He still thought of Ho Chi Minh City as Saigon, and had managed a brief walk into the centre of town before the connecting flight to Cambodia. It had all been there, from the newsreel memories of his childhood. This was it. He had finally made it to 'Nam.

Stepping out into the sunlight he looked around at the ramshackle buildings that made up Phnom Penh airport, wishing his assignment had been in Vietnam instead. Still, so long as they were paying him he didn't mind. He could work anywhere if he set his mind to it.

A figure scurried across the tarmac as Terry ambled off the steps.

'Mr Williams. Please come with me.'

'What about customs?'

'Never mind customs. The Minister is waiting for you.'

Too bad we don't have the same system at Heathrow, Terry thought, following the clerk towards an ancient battered car into which his suitcase and bergen were already being loaded.

Swinging out of the airport gates, the car turned towards the centre of town and set off at speed. From his seat in the front the clerk turned round and grinned at Terry.

'Welcome. We have been waiting for you, Mr Williams. The others are already here.'

'How many are there?'

'Three more.'

'Anyone I know?'

'Mr Colin Freeman from Australia, Mr Craig Samuel from America, and Mr Tommy Liu from Hong Kong. You know them?'

Terry smiled. 'Colin and I were in Africa together and I last saw Mr Samuel in the Middle East, although he called himself Joshua then. American citizenship's obviously had an effect. Who's this Tommy Liu?'

'He was in the Hong Kong Military Service Corps.'

Terry stared. 'What? Where the hell did you drag him up from? The HKMSC's a bunch of gate guards, little more than TA.'

'TA?' the clerk said doubtfully.

'Territorials, weekend soldiers.'

'He was also Special Branch, Hong Kong Police. Anti-Triad squad.'

'Now that's more like it.'

Easing back in his seat, Terry watched the city's outskirts go by. He was starting to like the look of the place. It had a vital feel to it. Turning into a courtyard, the car pulled up outside the decayed structure of what had probably once been a very smart hotel.

'This is the Monorom Hotel. You will be staying here.'

'Fine by me. I could do with a shower.'

But before he could even open the door the car was pulling away down the drive again.

'Later, please. You have a meeting with the Minister in fifteen minutes.'

'What's the rush?'

'Please, Mr Williams. The Minister will explain everything.'

Exactly fifteen minutes later Terry found himself being ushered into the presence of the small, bent figure of Yon Rin. After shaking him warmly by the hand, the Minister showed Terry to a chair. The other three mercenaries were already seated and two of them exchanged nods of recognition with their old comrade-in-arms. Only Tommy Liu sat apart, silently wrapped in his own thoughts.

'Gentlemen, I thank you so much for coming,' Yon Rin began. 'You have arrived at a crucial time in my country's history. You will have read the background briefing material that I sent you which will have clarified the position of the Khmer Rouge in the border jungle regions. As you can imagine, if you are going to penetrate the defences of Comrade Lon San and put a stop to his planned offensive, it is vital that . . .'

In his chair Terry had gone suddenly cold. He coughed politely.

'Mr Williams?'

'Erm, excuse me. I may have got the wrong end of the stick, but what's all this about penetrating defences? I thought we were here to train up a palace guard.'

Yon Rin looked puzzled. 'Oh no. No, no, no. You are to train an élite, certainly. But after that your contract requires you to lead them on this mission to stop Lon San.'

'Stop Lon San?' Terry asked, fearing the answer.

Colin Freeman turned and grinned at him. 'Roughly translated, "stop" means "wipe out", "blow away", "terminate with extreme prejudice".'

Yon Rin blushed. 'Believe me, we are not proud that one of our first acts as a newly elected democratic government is to hire men such as yourselves to carry out a – how do you say? – a "hit". But in these extreme circumstances, extreme measures are necessary.'

'And what will the UN observers have to say about it?'

'The UN won't give a damn,' Craig Samuel chuckled. 'They're too chicken to do it themselves. You ever heard anything so ridiculous as asking the Khmer Rouge to respect the will of the people?'

'I fear Mr Samuel is right,' Yon Rin continued. 'The

UN might not be happy with our arrangement, but so long as it's kept discreet they will do nothing to stop it.'

Terry shook his head.

'Is something the matter?' Yon Rin asked.

'Well, it's just come as a bit of a shock, that's all. I didn't realize I was going on a bloody suicide mission. In fact, I'm not sure I'd have come if I'd known the true nature of the contract.'

Yon Rin frowned. 'That's a pity. You were to head the training team.'

'I'm not saying I won't do it, mind,' Terry cut in.

'Come on, Dojo,' Colin said as he leaned across and patted him on the shoulder. 'We're in. Come with us. I've heard this Lon San's got whole bucket loads of gems in his camp.'

'It's true,' Yon Rin urged. 'He uses them to bribe the Thai border commander, General Sarit Chamonon.'

Terry stared at the ground. OK, so he'd been caught off balance. But then what had he got to lose? His life? It wasn't worth much at the moment anyway.

'I'll have to completely rewrite my training programme.'

Yon Rin heaved a sigh of relief. 'You can have the use of my personal secretarial facilities.'

'Attaboy, Dojo,' Craig Samuel beamed at him. 'Now we're in business.'

Yon Rin went on to outline the Cambodian contribution to the mission. They had already selected a company of the best troops in the entire army, each man hand-picked. To lead them Yon Rin had chosen Captain Manyuk Tron, but Terry would be in overall command, aided by the other three mercenaries.

'The chosen men all have a great deal of battle experience, but what they lack are certain . . .'

'Skills and drills,' Terry interjected.

'Exactly. Our battles with the Khmer Rouge have generally been messy affairs which we have won because of our superior numbers. But time and again they outmanoeuvre us. In low-level contacts they are the best jungle fighters in the business. We need your help please, gentlemen.'

Terry looked at the men flanking him. 'Well, Minister, it's not much of a training team, but we'll see what we can do.'

With the initial briefing over, Terry and the others returned to the Monorom Hotel. After a shower, he unpacked, taking out the planned training programme and tearing it up. He pulled up a chair, sat at the desk with a fresh sheet of paper, thought for a moment, and then set to work drafting a new programme. The list of lesson plans unfolded rapidly beneath the heading he had written in bold capitals across the top of the page: 'Jungle Warfare – Infiltration and Attack drills'.

When he went down to dinner that evening, Terry found the others already at the bar. He was particularly keen to get to know Tommy Liu but found him reticent and unwilling to open up.

'I was based in Hong Kong myself,' Terry said cheerfully. 'Whereabouts did you live?'

Tommy sipped a cold beer. 'I doubt you'll have heard of it.'

'Try me.'

'Diamond Hill.'

Terry whistled. 'I know it. Hard place.'

Tommy shrugged. 'Brits never go there. Only us Chinks.'

'Let's get one thing straight,' Terry said. 'Don't write me off as another pig-headed racist. As a matter of fact I know Diamond Hill well. I used to have a good friend there.'

Tommy eyed him suspiciously. 'Who?'

'Lee Won.'

Tommy's eyes started out of his head. 'Sifu Lee Won?'

Now it was Terry's turn to sip casually on his beer. 'Sifu, Sensei, it's all the same. I used to exchange a few tips with him on unarmed combat. How is the old buzzard?'

Tommy was impressed. Sifu Lee Won was one of the greatest Kung Fu masters in the Territory. 'I believe he's well. Eighty-three and still teaching.'

Terry smiled at him. 'One of life's survivors. Let's hope we all are, eh?'

The four men went through to the shabby dining-room and sat down to eat. As the meal progressed, their conversation became ever more lively as they recounted war stories, each man trying to outdo the others. Terry was grinning at one of Craig Samuel's yarns when he noticed a girl enter the room and make her way to a table on the far side. Japanese, he thought, probably one of the foreign aid workers of whom there were plenty in Phnom Penh. Petite and slender, she was the most beautiful girl he had ever seen. She had a reserve and poise that Terry had only ever seen in eastern women. However, watching her out of the corner of his eye, he noticed that she was wary, frightened of something, and when a tall, intense young man entered the dining-room with his eyes fixed on her Terry realized what it was.

She was halfway through her main course when Mandelson sidled up to her table and sat down. At once Terry noticed her nervous reaction to the man. Before long the American placed a hand on the girl's knee under the table. She angrily brushed it off, whereupon he leaned close and whispered something in her ear.

Pushing back her chair, the girl got quickly to her feet and left the dining-room, unnoticed by everyone except Terry and the young man, who sat back grinning. Then, with an unpleasant look on his face, the man got up and hurried out after her. Terry played with his food for a moment but, on an impulse, wiped his mouth and got up to leave.

'Won't be a minute, lads.'

Colin Freeman grinned. 'Don't think I haven't noticed what you've been looking at.' He elbowed the other two. 'Dojo's on a quest, boys. A one-man rescue mission.'

Terry felt himself blush. 'No harm in checking the little lady's all right.'

The hotel lobby was empty, so moving as silently as he could, he edged slowly up the stairway until he heard voices.

'Come here, you fucking bitch.'

The American's voice was hard and rasping. He sounded as if he had been drinking. There was the sound of a slap, followed by a scuffle. In three bounds Terry was at the top of the stairs and in the first-floor corridor. The man had the girl against the wall. A red bruise marked his cheek where she had just hit him, but now he had her arms pinned behind her and was reaching under her skirt with his free hand.

'Let me go!' The girl tried to wriggle free but was held fast.

'Stand still, you slut. You know you want it.'

'I think the lady asked you to let her go.'

The man's head spun round at the sound of Terry's voice, though he kept his hands firmly on his prize.

'Who the fuck are you?'

Terry had moved to within striking distance of the American, but stood in the relaxed open *shizentai* stance, his feet planted the width of his shoulders apart and looking, to the untrained eye, to be standing normally. His arms hung at his sides, hands open, but the focus of his balance had dropped to the *tanden*, the pit of his stomach, and his eyes were centred on his target.

He spoke again in the same neutral tone as before. 'Let the lady go, now. There's a good chappie.'

With a snort of derision the American held Suki firmly in one hand and with the other threw a punch at Terry's face. The Welshman's response was swift and to the point. Sidestepping the punch with a *tai-sabaki* body shift, he drove his elbow into the American's side, feeling the wind go out of him. Swivelling to face the crumpling man, he executed a simple footsweep, completing his counter-attack with an open-handed *shuto* rabbit punch to the side of the neck. Slamming into the nerves and muscles running into the skull, the blow knocked the American unconscious. Stepping deftly out of the way, Terry let the man drop heavily to the floor, his head cracking nastily on the worn carpet.

'Oh dear, now,' he said. 'What a silly boy.' He

turned to the girl, who was shaking, hugging herself with shock.

'Are you all right, love?'

'I think I'm going to be sick.'

'I have that effect on some people,' Terry said smiling. 'Here, let me help you.'

Putting his arm round the girl, he led her towards her room. She looked back doubtfully at the body of Mandelson.

'Oh, he'll be all right,' Terry reassured her. 'Although of course he needn't be, if you want me to finish the job properly.'

'No, no,' she stammered. 'You've been very kind. If you hadn't come along I don't know what I'd have done.'

'Well, if he ever troubles you again, just let me know and I won't go so easy on him next time.'

Letting herself into her room, the girl went in silence to the bathroom and splashed cold water on her face. Standing awkwardly in the doorway, Terry was making a move to go, when she spoke.

'Would you mind staying a moment. I need someone to talk to. My name's Suki. Suki Yamato.'

Terry introduced himself.

'What brings you to Phnom Penh?' Suki asked. 'Are you with the Red Cross?'

'Not exactly. I'm working for the government, though.'

'Oh? Who?'

'A guy called Yon Rin.'

Suki's expression chilled. 'The little man in the Security Ministry?'

'You know him?'

'Yes.'

From her previous warmth, Terry noticed that Suki's manner had become more distant and formal at the mention of Yon Rin's name.

'Have I said something wrong?'

Suki dried her face on a towel. 'No. I'm very grateful to you for helping me, Mr Williams, but I'm afraid that as a member of the UN team here, I can't condone the use of mercenaries. We know all about Mr Yon Rin's plans and we consider it a gross misuse of aid money.'

'Ah. I see. And the Khmer Rouge? How do you suppose they would use the aid money?'

'It is our intention to bring the Khmer Rouge into the democratic process.'

Terry smiled sadly. 'I wish you the best of luck. But I think you stand as much chance of succeeding as you did in convincing your chum on the floor outside that you wanted to be let go.'

Suki dropped the towel on the bed. 'Then we must agree to differ.' She held out her hand. 'Thank you all the same for your help.'

Terry took her hand, her palm soft and warm but the grip firm. Here's a girl who knows her own mind, he thought. Too bad she works for a bunch of wet fish. She's wasted on them.

He was just going out of the door when she called after him.

'By the way, where did you learn to fight like that?'

'Okinawa.'

'Really?' She smiled, then added: 'We're not all Bruce Lees, you know.'

Terry grinned at her. 'I never thought you were.'

On the way down the corridor, he passed Mandelson,

who was getting shakily to his knees. Terry grabbed him by the lapels and grinned at him menacingly.

'Hello, boyo. Now you listen to me. I've never liked bullies, see. Stay away from that young lady and you won't get hurt.'

He tightened his grip on the American's collar.

'Night-night.'

At the head of the column, Tommy Liu jogged easily in the early-morning heat. He knew it would get considerably hotter as the day wore on but he was used to the humidity. Behind him, he could hear the rhythmic crunch of a hundred or so pairs of boots as the Cambodian company followed him out of the training compound on the edge of town and headed out along the road through the paddy-fields. Raised above the level of the billowing green rice, the dusty road curved gently between a mixture of paddy and thick secondary jungle. Tommy breathed deeply, happy to be into the training at last. The programme that Terry Williams had devised was demanding, but then it would have to be if the little force was to have a chance of absorbing everything it needed to survive when it went up against the Khmer Rouge.

It seemed to Tommy that Terry had thought of everything. They had started with basic weapon training and range work, and then moved on to jungle navigation and contact drills. Next Terry had put them all through a period of live firing on a close-quarter jungle shooting range that he had designed himself, with targets popping up all over the place and simulated explosions going off to give the soldiers the proper feel of battle. This morning they would all go through the last such range practice before turning to patrolling and attack lessons. Then it would be up to the men themselves and to the leadership of Terry, the other two westerners and Tommy himself.

Tommy had been given charge of the physical fitness side of training and of the close-quarter battle instruction. In the jungle, where the average enemy engagement happened at only a few yards' distance, it was essential that the men's reactions should be both instantaneous and deadly. Tommy's experience of fighting had mostly been in the urban jungle of Hong Kong, but in the narrow backstreets of Kowloon exactly the same principles applied.

The run to the training area took a good half hour, but by the time the company arrived everyone had warmed up and was raring to go. The soldiers had taken to Terry's programme like fish to water and even their grim commander had started to show his appreciation. But it had been hard going at the start. Captain Tron had obviously had his nose put out of joint by the employment of foreigners, and Tommy could sympathize with him. It had often irked him having Brits running all the key police and military posts in Hong Kong. But whereas that was partly an accident of history, this could be construed as a direct insult to the competence of the Cambodian officer corps.

Nevertheless, Tommy had been amazed by the change in Tron. The man had seen the value of the extra training his men were receiving and had appreciated at last that Terry Williams was a man with a great deal to offer.

Arriving at the jungle range, the Cambodian company was met by Terry, Colin, Craig and Captain

Tron. Colin and Craig each took a thirty-strong platoon to carry out separate training exercises, while Terry led the third platoon to the preparation area and briefed them on his own exercise. The platoon would split down into its three sections, each of which would then go through the jungle battle shooting range. With live ammunition and explosives, it would be a realistic morning's training at the end of which the men would have a firm grasp of Immediate Action Drills.

While Terry and Captain Tron took the first section through, Tommy took the remaining two sections for weapon drills, stripping and assembling the machine-guns, practising stoppage drills, reloading drills and the like. Half an hour later, the second section was called forward, the first one returning in a state of high excitement, full of praise for Terry's range design.

As the sections carried on under their own instructors, Tommy drifted to one side and gazed out across the paddy-fields. It was so peaceful that it seemed a shame to be letting off explosions and firing rifles on a day like this. A man cycled by, waving merrily. He grinned at the soldiers and, a little further along the track, got off his bicycle, leaned it against a tree and disappeared into the bushes to enjoy his morning bowel movement.

The second section had finished their practice and it was now the turn of the last section. Terry and Captain Tron were flushed with the heat, but even more so with the enjoyment of an exercise that was going well and from which all the soldiers were benefiting. Tommy noticed how well they were now getting along together, and as the Cambodian instructors continued with their lessons, Terry and Captain Tron led the final section back into the jungle to put them through the exercise. Tommy estimated that it would be about half an hour before he could signal to Colin to bring the next platoon forward.

The drone of the unfamiliar Cambodian language had lulled Tommy into a state of complete relaxation. Glancing down the road, he saw the cyclist re-emerge from the trees and, after hitching up his sarong, mount his bicycle and set off down the road, wobbling from side to side to gain his balance. Tommy frowned. There was something strange about the way he rode that Tommy didn't like. A sudden chill shuddered through his entire body. The cyclist was no longer riding with the same carefree ease as before, but rather he was hurrying, peddling away from the scene as if his life depended upon it.

As Tommy started to run, he shouted at the top of his voice.

'Dojo!'

There was a good two hundred yards to cover and already Tommy could hear the first bursts of fire from the troops as they started down the jungle battle lane. Reaching the fringe of the jungle, Tommy flung himself through the undergrowth towards the sound of the firing. Machine-guns fired in bursts and the blast of shotguns echoed through the trees as lead scouts engaged the variety of pop-up targets that Terry had laid out. Any minute now, Tommy thought. Any minute now.

Bursting into the open, Tommy found himself in a dry river-bed. Fifty yards ahead, Terry stood with his back to him, a pair of ear defenders muffling the sound of the shots and of Tommy's shouted warnings. Captain Tron looked round and saw him, his puzzlement turning to alarm as Tommy covered the final yards and flung himself bodily at them just as Terry reached down and tugged at the hidden cord that he had rigged to the simulated explosives.

Terry had set it himself, a single half-pound stick of plastic explosive at the side of the track. When the cord was pulled it would detonate the charge, showering the soldiers harmlessly with dust but adding to the sense of realism that created a worthwhile exercise.

As Tommy hit Terry in the square of the back, knocking him to the ground, the cord was already tightening, sending the required signal to the detonator that should have been buried in the heart of the PE. But instead of a harmless shower of dust, the detonator triggered a claymore directional anti-personnel mine, shattering the plastic matrix and rocketing a jet of seven hundred steel ball bearings across the river-bed where, a split second before, Terry had been standing.

In the eerie silence that followed the explosion, Terry got to his knees and shook his head to clear the humming.

'What the fuck was that?'

'Claymore.'

Behind him, Captain Tron got shakily to his feet, staggering towards the bodies of two of his men lying in pools of blood. Beyond them, another man groaned.

'I saw the guy who did it,' Tommy said. 'I thought he was just having a crap but he must have sneaked in here and rigged it up while you were changing the sections over.'

Wiping the dirt from his face, Terry went quickly to help Captain Tron apply field dressings to the wounded man. The other two were beyond help.

'I owe you one, mate.'

'Forget it,' Tommy shouted over his shoulder as he jogged away. 'I'll see if I can catch the fucker.'

As he prepared a syrette of morphine for the wounded soldier, Terry glanced up to see Captain Tron watching him.

'I am sorry, Mr Williams. This is my fault.'

'How's that?'

'My security arrangements should have been better.'

'We live and learn.'

Terry sat back on his heels and looked up at the sky between the overhead branches. 'At least we've discovered one thing. Lon San knows we're coming.'

'It's the very least I could do,' Captain Tron said as he led the four mercenaries up the drive of his family's villa in Phnom Penh. 'I'm afraid that our hospitality won't be what it was in the old days, but my sister and I very much want you to enjoy some real Cambodian cooking after the slop at the hotel.'

'I thought it was very nice slop,' Colin remarked as he admired the façade of the impressive building before him.

'Does your sister know what we're doing here?' Terry asked.

'I have only told her that you are here to assist us with a training programme. She knows nothing of our mission concerning Lon San.'

'Good.'

They had caught the saboteur on the bicycle but had failed to detect the cyanide capsule in time to prevent his suicide. Robbed of the only source of intelligence, they could not know how seriously their mission had been compromised. Terry hoped that although Lon San knew they were coming, he did not yet know the time, the route or the other details of their plan. Even so, from now on they were obviously targets and would have to exercise extreme caution.

Coming out on the top of the steps to meet the guests, Sitha greeted them with flowers, offering a small white lotus to each of them in turn. As each man received the gift he followed Captain Tron into the house. When Sitha finally came to Tommy Liu, they were alone on the steps, the voices of the others audible in the depths of the echoing vestibule, admiring the splendour of the building.

Accepting the white blossom, Tommy felt that he had never seen a girl as beautiful as Sitha in his life. A radiance seemed to emanate from her and their hands brushed as she gave him the flower. She too seemed confused by feelings that she couldn't account for.

'You live in a beautiful home,' Tommy said, reluctant to follow the others into the house.

'Thank you. I am sorry there are not more of my family here to greet you.'

Tommy nodded. 'I understand. Your brother's explained everything. I'm sorry. In Hong Kong, though, we feel that the spirits of the dead are all around us.'

Sitha smiled. 'Really?'

'Sure. Mind you, we never had quite as much space as this at home, so it was pretty cramped even without the spirits.'

Sitha laughed. 'That's all right. They don't take up much room.'

For the first time since Sitha and her brother had returned to the house, the places at the dining table were all taken that evening and the room was filled with the sound of laughter and conversation. Sitha had spent the day visiting the markets and had prepared traditional Cambodian dishes that had not been seen in the house since 1975.

'So tell me,' Manny said to Terry after the meal, when the plates had been cleared away and Sitha had poured them cups of strong black coffee, 'where did you meet Craig?'

Craig grinned from across the table. 'I'm not sure he'll want to tell you that one.'

'Oh?'

Terry squirmed. 'OK, go on. Tell him.'

'We were employed by an organization that was trying to get Israeli military hostages out of Beirut. God knows what Terry was doing there, but he turns up in the oddest places. Anyway, we'd just sprung a pilot free who'd been imprisoned for two years since being shot down over the Bekaa valley. But then the whole local militia came down on us like a ton of bricks.'

'What happened?'

'Well, we got away, but in the process Terry stopped some grenade fragments in a very sensitive part of his anatomy. We spent an uncomfortable night on a hillside before we were supposed to be picked up the next morning by helicopter. However, the cloud came down and the helis couldn't get to us, so we had to walk out. But before we could do that, someone had to remove the grenade splinters from Terry's . . .'

'All right, Craig, spare them the details,' Terry interrupted, his face scarlet.

'I'll leave the rest to your imagination, suffice it to say that I drew the short straw. But believe me,'

79

the American concluded, sipping his beer, 'he's got a lovely ass!'

Noticing that Sitha had left the table, Tommy excused himself and went to look for her. He found her on the veranda.

'I'm sorry about that.'

'Oh, that's all right,' she replied easily. 'It's nothing really.'

Remembering what she must have been through during her years of captivity, Tommy felt suddenly stupid for thinking that something as harmless as Craig's anecdote could upset her, but, seeing his confusion, Sitha placed a hand on his arm.

'But it's very nice of you to think of me. Thank you.'

They were silent for a while, listening to the cicadas and watching a full moon come out from behind the clouds.

'You know,' Tommy said at last, 'in Hong Kong you can hardly see the moon. The city lights blaze all night and it's only in the morning that you can catch a glimpse of it, pale and fading.'

'What's the name of your village?'

Tommy smiled. 'We don't really have villages any more, just a few in the New Territories. I come from a place called Diamond Hill.'

'That sounds very beautiful,' Sitha said wistfully. 'I can picture it.'

'I doubt that,' Tommy replied, suddenly embarrassed. 'It's a hell-hole. Tens of thousands of people crammed into a square mile of towering concrete.'

'Oh, I see. And you live there?'

'I'm not sure.'

'I don't understand.'

Tommy sighed. 'There are some people there who want to kill me if they see me again. Sort of like the Khmer Rouge, I suppose.'

'Ah.'

Sitha looked at his face in the pale light. It was surprisingly gentle for a soldier. In the space of the last few hours she felt as if parts of her, long denied, had reawoken in his company, and she had started to feel things for this strange, quiet man that she had thought herself incapable of feeling again.

'Then perhaps you had better stay in Cambodia.'

5

The programme that Terry had devised was so thorough and intense that after a week the results were already plain to see. After a further week, the Cambodian company had reached a standard where he was prepared to take them out on a prolonged exercise to put into practice all that they had learned so far. He had built on the firm foundation of their cumulative battle experience, but there had been a number of bad habits to expunge. On their mission to seek out Lon San they would be unable to call on the heavy fire support that they had grown used to. Also, stealth would be far more important than in the past, when they had operated with overwhelming superiority of numbers, for they were about to move into the depths of Khmer Rouge country, where it would be the enemy who were in the majority.

Pushing their way slowly through the dense bush, Terry's patrol was nearing the end of its final exercise. Terry, Colin and Craig had taken a platoon each, and the aim that Terry had set was that his own platoon should penetrate an area of jungled hill country outside Phnom Penh while Colin and Craig's platoons had to seek them out and stop them. So far all had gone well. Terry had been favourably impressed by the fieldcraft of his soldiers. They were quick learners and moved silently through the jungle. Captain Tron and

Tommy Liu had both remained in camp to co-ordinate the arrival of new weapons and the final preparations for the mission. Terry had been amused to notice how Tommy had leapt at the chance as an opportunity for furthering his growing friendship with Sitha Tron. He himself had tried to get reacquainted with the Japanese UN girl, but so far with only limited success.

Walking through the bush in the rear of the lead section, Terry found his mind wandering back to Suki Yamato whenever he allowed it to. They had had dinner together on one occasion, but Terry was afraid that Suki had only agreed out of a feeling of gratitude to him and not from any sense of attraction. Perhaps he was getting too old to pull the birds, he thought. It had to happen sooner or later.

Distressed at the thought, he was taken by surprise when the lead scouts hand-signalled an enemy sighting, dropping silently into cover. Crawling forward on all fours, Terry drew alongside the point section commander, who indicated the direction and range of the contact. A flood of satisfaction swept through him as he noted how, on halting, every man in the long, snaking single file had gone to ground, facing outwards to left and right alternately down the line, the gun team at the rear covering the way they had just come. Good, he thought. That's good. If anyone hit us now they'd find us ready and waiting.

Giving the signal for an immediate ambush, he noticed with further pleasure how each of the three sections slid effortlessly into its prearranged place. While the point section fanned out to provide the maximum amount of fire to the front in the direction of the approaching enemy, the second and third sections moved up to right and left forming the sides of a triangle. The whole effect was to provide a solid defensive position that could lay down fire with equal effectiveness in any direction. Terry was impressed.

Waiting until the enemy closed to within ten yards, Terry gave the order to open fire, springing the ambush. Using blank ammunition, the soldiers unleashed a withering fire and seconds later Colin's platoon was in turmoil.   However, Terry was glad to see that rather than run like rabbits as they had done on the first such exercise, they now scattered from the immediate danger of the killing ground and then returned fire while their two rear sections put in a flanking counter-attack. Terrific, he thought with delight. These boys are getting better and better. If only we had more time I could form them into a cadre of instructors and pass on this knowledge to the rest of the army. We'd have the Khmer Rouge licked before they could say, 'What the fuck?'

With the ambush sprung and the counter-attack driven off, Terry set about withdrawing his platoon in good order. But they had gone barely a hundred yards when they ran into Craig's platoon. Swinging into the Contact Front battle drill, they again formed a triangle and laid down another blast of withering fire before executing a perfect withdrawal in contact, leapfrogging backwards by sections using the fire-and-manoeuvre technique.

When all three platoons finally emerged from the jungle at the rendezvous where the transport was waiting to pick them up, there were bashful smiles on every face. They knew they had done well. Forming the men up in front of him, Terry gave them a few well-chosen words of congratulations and encouragement. Then, after piling into the convoy of vehicles, they sped back towards the training camp, singing for the first time as the day drew to an end and the sun went down.

'Did you see how the boys performed today?' Terry said admiringly in the bar of the Monorom Hotel later that evening after a shower and dinner.

'Of course, we heard you coming a mile away,' Craig answered casually, swigging his ice-cold beer. 'Pull the other one.'

Terry was just about to order another round when Colin coughed and indicated that they had company. Turning round, Terry saw Suki in the doorway of the bar. He beckoned her forward to come and join them but she shook her head.

'Won't be a minute, lads.'

'Like hell you won't.'

Going across to Suki, Terry drew her aside.

'What's the matter? You're looking pale.'

'It's Jerry.'

Terry sobered instantly, his jaw setting into a firm line. 'What's he done?'

'Nothing. At least not yet. He tried to get into my room earlier but I locked it just in time. He went round into the garden and shouted up that he was going to get me. He said he was going back to the office to get a gun.'

'Has he got one?'

Suki shrugged. 'I didn't think so, but perhaps he's bought one.'

Terry thought for a moment and then darted away up the stairs.

'I won't be a minute. Stay where you are.'

Going quickly to his room he took the Browning 9mm pistol from his suitcase and stuck it in his belt under his jacket, putting a couple of spare ammunition clips in his pocket as an afterthought. Back in the lobby he took Suki by the arm and led her out of the hotel.

'I'll need you to show me the way to your office but when we meet your friend, make yourself scarce and leave him to me, OK?'

'Why can't we wait here?'

'Best not to have a scene. Besides, there are too many people here. Someone might get hurt.'

Once out of the hotel grounds, Suki led the way through the streets of Phnom Penh towards the UN office block.

'Is this the route Jerry will have taken?'

'Yes. It's the most direct,' Suki replied nervously.

Terry reached across and took her hand. 'It's OK. I won't let him harm you.'

'You sound very sure.'

'I am.'

After walking for some time, Suki indicated that they were nearing their destination. They had entered a quiet part of town where the streets were deserted at this late hour. The last of the shops had pulled down their steel shutters and the bicycles that filled the streets in the daylight hours had disappeared.

'A regular ghost town, isn't it,' Terry observed.

'Shh!'

Pulling him into the shadows at the side of the pavement, Suki pointed to the office entrance. A light appeared briefly as someone slipped out of the building.

'It's him,' she whispered.

Terry pushed her gently aside.

'OK, sweetheart. Time to play. Stay here.'

Judging the route that Mandelson would take,

Terry nipped across the street and took cover behind a pile of rice sacks outside a food shop. Crouching down, he removed his jacket to allow himself greater freedom of movement. Peering through a narrow gap he could just make out the approaching figure of the lanky American.

Waiting until Mandelson was almost upon him, Terry suddenly shot his foot out in a *mawashi-geri* roundhouse kick, driving the ball of his foot deep into his solar plexus, jarring the vulnerable nerve centre and knocking the wind out of him. Mandelson dropped to the ground and curled into a tight ball, gasping for breath and retching violently.

Darting from behind cover, Terry spun the fallen man on to his stomach, yanked one hand behind his back in a half nelson and frisked the pockets of his jacket.

'Well, well, well, what have we here?'

Holding the gun up to the light, Terry examined the 9mm Beretta pistol.

'Nice hardware.' He cranked Mandelson's arm higher up behind his back until he cried out in pain. 'But what were you going to do with it?'

'Get your stinking hands off me!'

'Now, now. Mind your manners.' Terry tightened his grip on the American's arm, cranking it up even higher.

Suki came up beside them. Mandelson turned his head painfully to look at her.

'You fucking bitch. So this bozo's screwing you now, is he?'

There was a loud smack as Terry's free hand whiplashed into the side of Mandelson's head in a backhanded *uraken* blow.

'If there's one thing I can't stand it's a man who doesn't know how to speak to a lady.'

Pulling the semi-conscious American to his feet, Terry decided to take him back to the hotel.

'There's no point trying to find a copper at this hour. The lads and I will take care of him until the morning and then hand him over to the authorities. He'll be out of the country and out of your life by tomorrow lunchtime.'

Suki tried to smile but the sight of her tormentor, albeit in the firm grip of Terry Williams, was unsettling.

Half-dragging, half-carrying the limp figure, Terry and Suki set off for the Monorom Hotel.

'So what's the story between you two, then?' Terry asked as they turned down a side-street to try out a short cut.

'We all make mistakes.'

'True, but this one's a real humdinger,' Terry said, jerking roughly on the American's collar.

'He seemed so sweet. It's odd how you can trust someone and yet be so wrong.'

Suki was silent for a while, but then asked: 'Are you married?'

'Sort of. My wife and I are separated.'

'I'm sorry.'

'So was I.'

Terry was just about to tell her about Liz, when he noticed a small, trim Cambodian man walking briskly down the street towards them, smiling broadly.

'Miss Yamato! Terry! I've been looking everywhere for you.'

Without taking his eyes off the man, Terry whispered to Suki.

'Friend of yours?'

'I've never seen him before in my life.'

As the man closed to within thirty yards of them, something caught Terry's eye, the slightest movement of shadow from the side of the street, undetected by Suki but to Terry a clarion call to arms.

Swinging the limp body of Mandelson in front of himself and Suki, Terry used the American as a shield just in time to stop a burst of sub-machine-gun fire. Feeling the rounds impact on the juddering body, Terry thanked his lucky stars that his attackers were not equipped with high-velocity weapons whose bullets would effortlessly have cut through all three of the people in their line of fire.

'Stay behind me!' he shouted at Suki.

Holding fast to his human shield, Terry backed away towards the side of the street. Further rounds now being directed at him from another angle indicated the presence of at least three attackers. When he was within striking distance of the nearest side-street, Terry threw Mandelson forward and, dragging Suki by the arm, dived into the protective shadows.

Breaking his fall, he rolled aside, drawing his Browning in the same fluid movement.

'Take this,' he shouted, tossing Mandelson's Beretta to Suki.

Catching it, she stared dumbly at the large black handgun.

'I don't know how to use it.'

Terry reached over, cocked the Beretta and flicked off the safety-catch.

'Just point it at anyone you see and pull the trigger. It'll give you fifteen shots.' He demonstrated the two-handed combat grip. 'Hold it like this. You've seen the movies, haven't you?'

Uncertainly, Suki aimed the pistol at the far side of the street.

'Open your eyes, for God's sake!'

When she fired, the barrel of the gun flipped up in the air, but bringing it back into the aim, she squeezed off a second round and Terry saw splinters fly from the wooden shutter next to the muzzle-flash of one of their attackers.

'Good girl!'

Further down the street another man decided to change his fire position to get a clearer shot at the British mercenary. It was the last thing he ever did. Steadying his aim against the corner of the wall, Terry fired a rapid double tap and the man crumpled and lay still.

But even as he was engaging the moving target, Terry's mind was working hard. It sometimes seemed to him that he functioned best under extreme pressure and now, once again, his mind was identifying and sifting the options, balancing them against the threat, evaluating and selecting. The enemy knew his exact location and although they could no longer get a clear line of fire on to him or Suki, Terry knew that they would soon sort that out. They were probably keeping him pinned down while others in the ambush team worked their way round the back. If Terry stayed put he was dead. Of that he was certain. He had taken out one of his attackers but complacency would be his death certificate. He had to keep ahead of the game and try to seize back the initiative. He had to move.

Checking behind him, Terry noted a dark alleyway leading deeper into the maze of narrow streets. It would lead him away from the Monorom Hotel, but also away from the ambush killing ground. But then it could be a come-on, an escape route purposefully left open to lure him into the real killing ground. That was a chance he and Suki would have to take.

'Follow me,' he shouted, doubling back past Suki into the alleyway.

'Where are you going?'

'Just do as I say!'

Impressed by Terry's confidence, Suki darted after him, glancing back over her shoulder and loosing off a single wild shot for good measure at the gunmen concealed opposite. But her head was still reeling from the shock of the ambush, coming as it did on top of Mandelson's threat. Amidst the blur of emotions she realized that she didn't feel any sorrow at his death; he had threatened to kill her and Terry had found a gun on him. She had no doubt that he would have carried out his threat. She owed her life to this strange man in front of her, moving like a snake along the side of the alleyway, his senses taut for the first sign of the enemy.

But who were the attackers, and was it Terry or herself they were after? Suki was just about to ask Terry where he was taking her when he signalled for her to freeze. At first she heard nothing. The firing from behind had ceased and the air was still and humid. Looking down at the front of her blouse, she saw that it was soaked with sweat and smeared with dirt from the street.

Then, as she opened her mouth and tuned her ears into the silence, she heard the barely perceptible sound of shuffling feet, sliding towards them from around the corner some yards ahead. Whoever it was, they had also heard her and Terry, for a second after the two of them stopped to listen, the sound stopped also. Terry dropped silently on one knee and brought his pistol into the aim. To Suki, he appeared to move with the ease of a big cat close to its prey, and she was comforted by the thought that from being hunted they had, for the moment, become the hunters.

Suddenly, everything happened at once and for Suki it was as if time had stopped. Seconds could no longer keep pace with the speed of the close-quarter battle that erupted in the confined space of the back alley. A head appeared tentatively round the corner and with an instant double tap, Terry removed the exposed right side of the face. Toppling into the dirt, the body fell still clutching its sub-machine-gun, but it had hardly hit the ground before two more men burst from cover and began spraying wildly from the hip. But Terry had foreseen this possibility and was rolling away before the second round had left his pistol.

The men had fired without acquiring their targets and Terry knew that it would be a few rounds before they were able to bring their guns on line. In that brief space of time he took out the first man and then, switching targets and ignoring the bullets snapping ever closer to him, calmly shot the second through the centre of the chest. He seemed as cool as if snap-shooting on a thirty-metre range in Aldershot.

Although he had been counting his rounds and knew that he had enough for perhaps one more short engagement, Terry prepared to reload. Taking a full magazine from his pocket, he held it ready and then snapped the old magazine out of the butt of his Browning. He was sliding the replacement into the butt when the top round sprang free, jamming the mechanism. Cursing himself for trying to rush it, Terry shook the round loose. But before he could complete the reload, a shadow flickered across his peripheral vision and he flung himself instinctively forward, clasping the unloaded weapon to his chest as he tried to execute another forward roll.

A gun roared from behind him and in the moment's confusion he thought they had been surrounded. But then he remembered Suki and glanced back to see her blazing, the Beretta tight in the two-handed grip that he had shown her.

'Terry, look out!'

Jerking his head back, he felt the rush of air as a machete scythed past his face and buried itself in the wall. Still on his knees he steadied himself and then drove forward with an *empi* elbow strike. In the process he dropped his pistol but the fight had progressed beyond a shoot-out now. With his hands suddenly free, Terry went into action. His elbow strike had made contact with his attacker's ribcage. However, Terry had reacted hastily and the focus and distancing were wrong. A blow that should have shattered the ribs and incapacitated his opponent did little more than wind him and there was no time for a follow-up because a second figure was already upon him.

Jesus, Terry thought, how many of the buggers are there? Unable to get a clear shot and fearing she might hit Terry by mistake, Suki watched helplessly. There were now three men around Terry and as the mêlée swung across the alley, she shifted to left and right for a clear line of fire.

One of the Cambodians had grasped Terry round the body, pinning his arms to his side, but instead of waiting for the other two to begin the beating that they intended, Terry leaned back, allowing his captor to take his full weight, and shot out both feet, simultaneously hitting the two men facing him. Once again he had been unable to give the blows the necessary focus but it was enough to buy him valuable breathing space.

Turning his attention to his captor, Terry raked his boot down the man's shin and at the same time drove his head backwards into the man's face. The assailant grunted with pain but before he had quite released his grip, Terry locked hold of his arm and bending forward from the waist, flung the man over his shoulder in an *ippon seoinage* one-arm shoulder throw.

Before the other two could recover, Terry was upon them. The first received a rapid double punch, first the left fist and then the right powering into his face, dropping him unconscious to the ground. By now the third man was on his feet and spinning into a backkick aimed at Terry's head. Swiping it easily aside with a palm-heel block, Terry executed a *kansetsu geri* stamping kick on the knee of the attacker's supporting leg. With a sickening crack the joint gave way. The man screamed out in pain and as he toppled to the ground, Terry dropped a *tettsui* hammer blow on the crown of his head.

Retrieving his pistol, Terry snapped the full magazine into the butt and cocked it.

'You OK?' he asked Suki as he checked on his fallen opponents.

She stared at the bodies dumbfounded. 'Jesus, Terry. You're a one-man disaster area.'

'Only to those who get in my way.'

'Who were they? What did they want with us? They knew our names.'

'That's what I intend to find out,' Terry said as he rifled through the men's pockets for any signs of identification.

'Hello, what's this?' He pulled out a small plastic wallet containing various papers. 'Bingo.'

He was just about to resuscitate the men to take them prisoner, when he heard the sound of running feet from the street behind him. Realizing that there could still be others unaccounted for, he quickly retrieved another wallet and then, pulling Suki by the hand, led her down the alleyway and away from the ambush site.

'We can't just leave them here. They tried to kill us!' Suki protested.

'I don't like it any more than you do, but let's just be thankful we're still alive.'

Back at the hotel, Terry checked that Colin, Craig and Tommy were all right, telling them of the ambush and warning them to stay alert and watch their backs. Then he telephoned Captain Tron to ask him to come over as a matter of urgency, and waited while a search party was hurriedly assembled. But when they returned to the site of the ambush all evidence of the attack had been removed, including the body of Jerry Mandelson.

'We'll probably find him floating in the river tomorrow morning,' Manny Tron observed laconically. 'The story will doubtless be put around that he tangled with the brothers of one of his prostitutes.'

Reluctant to give up the search, Manny had the backstreets combed until even he was convinced that the attackers had escaped, and with the first dawn light appearing in the sky he escorted Terry back to the Monorom Hotel.

'My Intelligence boys will have a good look at the documents you seized. I'll let you know the results in the morning.'

Terry rubbed his eyes sleepily. 'It is the morning.'

Manny smiled. 'You did a good job out there last night. I'm glad I'll be on your side when we get into the jungle.'

When Manny had gone Terry slipped off his shoes and collapsed on to the bed, but as he was sliding into sleep a knock at the door jerked him awake. He grabbed his Browning and stepped quickly across the room.

'Who is it?'

'Me. Suki.'

'One minute.'

'Can I come in. I can't sleep,' Suki said, as Terry opened the door.

'Oh?'

'Be reasonable. It isn't every day you get ambushed. At least I don't.'

'No, I suppose not.'

She stood in the centre of his room. 'Can I sleep with you?'

'Now that's what I call an offer I can't refuse.'

'I mean here, on the couch.'

'Oh,' Terry said. 'I tell you what. You have the bed and I'll take the couch.'

Switching off the lights, Terry punched the cushions, wrapped himself in a thin sheet and curled up on the sofa with his feet sticking off the end. From the bed Suki's sleepy voice called across.

'Are you all right over there?'

'Couldn't be better.'

'Terry, I haven't said thank you. You saved my life.'

'All part of the service, love. All part of the service.'

The following day Captain Tron arrived early at the hotel and confirmed that the men who had ambushed Terry and Suki were Khmer Rouge.

'I've spoken to Minister Yon Rin and we both think that we should advance the timing of the operation. The next assassination attempt might succeed.'

Sitting round a table in the hotel bar, the four mercenaries and Captain Tron weighed up the options.

'But now they know we're coming,' Colin said, 'surprise has been lost. Whenever we go we're likely to walk into a trap.'

'You're very quiet, Terry. What do you reckon?' said Manny.

'Colin's right. However, they can't cover every approach. Even the Khmer Rouge haven't got the manpower for that, especially after the success of the army's latest offensives.'

'What are you suggesting?'

Terry sipped his beer. 'What we need are diversions. Lots of them. Tell Yon Rin to send out company-sized groups identical to ours, in all directions. We'll disguise the exact time of our departure and route. If we weave ourselves in among the patrol routes of all the other companies, the Khmer Rouge won't know which one's the real assault company or which direction we're going to hit them from.'

Manny sat back. 'I like it. I'll speak to Yon Rin today.'

Getting up to leave, he asked how Suki Yamato was doing. Terry smiled. 'She's a bit shell-shocked but otherwise OK. She's quite a girl that one.'

Craig nudged Colin and grinned. 'I never thought I'd see the day. Dojo's in love.'

'Shut it, you two.'

'Well, in that case you'd better bring her with you when you all come to dinner this evening,' Manny said as he pushed back his chair and got up to leave.

Knowing this would be the last visit of the mercenaries before they left for the north, Sitha had prepared a special meal of spiced fish and curried pork. When she heard their voices coming up the driveway she hurriedly checked her dress before going to greet them at the front door.

'Hi there. Sitha, this is Miss Suki Yamato,' Terry said, introducing his companion. 'She's a UN observer but tonight it's me that's observing her.'

Sitha shook Suki warmly by the hand, and then showed everyone inside. Hanging back, Tommy Liu self-consciously handed her a small bunch of flowers.

'They're not much but I'm afraid they're all I could find.'

Sitha smelt the brightly coloured petals. 'You couldn't have known it, but these are my favourites.'

Tommy's face brightened and as they entered the hallway he slipped his hand into hers.

All through the meal Sitha could feel Tommy's eyes on her and whenever she met them she smiled, the joy surging through her, oblivious to the conversation around the table. Craig and Colin had each brought a bottle of brandy and when the meal was over the little party retired to the veranda to continue their talk and to drink the brandy in the cool night air.

As Craig and Colin were discussing the finer points of patrol techniques with Manny, Suki leaned closer to Terry.

'Have you noticed Tommy and Sitha?'

'What about them?'

Suki stared at him in exasperation. 'You men are incredible. You can detect the signs of an ambush but when two young people are falling in love in front of your very eyes, you're as blind and as deaf as the dead.'

Terry blinked in surprise. 'Who's falling in love?'

Suki dug him hard in the ribs. 'Look, you idiot!'

Following her eyes, Terry glanced across to the end of the veranda, where Tommy and Sitha were standing side by side.

'They're just having a chat.'

'A chat?' Suki said, incredulous. 'They were gazing into each other's eyes all through dinner. You were too busy eating to notice.'

'You bet. I'll leave it to you girls to natter away about love and all that.'

Suki eyed him shrewdly. 'You said your wife was divorcing you. I bet you've no idea why, have you?'

Terry shrugged. 'Irreconcilable differences, she said. Couldn't have put it better myself. We just wanted to go in opposite directions, that's all. Quite simple, really.'

'And what do you think it must have been like for her, being married to a mercenary?'

'I know it wasn't easy,' Terry replied. 'But it's all I ever wanted to be. A professional soldier.'

'Then why didn't you stay in the army?'

'The peacetime life of a garrison soldier wasn't for me. It's hard to explain.'

'Try.'

'Well, take the fight we had in the Phnom Penh ambush. It sounds kind of odd, but you know you're alive at moments like that.'

Suki laughed. 'It sounds bloody mad, not just odd.'

'Well, you asked me. And there's another thing which I don't tell many people.'

'What's that?'

Terry felt a blush rising in his cheeks. 'It feels good to be able to help folks like these. I mean, the Khmer Rouge are a bunch of murderous butchers and I really believe in what we're doing here.'

'So do I,' Suki replied. 'That's why I joined the UN. You don't have to kill people to help the world, you know, Terry.'

Terry poured himself another brandy. 'Are you sure about that? The Khmer Rouge don't give a damn about the UN. It's the same with the Serbs in Bosnia. There are some people who only respect force. The world's not a simple place. With some people, it's no good simply asking them to stop the killing and put down their arms. They just won't listen to reason.'

'And that's where you come in?'

'Yes.' Terry swirled his brandy, staring into the glass. 'I'm not always proud of what I do. It's a dirty job but someone's got to do it.'

Suki reached across and took his arm. 'A little while ago I would have argued you into the ground.

But after last night I'll call it quits and let you off the hook.'

Terry looked at Suki and smiled, raising his glass in a toast.

'This could be the start of a beautiful friendship.'

6

As the preparations for the expedition entered their final phase, Terry and Captain Tron discussed with Yon Rin the deployment of the decoy companies. It was eventually agreed that ten of them would be enough and as the mission to destroy Lon San was a top priority, the army was ordered to provide the extra companies and anything else that Captain Tron required.

One final shipment of arms completed the equipment that Terry had deemed necessary for success, and when the last-minute familiarization training was complete all the soldiers of the company were given a forty-eight-hour period of rest before departure. Some of them had asked for leave so as to visit their families, but reluctant to risk any further compromise of security, Terry ordered everyone to remain in camp.

On the morning of departure, Suki and Sitha came to see the men off. Giving Tommy a small pendant, Sitha said: 'I wish it had been a family heirloom, but the truth is the Khmer Rouge took everything. I went to the market especially and found it there.'

'It's beautiful,' Tommy replied, holding the chain in his hand and watching the pendant catch the light as it turned.

'It's engraved with a picture of the Buddha,' said Sitha.

Nearby, Suki smiled playfully at Terry. 'I only came because Sitha needed a lift,' she said.

'Sure,' Terry laughed. 'Why else?'

'Be careful,' she said as she reached up to kiss him lightly on the cheek.

'That's how you'd kiss your grandad. Come here.' Putting his hands on her shoulders, Terry kissed her on the mouth. Behind him Craig and Colin whistled.

Suki blinked in surprise. 'God, a romantic as well as a mercenary.'

'That's me. And when I get back we'll have dinner without all these grinning idiots leering at us.'

'I'd like that. I'd like it very much.'

Once aboard the trucks, the company joined a military convoy heading north along the main road towards Battambang. One decoy company had been flown by transport plane direct to the main Battambang airfield and had then made its way into the countryside, while another had flown to Angkor Wat, north of Siemreab. It was hoped that the Khmer Rouge would assume that the real assault company was one of these and not part of the large military convoy on the long overland slog up towards the border.

In the other trucks, the remainder of the decoy companies travelled with their equipment, arms and spare ammunition. Once they reached Battambang, they would fan out into the jungle and head in a broad swath towards the Khmer Rouge territory along the Thai border, but here on the road they provided some welcome extra protection in the event of a major ambush. Terry was happy with the plan and sat back in the rear of his truck; it had been decided that the four mercenaries should all keep out of sight on the road, only emerging at night. It was a sure bet that the Khmer Rouge would have spies watching the main routes and reporting on all troop movements. The sight of one white face would give the whole game away.

Peering through a hole in the truck's canvas canopy, Terry looked out at the passing countryside. It looked a rich land. The rice paddies were carefully tended and as the convoy wound its way along the banks of the Great Lake of Tonle Sap, Terry could see the fishermen in their boats and the busy steamers carrying trade from one end of the country to the other.

'You see,' Manny Tron said leaning across, 'it's as if we have all emerged from the Dark Age of Pol Pot and his henchmen. For us, it has been like waking up after a horrific nightmare.'

He ran his hand almost lovingly over his holster. 'They will never return,' he said with finality, his jaw set and the glint of battle in his eyes.

'Not if we can help it,' Terry added.

When darkness fell the convoy halted on the banks of the lake and as soon as Manny had checked that there were no locals about, the four mercenaries jumped out of the truck and stamped up and down to loosen their stiff limbs.

'We'll harbour here for the night,' Manny said.

'Fine by me.'

Terry had seen enough of Manny Tron to know that he would already have deployed clearing patrols and posted sentries. He had been impressed with the Cambodian's dedication and readiness to learn, and Manny's initial resentment at the employment of foreigners had vanished when he had seen how Terry and the others passed on their expertise without ramming it down anyone's throat or ridiculing the Cambodians' lack of polish.

When the food, cooked on open fires, was ready, Manny sat down beside Tommy to eat. It wasn't long before he found the chance to broach the subject of his sister.

'I haven't seen her like this since . . . well, never, come to think of it. Before the Khmer Rouge came she was just a child, and afterwards we were simply happy to be alive. You've become very important to her, you know.'

'She's important to me as well,' Tommy replied.

Manny pushed his food round his plate. 'It's just that I don't want to see her hurt. She couldn't take it. Not after all she's been through.'

'It's OK, Manny. I know what you're trying to say. I'm not good enough for her, is that it?'

'No! I don't mean that at all.'

'You mean that as a soldier I might get killed at any time?'

'Partly that.' His appetite gone, Manny put down his plate. 'I don't know what I mean. I suppose I'm just trying to say, don't go and get yourself killed, that's all.'

'That's all right, then. I've no intention of doing that.'

In his jungle base of Rurseng, Lon San was evaluating the latest intelligence reports from his agents in Phnom Penh. The fools had completely bungled two attempts to assassinate the leader of the mercenaries and now they had lost track of the entire blasted company. It was quite beyond Lon San how one man and his whore could escape a deliberate ambush and, what is more, eliminate a handful of his top men. Whoever this Dojo Williams was, he was proving to be a tricky opponent.

Lon San unrolled a large map on the bamboo table in his living quarters and scrutinized the various routes that branched out of Phnom Penh towards his base on the Thai border. His agent in Battambang had reported faithfully that the company had arrived there that morning by transport plane and Lon San had been on the verge of believing him, when his man in Siemreab had sent a similar message about the arrival of troops at Angkor Wat.

Then a convoy had been reported leaving Phnom Penh on the northwards route, bringing an estimated one thousand troops into the region. Balancing all the conflicting evidence, Lon San was desperately trying to work out the government's plan. It was obvious that most of the troops were decoys, but which ones?

Calling in his commanders, he briefed them on the situation and ordered an increase in patrolling.

'I believe they're going to hit us in the next few days. We can't be sure from which direction but it'll be your job to find out. I want ambushes on all track networks and junctions, on rivers, clearings and villages. If they try to come through the jungle itself they'll be harder to intercept, so I want saturation patrols criss-crossing the jungle in between all the main ambush sites.'

Turning to a model of the camp itself, he began to outline his plan for the defence.

'The airstrip runs along the eastern side of the camp. It's too big to defend but we can cover it with machine-gun fire. Anyone trying to cross it will enter a killing zone and be cut to ribbons. I want ditches dug around the actual camp itself and filled with bamboo panji stakes. We'll build sangars of timber and earth at each corner, and in the middle around the command complex I want more fire trenches and sangars. Any questions?'

As the commanders studied the model in silence, each focusing on his own particular task, Lon San surveyed them carefully. Each man was a hardened fighter who had grown up in the jungle. Like himself, they had never known a settled life or the peaceful routine of a village farm. For them the seasons broke simply in two, the campaign season and the rest period when the rains drenched the landscape, making warfare difficult. However, with government pressure increasing they were now obliged to fight all the year round. But with the arms from Colonel Kon that would soon change.

Looking out of the window, Lon San glanced at the airstrip. It wasn't as large as Sarit Chamonon's but then the General had no need of secrecy in the safety across the Thai border. Here in Cambodian territory the airstrip had to be concealed by a covering of young saplings and scrub. It was a laborious task removing them and preparing the strip to receive aircraft, but with the roads no longer completely in the hands of the Khmer Rouge the arms would have to be flown in. They were far too important to risk losing.

'Is everything clear?' he asked, bringing the briefing to a close. When no one moved Lon San picked up his Kalashnikov and strode to the door.

'Good. Follow me. I'll take you round the perimeter and show you exactly where I want the sangars built. This is going to be the final test of strength, comrades. If the government defeat us this time it will encourage the Thais to desert us. Even that bastard Chamonon.'

*　　　*　　　*

General Sarit Chamonon had given orders that he was not to be disturbed. Outside his private quarters, the sentries had been removed to an appropriate distance so that the General could enjoy the full pleasure of the afternoon without being overheard.

For an operational base, the General's border head-quarters was a sumptuous affair. The furniture had been flown in from Bangkok and the centre-piece of the main bedroom was an enormous bed with a cover of Chinese silk, embroidered with a golden dragon. It had been a gift from Eddy Passenta, along with the Burmese girl on top of whom the General was now grunting.

The beautiful cover was flung halfway across the bare wooden floor and, naked on the mattress, Sarit Chamonon's buttocks convulsed rhythmically. With her legs spread wide, the Burmese girl clutched at the bedsheet with her fists, rolling her head from side to side in a pretence of ecstasy. But the sweat that covered her light brown skin was the sweat of fear rather than sexual arousal, for when the General had last raped her she had been beaten for making it obvious that she had not enjoyed his lovemaking.

Pulling himself from the girl, Sarit Chamonon bent over her breasts and took a nipple in his mouth, running his hands the length of her smooth body, marvelling at the beauty of the Burmese village girls that he was using to restock his brothels. His business had suffered from the Aids scare, so the influx of new blood was a welcome lure to his customers. Of course it would only be temporary; even these beauties would be infected soon, but by then he would have discovered a new source of supply. For the moment, however, everyone was asking for the Burmese, and Lalin had seemed the loveliest of the lot.

The General had no idea how old she was but she had been untouched when Fat Eddy had delivered her. In fact, Sarit Chamonon had almost thought that he might keep her for himself, although he had decided against it in the end. She didn't have a clue what to do, but just lay back like a corpse and let him get on with it. It was no fun at all and he had resolved to be rid of her, packing her off to Bangkok when the next batch of girls arrived from Chiang Mai. Then he would select a new one and Lalin could perform her miserable act for the German businessmen.

He put his mouth close to her ear. 'Do you love me, Lalin?'

'Yes. I love you,' she answered woodenly.

'Good girl.'

Rolling over, the General took her by the waist and pulled her on top of him, wriggling his pale hips until he was inside her again.

'Now, Lalin, now,' he commanded.

Bucking mechanically, Lalin forced herself to groan as she felt the Thai General push upwards. Not daring to look him in the face, she clenched her eyes tightly shut, blotting out the pain and the sight of the man she hated most in all the world. She threw back her head and moaned, her tongue moistening her lips as he had shown her. But that had been in another world, when she had been new and unsoiled by the monster who had defiled her.

Feeling the General tighten under her, Lalin waited for the burning rush deep in her loins before faking her own orgasm, gripping the General's thighs with her knees and dropping slowly forward on to his chest with convulsive shudders. Opening her eyes, she glanced sidelong at the Thai commander, oblivious in his own private ecstasy. Wondering at his momentary vulnerability, she fought to suppress the flood of hatred burning beneath her fear and disgust. If there had been a dagger to hand she would have been unable to prevent herself from using it. But it wouldn't even take that; a shard of glass would do.

Terrified by her own thoughts, Lalin slid from the General's embrace. He would expect her to be gone by the time he awoke.

The moment they entered the bush Terry insisted that full movement discipline was observed. They had debussed from the trucks at a bend in the road where the jungle came right up to the verge. Barely stopping, the convoy had disgorged the company and then sped away to disembark yet another company five miles further on in equal secrecy. By repeating the process throughout the region, it was hoped to confuse the Khmer Rouge still more. Each company was treated with equal care as anything less would have stood out to a professional observer as a set-up.

The company marched for a full half hour before halting to sort itself out. Wanting to put a good distance between themselves and the drop-off point, Terry waited until they reached a heavily wooded crest line before signalling the company to go through the triangular harbour drill.

Once everyone was in position, each of the three platoons forming one side of the triangle, Terry ordered out the clearing patrols and only when these had returned to report the area free of enemy were the sentries posted. With practised ease, a machine-gun

110

team moved out from each corner of the triangle, walking until just beyond hearing range before taking cover and setting up their guns.

At last, with his defences set, Terry called in the commanders, secure in the knowledge that they could converse in whispers without any risk of being overheard by the enemy.

'Right then, lads, from now on I want everyone to stay alert.'

'What's a lert?'

'Ha, bloody ha. Thank you, Colin. For that your platoon can take point for the rest of today. Thereafter I'll rotate the order of march to give everyone an equal share of the burden. I'll travel immediately behind the point platoon. Manny, you stay with me, right?'

'Right.'

'Tommy, your platoon will go in the centre for today, while Craig brings up the rear. You should all be happy about the Immediate Action Drills: we've rehearsed them bloody often enough.'

There was a chorus of moans from the group.

'Lovely. Nothing like a bunch of happy campers. What's the matter, Colin? You look as if you're about to give birth.'

'What if we do have a contact? We can't just turn back. I mean, it's pretty likely that we'll bump into the Rouge at some time or other before we reach the camp.'

'I'll be surprised if we don't. In fact, I hope we do. The lads can use the practice. But the ten other companies are going to be having contacts as well. With luck we'll keep Lon San guessing until the last moment.'

'When do we make the hit?'

'Three days' time. That's when the arms are being flown in. The plan is to take the lot. One day late and we'll be walking into a hornet's nest. And a well-armed one at that.'

For the rest of the first day Terry led the company on a straight line towards the camp at Rurseng. When they got closer he would start to dog-leg, but for now his main concern was to put some distance behind him; the more ground they covered now, the slower they could go when they neared the objective, and in that last vital stage stealth would be of the essence.

Harbouring for the night, he again waited until the clearing patrols had checked the perimeter and sentries had been deployed, before allowing the men to rest and eat, and before calling in the commanders to go through the next day's march. But halfway through the briefing, one of the sentries gave the signal for enemy sighting.

A stand-to was ordered and every man rolled over into the shell-scrape that he had prepared, brought his rifle into the aim and prepared for a contact battle. Crawling forward to the corner of the triangular harbour that had signalled the contact, Terry peered through the dense undergrowth. Luckily the company had had time to complete the camouflaging of the position and Terry knew that the enemy would virtually have to trip over them to see that they were there.

For two minutes all was still and he began to wonder if the sentry had been imagining things, spooked by his first night back in the jungle. But then something caught his attention. High above the jungle floor the top of a sapling moved suddenly, and a moment later Terry heard the unmistakable sound of a human footfall. But whoever they were, they were good. There was no sound of voices and they were moving as quietly as anyone could in the jungle. Then everything went silent. Nothing moved, nothing stirred and no one breathed.

This is it, Terry thought. The listening game. He played it himself every day, halting the column for ten minutes of every hour simply to listen to the sounds of the jungle. It was the best way to detect another human presence, but in such close proximity to the enemy it became a battle of discipline and nerves. He was certain that the Khmer Rouge, only yards away yet still invisible, were unaware of his presence. But all it would take to give him away was for one frightened soldier to panic and open fire.

The minutes passed and still no one stirred, and Terry admitted to himself that he was impressed. The intensive training had paid off. High above them in the treetops a monkey hooted and swung away, and all around the jungle hummed gently with the sounds of nightfall. Then, when the tension had become almost unbearable, another sapling waved, the footfall sounded softly again and the Khmer Rouge patrol moved off.

Terry looked at the soldier next to him, who broke into a huge grin of pride and gave him the thumbs up. Terry winked in reply and crawled back to the centre of the harbour.

'Manny,' he whispered, 'give it ten minutes and then prepare to move.'

Manny looked at him in surprise. 'Move? But it'll be dark soon.'

'I don't give a damn. Just because they didn't attack doesn't mean they didn't detect us. There might have been only a couple of them and they decided to go for reinforcements. I don't intend to wait to find out. A comfortable night's sleep isn't worth dying for. Always assume the worst and act accordingly – that way you'll live longer.'

As the company repacked its equipment and snaked out of the harbour position, Terry ignored the glares of resentment. They would find another harbour in an hour or so, but only once he was happy that they were in the clear. Then he would insist on going through the whole procedure of patrols, sentries and the myriad other standard harbouring drills. They had been worked out and tested in battle. He was damned if he was going to ignore them just because the men were tired. Jungle warfare was an exhausting business of meticulous attention to detail. Against a capable enemy, the slightest slip could lead to disaster, and whatever else they were, the Khmer Rouge were certainly capable.

The city of Kunming had grown considerably since Colonel Leonard Kon had lived there as a boy. It was hard to believe the extent of the changes that had taken place in China since the death of Mao and the fall of the Gang of Four. The opening up of the country to foreign investment had gone slowly at first but by the mid-1980s the trickle had become a torrent. It had taken a while to filter down as far as Kunming in the far south-western province of Yunnan, but it had arrived eventually, and with it the greatest of all of capitalism's benefits: corruption.

From an insignificant officer in the Chinese People's Liberation Army, Colonel Kon had become a key player in the illegal arms trade. He had started off shipping arms to the Khmer Rouge when it had all been legitimate. Then Beijing had been obliged to distance itself from its erstwhile allies. Trade with America and financial aid from western businesses had become more important.

For his part, Colonel Kon didn't give a stuff. The Khmer Rouge were murderous thugs and as far as he was concerned they could rot in hell, if there was such a place. But taking note of the new directive to diversify the Chinese economy, he had set up his own arms smuggling business: since the PLA had been cut by up to a million men, there was a vast stock of surplus weaponry available, and as an officer in the army's Supply Branch, Colonel Kon had been the right man in the right place at the right time to take full advantage of the opportunity, channelling the hardware into the illegal arms market.

In a very short time he had become both wealthy and powerful. Of course, he kept his sideline as secret as he could, but whenever any official poked his nose in Colonel Kon simply paid him off with handsome bribes. As well as getting them off his tail, it gave him a certain future blackmailing leverage until eventually he owned a network of corrupt party officials all securely in his debt.

Strolling through his warehouse, Kon ticked off the latest Khmer Rouge shipment on his millboard, thinking all the while of Lon San. The man was as cold as a fish. It was like talking to a sheet of glass; there was nothing there at all – certainly nothing human. He wasn't too happy with the idea of flying the arms directly into Cambodia but Lon San had been adamant that he needed them at Rurseng. The Colonel always enjoyed the usual run to General

Sarit Chamonon at Paksaket; he always went himself and the General took good care of his needs during the stopover. But he was damned if he'd stay at Rurseng more than the time it took to unload the crates. He was confident that Lon San would have the airstrip secured, but he doubted if the girls would have been arranged. He laughed at the thought. Lon San was probably a virgin. He probably thought that insemination was a type of political indoctrination.

Coming to the last of the crates, he ticked it off on his list, totalling up the separate weights to ensure that the single transport aircraft would be able to manage. It was a long haul to Rurseng and to allow for the necessary extra fuel he would be unable to provide quite everything that Lon San had ordered. Still, he would leave it to the Cambodian to find out. With luck he would only discover it once he had parted with his payment.

The thought of the gems made Kon's head spin. He had already prepared the channel to Hong Kong, where he would sell the majority of them, but he would keep a nice little reserve for himself as insurance against a rainy day. It was always hard to tell when things might change, and if the government in Beijing ever clamped down, as they did from time to time, he might need a ready source of finance to get out of the country in a hurry.

But for now escape was far from his mind. The shipment was ready and the plane would arrive tomorrow for loading. Then the quick flight in and out of Cambodia, and Colonel Leonard Kon would be very much the richer. Emerging from his warehouse into the sunlight, he stuck the millboard under his arm and smiled to himself. The new China really was a land of opportunity. If things went on as they were, then one day it would swamp America, the European Union, and even Japan. With the combination of an endless supply of manpower, a dynamic economy, a ruthless government and no scruples, who could say where it would end?

When the point section ran straight into the Khmer Rouge patrol there was a moment's stunned surprise on both sides. A second later all hell broke loose. Moving slickly into the Contact Front Drill, Craig's platoon, which had been in the lead, deployed to provide covering fire for the point section to extricate itself from the fire-fight, while Craig himself crawled forward to try to ascertain the strength of the enemy. Further back down the column, Terry listened to the reports coming in on the radio and, drawing on his years of experience, began to get the feel of the battle. Then, after ordering Tommy and Colin to shake out their platoons into a stop line a hundred yards back, he went forward to find Craig.

'Hang on here for five minutes and then fall back through Tommy and Colin. Slacken off your fire towards the end. We'll give the Rouge a come-on. When they try to rush you they'll find a whole company waiting for them.'

Craig hugged the ground as the branches above his head were shredded by machine-gun fire. 'Wilco! Tell them to get a shift on. This lot's fucking aggressive.'

Doubling back to the stop line, Terry found Manny in firm control.

'Everything's set. I've put a section on each end as flank guards.'

'Nice work, Manny. Signal Craig to break clean.'

117

Hearing the fire from Craig's platoon begin to tail off, Terry checked the magazine on his Colt Commando and flicked the selector switch to automatic.

'Come on, my lovelies. Let's have you.'

As the first of Craig's men appeared through the undergrowth, Manny counted them off. Bringing up the rear, Craig darted past, shouting to Terry as he went.

'Last man. Give it to 'em!'

He had barely disappeared when Terry heard a crashing in the undergrowth to his front. With shouts and whoops of triumph the Khmer Rouge had fallen for the trick. Thinking they were up against a demoralized government patrol that had broken and run after token resistance, they had followed up in hot pursuit, the smell of blood blotting out caution, the jungle soldier's friend.

'Fire!'

Terry's screamed command carried the length of the stop line and the air was shattered by the thunderous roar of the automatic fire from two platoons. In front of him, Terry saw the jungle disintegrate, the tumbling bodies of the Khmer Rouge jerking in mid-run, crumpling to the blood-soaked floor.

Having emptied his first magazine into the bushes, Terry dropped it out and slammed in a replacement, cocking the weapon in the same movement. The second magazine he fired in controlled, aimed bursts, directing his bullets at any returning fire that the Khmer Rouge were sending back. By the time he got to his third magazine his barrel was smoking and he engaged only identified targets. But the ambush had already done its work and when he gave the order to cease fire, nothing moved in the killing ground. Not a single man had escaped the iron fire control and ruthless battle discipline of the company.

Returning from his tour of the defences, Lon San was unhappy with the rate of progress. His men had been unsettled by the recent government successes and would rather have been across the border in the safety of Thailand. Even Lon San himself had experienced moments of doubt when he had wondered whether they should indeed withdraw and embark on a period of retraining and re-indoctrination. There, in the seclusion of the Thai border zone and under the protection of General Chamonon, they would be able to rest and plan their future campaign, but as soon as the thought entered his head Lon San eradicated it. Any withdrawal would be an admission of defeat and would be seen by the junior commanders as weakness. There were plenty of them jockeying for position and it was not inconceivable that Lon San himself might be ousted. And in the Khmer Rouge, being ousted meant being dead.

Walking back towards his quarters, Lon San was suddenly confronted by a young woman in black combat fatigues.

'Comrade, would you like to inspect the sangars in my sector?'

Lon San nodded formally. Once again, he was uncomfortable to notice the shyness that came over him whenever he was near to Comrade Mi Vi. He could feel the sweat prickling and he scowled at her to conceal the throbbing in his chest.

'Well, all right. But be quick about it.'

Dropping slightly behind Mi Vi, Lon San cast his eyes over her, the contours of her narrow body hidden by the shapeless tunic and trousers. Reaching the first of the sangars, Comrade Mi Vi went down the steps into the stuffy underground bunker.

'You will see, Comrade, that the firing slits give on to the airstrip. From here we can slaughter anyone who approaches.'

'Excellent, Comrade,' Lon San nodded. 'Show me the extent of your fields of fire.'

Leaning out of the firing slit, Mi Vi stretched forward to indicate the edge of the jungle.

'It's just over there.'

Lon San stood back in the dark shadows. He was barefoot and the feel of the damp earth was soothing and strangely sensual. An expanse of naked skin had appeared between Mi Vi's blouse and the top of her trousers. A drop of sweat ran into Lon San's eye. He swallowed hard.

'Right.'

He could hardly breathe. Though he would take the secret to his grave, he had never had sex with a woman. Until Mi Vi he had been able to dispel women from his thoughts, dismissing sex as an unnecessary bodily function, avoidable, unlike the other functions such as defecation. But Mi Vi was different. Somehow thoughts of her invaded his concentration and, what was more, he was certain that she felt the same. Why else did she follow him around like a lost dog, seeking his advice when any other commander would have sufficed?

'You have done well, Comrade,' he said stiffly, attempting a smile.

The young woman saluted, then looked around awkwardly, searching for something else to say. 'My work detail will have the other sangar finished by tomorrow night. Perhaps you would care to inspect it now as well?'

Lon San's heart leapt into his mouth. His lips went dry and when he answered it came out as little more than a croak.

'Er . . . I . . . of course, Comrade.'

Fighting to subdue the swelling that he felt stirring in his trousers, he coughed and cleared his throat, urging himself to speak, ashamed of his shyness.

'It might be better if I inspect it when it is ready then. The day after tomorrow, say. Then I can see the arcs of fire.'

Watching Mi Vi as closely as he dared, Lon San detected the flicker in her eyes.

'Good, Comrade,' she answered. 'I will wait there until you come.'

'Right. Good. I . . .'

Lon San could barely keep himself from passing out with the anticipation.

'Once the watch has changed and the morning meal is in progress.' He hesitated. 'But of course, you will be eating then.'

Mi Vi rushed to reassure him.

'My duty has always come first, Comrade. I will not eat until we have inspected the sangar.'

She paused. 'I will arrange to be on guard myself,' she said, dropping her voice, gauging Lon San's reaction. 'It will be quiet and . . .'

'Good!' Lon San said forcefully, turning quickly to go, his hands clasped in front of his groin as devout as a statue of Lenin.

7

Parting the tall grass Terry looked down on the thin bare line of the airstrip a quarter of a mile away.

'Rurseng,' Manny stated bluntly, his voice devoid of emotion. 'That's where the bastard lives.'

Identifying the adjacent camp through his binoculars, Terry examined the fortifications.

'He may be a bastard, but he's been a busy bastard.'

Counting the sangars and bunkers, noting the mutual support and interlocking machine-gun arcs, Terry whistled softly. From the colour of the spoil he could see that many of the fortifications were recent. The loose dirt from the new trenches and dug-outs had been used either to build ramparts or to fill the sandbags that had been stacked to form thick walls around the many machine-gun emplacements.

'This is going to be fun.'

Manny looked at him doubtfully. 'Do you think we can do it?'

'Every defensive position has its weak point. It's just a matter of finding it.'

Terry rolled on to his side, took out a sketch pad and started to make a plan of the camp's layout.

'The trick is to match your weapon systems very precisely to each part of the enemy's position exactly as required. In one place for deception, in another to create a breach, and in another to exploit the breach and establish a break-in. It's like precision engineering, except that instead of building something, we're going to blow the fucker apart.'

Manny watched with admiration the short sharp strokes of Terry's pencil depicting with the symbols of military shorthand the deployment of the Khmer Rouge defences. Between every few strokes, Terry peered through his binoculars at the distant camp until he had recorded everything that was visible from the vantage point. When he had noted down all that he could, he and Manny moved with their escort to another thickly jungled hillside and began the process all over again, each new vantage point giving an altogether different perspective. Bunkers that had appeared to be in close proximity to one another turned out to be further apart; a line that Terry had supposed to be a simple communication trench linking one sangar to another proved instead to be a complex defensive network; and harmless stretches of open ground were revealed as killing areas covered by overlapping machine-gun arcs.

When he had seen all that he could from the relative safety of the surrounding hills, Terry covered his face and hands with camouflage cream and went forward for a close recce. Accompanied only by Manny for protection, he left his Colt Commando behind, relying on his Browning pistol to get him out of trouble. It was essential for the close recce that he should travel as light as possible, unencumbered by weaponry and other equipment, trusting to stealth, skill and silence instead. In the event of trouble Manny would provide fire support to extricate the two of them. But compromise was out of the question, not just because it meant certain death, but because Terry was a master of the close recce, a trained sniper used to long, gruelling stalks. If he could manage to remain undetected on the bare features of Salisbury Plain, he told himself, he was buggered if he'd allow himself to be spotted in the dense jungle.

Crawling forward to within a hundred yards of the perimeter wire, Terry circled the camp on his stomach, venturing in from each point of the compass until almost able to touch the defences. Memorizing the detail, he then withdrew and noted it down before crawling further around the circumference to the next selected compass point and closing in again. After six hours of painstaking stalking he was satisfied that he had seen all that he could. Ideally he would have liked to set up an OP to watch the camp over a period of days to establish the enemy's routine and to identify, if possible, Lon San's private quarters, but there wasn't enough time and he would have to make do with the information he had. While he had been on the close recce he had left a four-man OP at one of the hillside vantage points; with luck they might have worked out at least part of the detail.

When he finally staggered into the company harbour, half a mile from Rurseng, Terry collapsed exhausted beside his bergen.

'I reckon you could use this,' Craig said, handing him some tea. Cupping the steaming mug in his hands, Terry sipped the hot, sweet liquid with closed eyes. A hot brew was the best thing in the world at times like this, no matter if you were freezing your nuts off in the slanting rain of the Brecon Beacons or sweating like a pig in the heart of the jungle. The sugar flowed straight into the bloodstream and with every sip Terry could feel the strength pumping back into his limbs.

'Cheers, mate. Give me half an hour to sort my thoughts out and then get the others together for an O Group.'

'Do you want me to make a model?'

'Manny's doing it.'

Craig smiled. 'He's a fast learner that one, isn't he?'

'One of the best.'

Balancing his mug on a tree root, Terry read through his notes. He had never imagined that the attack would be a walk-over but now he had seen the camp for himself he realized just how much he had bitten off. Under normal circumstances he would only have attacked it with at least a battalion, possibly with a second battalion to provide a cordon of ambush positions to catch anyone who might escape. But then in Cambodia things were far from normal. With luck and a good deception plan he reckoned he might be able to convince the Khmer Rouge that they were being hit by a much larger force than simply a company.

Studying his sketch plan of the camp, Terry focussed his attention on the one corner that he had identified as a potential weak spot. On every other sector the bunkers were mutually supporting; thus anyone attacking one position could expect to be fired upon by machine-guns from at least two other flanking bunkers. However, at the far left-hand corner the defenders had failed to take account of a rise in the ground and Terry was confident that it would be possible for an assault team to crawl to within ten yards of the bunker without being engaged by its neighbour. To all intents and purposes the bunker was in dead ground. Its fields of fire would have to be severely limited and furthermore it appeared to be the key to the whole defensive layout. Once it fell, an attacking force would be able to penetrate into the very heart of the camp and take on the remaining bunkers from the rear.

A slow smile spread across Terry's face as he growled: 'Gotcha, you buggers.'

With practised speed he flicked open his notebook and jotted down his plan and a set of orders, checking his watch to work out the co-ordinating timings. By the time the others had gathered to receive the orders Terry was ready. By digging in the soft earth with his jungle knife, Manny had constructed an accurate model of Lon San's camp. Twigs, leaves, threads of coloured material, bullets, matches and ammunition magazines had been used to represent the wire fences, huts and defences that in a few short hours would be the various objectives of their attack.

'We'll divide into three groups,' Terry went on after outlining the general scope of the operation. 'Colin, as well as being the Fire Support Group, I want your platoon to provide a single cut-off ambush on the main track leading towards the Thai border. I expect the Rouge to stand and fight but if any of them decide to try for a getaway, I want a section of your men waiting for them.'

'Roger.' Colin studied his map, comparing it to the model, selecting a location for his Fire Support teams. Ideally it would be at right angles to the assault so that they could fire on the enemy bunkers up to the last moment without endangering their own troops as they closed for the assault.

'Craig, you've drawn the short straw. Your platoon

will be the Breaching Group. Once you've established a break-in, Tommy's platoon will pass through as the main Assault Group to exploit the breach and carry out the destruction of the camp. As soon as they're through, Craig, I want you to reform your platoon as my reserve and be prepared to take on any surprises that Lon San might have in store.'

'What about me?' Colin asked. 'Once you're inside there'll be precious little I can do from the hill.'

'Correct. Once you see us through the perimeter defences, I want you to give the camp depth positions a good shoot-up and then move down to the airstrip. If our intelligence is right, the Chinese arms shipment is coming in sometime tomorrow. We'll attack after their morning stand-down. With luck we might be able to destroy the arms plane as well.'

'Got it.'

Terry went round his commanders checking that everyone knew his allotted task. When he came to Manny he had something special in mind.

'I want you to stay beside me throughout. You'll be my troubleshooter. Also you're the only one who'll recognize Lon San.'

'Do you want us to try and take him alive?' Tommy asked.

'Do I hell! Shoot the fucker on sight. With him dead it's likely the rest'll cut and run.'

When he was satisfied that he had covered everything, Terry dismissed them and with a final check of his notes, curled up in his lightweight blanket and tried to sleep. Elsewhere around the company harbour position the individual commanders were now busy studying the orders given to their particular platoons, extracting the details relevant to themselves and preparing their own sets of orders for onward transmission to their own section and fire team commanders. But with his part of the battle procedure complete, Terry finally closed his eyes upon the overhanging jungle canopy and a short while later the sounds of the nocturnal insects dulled in his ears as he slipped into sleep.

Tossing and turning on his bamboo cot, Lon San had hardly slept a wink all night, not so much from thoughts of the many contacts with government troops that had been occurring throughout the region, but more because of his impending liaison with Comrade Mi Vi in the morning.

Ever since the disappearance of the mercenary-led company from Phnom Penh, it had been clear to him that the camp would be the eventual target of any attack. However, he was not too concerned: government forces had approached within relatively close proximity on past occasions and been repulsed. They rarely penetrated the network of patrols that Lon San deployed in the surrounding jungle and he was confident that this latest threat would prove no more capable. The officers might well be foreigners but the men under their command would be as useless as all the rest. In the past they had been easily cowed into submission and it would take more than a bit of fancy training to convert them into worthy opponents of the Khmer Rouge. It would take more than reports of a few scattered fire-fights to unsettle him.

Comrade Mi Vi was another matter. Lon San was fully aware of the possible consequences of their meeting being discovered, but his mind had been completely taken over by desire. For the first time in his life he was allowing his heart to rule his head and it frightened him. But hidden amid the fear was a wild thrill. Never before had he tasted such sweet anticipation and throughout the humid night his brain had raced with images of their two bodies locked together on the cool earthen floor of the bunker. When he had finally dozed off he had dreamed of her, even smelling her fragrance and tasting the sweat of her skin. By the time the first light dappled through the mosquito-net to wake him, Lon San felt he was about to explode.

Slipping into his baggy trousers and combat shirt, he splashed his face with water and combed his jet-black hair stiffly in place with a worn brush. Baring his teeth in a small mirror, he checked for fragments of the previous night's food and then, gathering himself to his full height, strode out of his quarters and into the glare of the early-morning sun. It had hardly appeared over the tops of the distant trees but already Lon San could feel the heat that heralded another scorching day. But the sky was clear and the pale blue indicated that Colonel Kon would have a smooth flight into Rurseng.

As he crossed the rough clearing that served as a parade ground, Lon San acknowledged the greetings of several soldiers. The first light stand-to was under way, and rounding some of the bunkers, Lon San made a great show of inspecting his men's readiness. Peering out through the surrounding wire, he shaded his eyes at the glare coming off the yellow surface of the airstrip, now cleared of its camouflage of scrub. In the surrounding jungle everything was peaceful and still. A thin mist rose gently from the treetops and would hang in a low cloud until burned off by the strengthening sun. Across the dirt strip, a patrol was returning from the nearest village, laden with fresh vegetables, half a dozen chickens and a pig, and in the last bunker yet to be visited, Mi Vi was waiting for her commander.

From the open-sided hut that served as a cookhouse on the far side of the camp, a soldier banged wearily with the blunt edge of his bayonet on the metal casing of an old artillery shell. At the signal to stand down, men and women rose from the trenches and emerged from the bunkers, slinging their weapons over their shoulders as they made their way across the camp towards the smell of the cooking fires. Another day had begun, just like any other. Except for Lon San.

When he was sure that the farthest corner of the camp was deserted save for the single sentry high in a tower, Lon San strolled along the perimeter wire, whistling quietly to himself. The sentry looked down, met his icy stare and glanced quickly away. Dropping down into one of the communication trenches, Lon San worked his way along, stopping to check a sandbag wall on the way, displeased to find it insufficiently secure. Then, with one final glance around, he ducked down the steps into the bunker.

At first Lon San thought it was empty and that Comrade Mi Vi had had second thoughts and failed to turn up, but as his eyes adjusted to the gloom he picked out the shape of a figure pressed into the far corner. With a light cough, Comrade Mi Vi stepped forward. A shaft of light coming through one of the firing slits fell across her face. She looked pale and Lon San thought that he saw her shiver. Like himself, she was barefoot.

'Ah, Comrade. There you are,' he said awkwardly.

He tried to smile but in his embarrassment it came out more as a grimace.

'So then, I see your team has completed its work. They've done a fine job.'

He waved a hand miserably at the walls, his wretched shyness contrasting savagely with his erotic dreams of a few hours ago. Mi Vi took another step forward.

'You are too kind, Comrade. I only want to be of service.'

Lon San's mouth went dry as stone. Moistening his lips, he reached out a hand towards her.

'Here, let me congratulate you,' he said strongly, shaking the small young woman by the hand. Mi Vi added a second hand to make a threesome, on top of which Lon San planted a fourth until their handshake resembled a meeting of two world leaders. He broke into an open smile to which Mi Vi responded, but feeling suddenly ridiculous, she pulled her hands free and took the final step towards her commander.

'Comrade,' she muttered, more to herself than to Lon San.

'Mi Vi,' Lon San replied, reaching forward tentatively to touch a strand of her hair with one fingertip.

It was as if he had hit a trip-wire, releasing a chain reaction of booby-traps that exploded one after the other. Mi Vi raised her arm to his shoulders, and reaching up, kissed him on the lips. The taste of her mouth sent Lon San's head spinning and he almost staggered forward, colliding with Mi Vi and grabbing hold of her for balance. Her waist was slender in his hands and he felt he could almost make his fingers meet around it. Lifting the tail of her fatigue shirt, he stroked the smooth skin of her back, first with his fingertips and then with the whole palm of his hand, circling upwards along the spine until his hands were between her shoulder blades.

With racing heart and panting breath, Lon San circled his palms slowly round to the front, passing under her arms, the soft skin under the black tunic exposed only to his hands. Unable to contain himself, he covered the last precious inches to the twin mound of her breasts. Cupping one in each palm, he briefly closed his eyes, hearing Mi Vi gasp and press against him. Then he was fumbling for the buttons at the front of her tunic, pulling and yanking at them as Mi Vi leaned back against the damp earthen wall of the bunker, her arms limp at her sides.

Parting the cheap cloth as reverently as a temple curtain, Lon San gazed in awe at Mi Vi's small, firm breasts, the nipples hard and taut. Quivering with Mi Vi's every breath, they lured him forward, rising and falling as her stomach arched inwards, tight as a drum. But Lon San couldn't move. He was rooted to the spot, both from uncertainty as to what he was supposed to do, and because he wanted to gaze upon Mi Vi's naked chest for ever.

'Come,' she urged gently, taking his hands in hers and drawing them towards the cord fastening her trousers at her slim waist. The moment Lon San's fingers touched the rough material he began untying it, pulling the two frayed ends apart and then standing back as the trousers loosened, slipped and finally dropped to Mi Vi's ankles. In the dark of the bunker, her legs were a smooth deep brown, her groin a tangle of hair concealing the inner mystery.

Suddenly aware that he himself was still fully

clothed, Lon San tore at his own tunic, baring his chest and then fumbling with his trousers. But Mi Vi slipped softly to her knees and pushed his hands away, opening his trousers and taking him in her hand as tenderly as a bird.

Lon San stared down at her in amazement. He had never realized that it was possible to feel like this. After all the years of war and slaughter, he had come to this one moment as if it had been lying in wait for him from the very beginning of his life. With every stroke of Mi Vi's soft hand, Lon San felt himself grow. Reaching to a shelf for support, he leaned against it as Mi Vi caressed him with her tongue. A sudden flash of anxiety flooded through his body. Where had she learned such skills? How many men had enjoyed her in this same way, perhaps even in this same place?

But the thought died even as it was turning to resentment. She was lying back on the floor and pulling him down on top of her. For one more moment Lon San gave way to fear, imagining Mi Vi boasting of her conquest later to the other women, and of the titters they would all enjoy at his expense. But then she was parting her legs, revealing to him for the first time the hidden, tightly guarded place that he had so often scorned when hearing other men speak of it. As with them, so now with Lon San, the spell had been cast and he felt himself powerless to resist. Lowering himself on to Mi Vi, Lon San felt her reach between them and take him in her hand, guiding him towards the prize.

'Come,' she said again, her eyes half closed, her breath short and panting. 'Come.'

Landing within five yards of the bunker, the first mortar round drove deep into the earth before the delayed-action fuse detonated. Designed for attacking strong points and well-prepared defences, it seemed almost to lift the bunker out of the ground before setting it down again, the earth rudely torn from its carefully formed parapets and firing shelves and flung into the air like so much chaff.

On the floor of the bunker, Lon San fell heavily on top of Mi Vi as if pushed hard in the small of the back. With a grunt of pain, he rolled off her, scrabbling to hitch up his trousers just in time to be knocked sideways across the floor by the second round.

'What the . . .?'

Mi Vi was sitting up, her trousers round her ankles, tugging her blouse together, her fingers racing to find the buttons. Getting to his knees, Lon San peered gingerly out through the firing slit as another round whistled over the roof of packed earth and impacted in the heart of the camp behind him. Mi Vi was sobbing as she pulled up her trousers.

'Comrade,' she gasped helplessly. 'What is happening?'

But Lon San had no time for words. Within the space of seconds the habits of a lifetime had taken firm command of his soul. When he looked at Mi Vi again it was not as the novice lover but as the Khmer Rouge battle leader.

'Go immediately to your station,' he commanded coolly. 'Your fire teams will be on the way. They will need direction.'

Then, as she pushed past him, he held her back for a single brief moment and looked in her eyes.

'Mi Vi,' he said simply, enunciating the syllables of her name as if speaking of a great treasure. He stroked some of the dust from her hair and then she was gone.

Returning to the firing slit, Lon San took one more look at the sight that had yanked him from the arms of passion and chilled his blood to the core. Government troops were attacking the stronghold. But unlike the usual rabble who only ever won from overwhelming superiority of numbers, these men seemed different. He could tell it from the way they moved, rigidly abiding to the principles of fire and manoeuvre. They had been trained by professionals. The mercenaries and their company had found him.

As soon as Colin was in position on the low hillock overlooking the camp, he crawled forward to identify targets for his mortar team. Through his binoculars he could see the lead elements of Craig's platoon edging cautiously through the long grass towards the perimeter wire. As the first section closed up and the combat engineers started to cut a way through the first of the obstacles, Colin gave the order to start the fire plan.

At a nod from the mortar fire controllers, the mortar teams dropped the rounds into the barrels. Firing high above the treetops, the rounds reached the pinnacle of their arching flight, turned and drove mercilessly towards their targets. Unlike the normal rounds, which would explode on impact, the delayed-action fuses detonated only once buried underground. Huge gouts of earth cascaded into the sky, drifting across on the wind, mixing with the smell of cordite and burning timber.

'Left one hundred, add fifty, repeat!'

Calculating the adjustments from Colin's corrections, the mortar teams barked out the new bearings and elevations, reset their weapons and fired again. In the camp below, the rounds straddled the outer defences, bracketing the watch-towers and the bunkers.

'On target! Fire for effect!'

As the mortar bombs rained down on the camp, the combat engineers penetrated the outer defences and proceeded to the next line of wire. When they encountered a ditch filled with sharpened panji stakes, they checked first for booby-traps and trip-wires and then smashed the lethal fire-hardened bamboo tips aside with the butts of their M16 rifles. Immediately behind them, the second section directed short aimed bursts into the firing slits of the nearest bunkers to deter anyone from interfering with the operation. But there was no one around to try. After the morning stand-to the Khmer Rouge had felt secure enough to go for breakfast, leaving only the sentries in their watch-towers. Having grown used to the inadequacies of the government army, they had been lulled into a false sense of security. Only Lon San himself, caught in the perimeter bunker, had borne unwilling witness to this new and very different breed of opponent.

Rushing for their weapons, the Khmer Rouge broke from the cookhouse in panic moments before a mortar round scored a direct hit. Tearing through the eating area, one of the white-hot shell splinters pierced a gas cylinder which exploded in an orange ball of flame. Instantly the *atap* roof was alight, the fire fanned by a fresh breeze, blowing it towards the nearest of the living quarters.

At the perimeter wire, the combat engineers were almost through to the last line of defence. Seeing the Khmer Rouge guerrillas running for their bunkers, Craig directed the fire of his close support section on to them.

'Don't let them reach the sangars!'

But on the hill, Colin was also on to it and scarlet beads of tracer fire snaked down from the 7.62mm M60 machine-guns of the Fire Group, hosing the clearing inside the camp. Running smack into the deadly rain of bullets, the Khmer Rouge tumbled and jerked, stopped in their tracks.

Behind Craig's Breaching Group, Terry and Manny sat up to peer over the top of the undergrowth, gauging the exact moment to switch to the Assault Group and order Tommy's platoon to pass through and take over the battle. But Craig's combat engineers had encountered problems. Not for nothing had the Khmer Rouge acquired their reputation as fearsome fighters. A group of them had made it into a bunker and were now directing heavy, accurate fire on to the Breaching Group. Unable to crawl farther forward and to cut through the last line of concertina razor-wire, Craig turned to the section commander behind him.

'Get the Bangalores!'

The normal Bangalore Torpedo consisted of several lengths of metal tubing packed with PE, clipped together for easy carriage. When needed, the separate lengths would be unclipped and fitted together end to end, the newly elongated pole being slid along the ground underneath the wire obstacle to be breached. Detonated from a safe distance, the metal-encased length of high explosive would blast a cleared passage, through which the assaulting infantry could then crawl. However, unable to get the real things, Terry had improvised with several six-foot-long, right-angled iron pickets. After packing the crease of a metal picket with sticks of plastic explosive, he had

then put a second picket on top, wiring the two together
to form a long, square-section metal sandwich. At one
end he had wedged a primer, detonator and length of
safety fuse timed to ten seconds. Knowing that in a
close-quarter breaching engagement it would not be
possible for the combat engineers to withdraw to a
safe distance, he had selected a point in the perimeter
where a fold in the ground would provide just enough
cover from the jagged splinter fragments.

Having pushed three improvised Bangalores side
by side under the wire, Craig waited until his men
had crawled back to the safety of the depression and
then lit the fuses before wriggling back himself. On
the hillside, Colin watched the operation through his
binoculars, switching the fire of his M60s and mortars
on to any new group of Khmer Rouge that dared to
approach the scene of the developing breach.

'Keep back, you fuckers,' he muttered through
clenched teeth. Then, identifying an enemy machine-
gun team edging towards the protection of a sangar
he barked out a fire control order.

'Fire Team Charlie. Three hundred, watch-tower.
Base of tower, gun team. Rapid fire!'

Identifying the watch-tower at three hundred yards,
the men of Fire Team Charlie spotted the enemy crawling past the base of it, set their sights, and engaged the
new target with bursts of rapid fire. Underneath the
binoculars Colin's lips creased in a satisfied smile as
he saw the spurts of earth around the enemy soldiers,
dancing closer until all of them lay dead.

'Cease fire!'

The boys were performing well and he was proud
of them. The training was paying off and he could
sense that the soldiers themselves were on a high.

It was a feeling that came from being confident in your weapon systems, your leaders and your own abilities. Professional armies trained for years just to achieve it, but for the Cambodians of Colin's platoon it was a new experience, and one that they were determined to exploit to maximum effect against their hated enemies.

In the moment's lull before the explosion, Terry hugged the ground, catching Manny's eye as he pressed himself into the crushed grass.

'Nice 'ere, ain't it?'

Manny grinned doubtfully and opened his mouth to reply but his words were drowned in the deafening roar of the detonating Bangalores. Feeling the whole ground jump, Terry flinched and then laughed.

'It reminds me of my wedding night. I felt the earth move then, as well.'

In front of him, Craig was up and on his feet, rushing forward to seize the newly created gap before the Khmer Rouge gunners and riflemen could recover from the shock of the blast and bring aimed fire to bear.

'Come on!'

Screaming at the top of his voice, he hurtled on, blazing from the hip with his Colt Commando assault rifle. Immediately behind him the point section hurled smoke grenades into the heart of the compound, the dense fog of orange and red smoke building quickly into an impenetrable screen behind which the rest of the platoon closed up. As the combat engineers dragged the shattered ends of the razor-wire aside, widening the breach, Craig shouted for his depth section to move through and take the lead.

With a ferocious battle cry, the section commander

leapt forward, racing through the wire gap, followed by his fire teams. Once through they split to left and right, blazing at the bunker firing slits and hurling fresh smoke grenades to thicken up the protective screen. As Craig directed the supporting fire of the combat engineers and the rest of the platoon, the fresh fire teams closed up to the nearest of the bunkers, crawling on their bellies. They worked in pairs: as one man fired aimed bursts from his M16 through the firing slits, his partner crawled to the very side of the bunker, pulled the pin of an HE grenade, and posted it through the slit. Burying his face in the dirt, he waited for the booming subterranean thud of the explosion before getting to his feet and throwing himself down the steps into the smoking dark of the interior, fighting to keep himself from retching at the stench of cordite as he pumped his 5.56mm rounds into anything and anyone that he found there.

Meanwhile, on the hill, seeing that the Breaching Group was in, Colin ordered his platoon to switch their fire to the enemy's depth positions.

'Don't give the fuckers breathing space!' he screamed above the noise of the battle, pitching his voice to carry through the chatter of the machine-guns.

Down on the ground, Terry was moving forward, still on his stomach, the air immediately above his head alive with shell and grenade fragments and the snap and whine of high-velocity bullets. Reaching the gap in the wire, he spied Craig and his sections pushing on towards their objectives. The nearest of the bunkers were smoking and the timber roofs had caught fire, detonating the bullets in the rifles of the dead as though, even from their graves, the Khmer Rouge defenders were fighting back.

When he saw Craig hand-signalling and screaming at his farthest fire teams to go firm, Terry waited for him to turn and catch his eye. Unable to hear his voice above the noise, he could nevertheless read his lips and understand the message in his broad smile: 'Over to you.'

Craning over his shoulder, Terry looked back to the fringe of the jungle, where Tommy Liu was jogging forward at the head of his platoon. It was time for the battle to enter its next phase and for Terry to order the next platoon to pass through. Craig's Breaching Group had done their job and done it well. The Khmer Rouge defences had been breached. Now it was up to Tommy's Assault Group to carry the fight into the very heart of the enemy camp.

8

Soon after the attack had begun, Lon San ducked out of the bunker and sprinted across the open parade ground back towards the cookhouse, flinging himself flat as the mortar round landed, detonating the gas cylinder. As he picked himself up he screamed orders to the panic-stricken soldiers fleeing in all directions.

'Get to your posts! Repel the attack!'

Grabbing one of the men as he darted past him, Lon San shouted into his face: 'Where the hell do you think you're going?'

'But . . . but the enemy. They're in the camp!' he stammered.

Lon San slapped him.

'Forget the fucking enemy. It's me you should be scared of.'

One look into his commander's eyes was enough to bring the soldier to his senses. He had seen Lon San carry out summary executions of deserters before and he didn't intend to join them.

'Yes, Comrade. Of course.'

Staggering away, the guerrilla turned towards the sound of battle and ran to his assigned post in one of the bunkers.

When he had retrieved his Kalashnikov from his quarters, Lon San strapped on a canvas webbing belt and ammunition pouches, slipped into his sandals, and went out to try to regain control of the battle. Against all the odds the government troops had been able to seize the initiative and Lon San knew that unless he was able to take it back, he would lose the entire camp. What was more, the arms shipment would be lost with it, as well as any chance of restarting the offensive on Phnom Penh. With the campaign in tatters it would not be long before he himself was in danger of execution by a People's Court for incompetence.

On locating the enemy's fire support position on the overlooking hillside, the first thing he did was to order one of his subordinates to mount a counter-attack with whatever men he could muster.

'But they'll be in prepared positions,' the man protested, his eyes wide with fear. 'We don't have anyone to spare.'

Lon San pushed the man against a wall of sandbags and stuck the barrel of his Kalashnikov in the hollow of his throat, speaking through gritted teeth.

'Take the fucking cooks and the women if you have to, I don't care. You don't have to capture the hill – just distract them and stop those bloody mortars and machine-guns.'

When the man had gone, Lon San cursed himself for not occupying the hill with a piquet. They had posted a sentry up there but the government troops had obviously silenced him before he could raise the alarm. Why had he been so bloody confident that he was secure here at Rurseng? The blasted foreign mercenaries were to blame. If he ever caught up with them he would make them pay dearly for this humiliation. But then for that he would have to be alive.

Aware that he was presenting a clear target to the machine-gunners on the hill, he ran for the nearest communication trench and dropped into it, doubling along it until he came to a bunker. The men inside were busy pouring fire towards the centre of the battle on the perimeter, but when he peered out of the firing slit, Lon San noticed that their rounds were going harmlessly over the top. The actual breach that the enemy combat engineers were preparing was in a fold of dead ground. Again he cursed the mercenaries. How had they seen what he had missed? He had been round all the positions personally but when he had checked their arcs he had stood on the sangars' roofs. Only in one or two had he got down inside to look through the firing slits, to check the view and the field of fire that the occupants themselves would have. Mi Vi had prepared her sector properly. She had done her job well. If only he had more commanders like her.

Even in the midst of battle, the thought of her sent a wave of heat flooding through his loins, a strange and potent cocktail of combat adrenalin and lust. Mi Vi. Where was she now? He had sent her back to man her section of the perimeter defences, and with a sudden chill he realized that her fire teams held the area immediately in the path of the main assault. If the enemy was through the perimeter wire then Mi Vi's position would be the next to be hit.

'Get out on top, you idiots,' he screamed at the top of his shrill voice. 'What do you think you can hit from in here?'

Kicking and punching the men up the steps, Lon San deployed them on the roof of the bunker, grabbing hold of their smoking rifle barrels and directing them forcibly at the perimeter breach. Then he seized three or four other men and led them back across the parade ground towards the firing. Halfway across, one of them was hit, a burst of 7.62mm M60 rounds slamming him full in the face. The fallen mass jerked spasmodically on the ground and was still, the brains tumbling from the gaping back of the shattered skull.

'Get on, don't stop!'

Kicking and thrusting the men forward, Lon San fought against his own fear, converting it into a blind rage that blotted out any thought of injury to himself. Wounds and death were for lesser men. He was Comrade Lon San, commander of Khmer Rouge guerrillas, and when they eventually returned to power he vowed to wreak a bitter revenge on the people who had perpetrated this affront. No matter who they were, peasant, farmer, doctor, clerk. The people of Cambodia were his enemies and every one of them would pay for thwarting his plans and shaming him with this attack.

Throughout the break-in phase of the battle, Tommy Liu had kept his platoon well forward, close enough to the scene of the action to pass through when ordered, but not so close as to become involved in the savage fire-fights. That would come later. Watching from the fringe of the jungle, he had seen the development of the breach, admiring the cool nerves of the combat engineers as they inched their way through the rolls of razor-wire, panji stakes, booby-traps and mines.

Tommy couldn't help smiling whenever he looked at Terry. Good old Dojo was so far forward he was almost lead scout, but then it was only by having a feel for the battle and knowing exactly what was going on that a commander could make the right decision at the right time. It was a question of knowing when to switch from one phase to another, and when and where to commit your reserves, and in questions such as these Dojo was the master. He had an answer for everything.

In the few moments of waiting that were not occupied with thoughts of the battle, Tommy found himself thinking of Sitha: brief intense glimpses of her face that left him breathless with longing. Love and death, he thought, the two great intangibles that ruled one's life, and coming together in this remote jungle-covered country it seemed that both were closing around him in a contest to see which would take eternal possession of his soul.

'Sitha,' he said softly to himself, fingering her pendant at his neck. But in the last moments of peace he vowed that if he lived to return to Phnom Penh he would make her his own. He knew that she felt the same and if the two of them could salvage some harbour of love from the wreckage of their lives, then there was hope for all of humankind.

'Sir. We go.'

Tommy looked into the eyes of his platoon sergeant, following his pointing arm towards the breach where Terry was waving wildly at him, hand-signalling him forward. Tommy smiled at the anxious men around him, giving them courage with his own display of calm confidence.

'OK?' he asked.

A couple of them chuckled, some smiled to cover the fear gnawing at their guts, but most stared fixedly at the swirling smoke of the breach, beyond which lay the gods of life and death, each with their list of names, waiting for the soldiers to come and claim whatever personal destiny awaited.

'Move now,' Tommy said firmly, breaking from cover and jogging out towards the tattered wire.

Up on the hill, Colin spotted the single line of men snaking out of the far side of the camp.

'Here they come, lads,' he called. 'Enemy counter-attack force at two o'clock. Right-hand mortar, go right four hundred ... add two hundred ... adjust fire.'

After cranking the barrel of their weapon round to engage the new target, the mortar team dropped a bomb into the weapon, listening to the rasping sound of metal on metal as it slid down the tube towards the fixed firing pin at the base. Cringing back in readiness for the explosion, they stuffed their fingers in their ears. Nothing happened.

'Misfire! Unload!' the number one shouted.

Colin watched as they tilted the barrel forward, sliding the round gingerly out.

'Hurry, lads, hurry. They'll be in the cover of the jungle in a minute.'

Tossing the dud round to one side, they relaid the mortar on line and slid in another round. Shooting from the barrel, the bomb arched towards the Khmer Rouge counter-attack force.

'Fuck the adjustment,' Colin roared. 'Fire for effect. Now! Before we lose them!'

With the enemy force close to the jungle at the foot of the hillock, Colin realized that he couldn't afford the luxury of accuracy. He would have to trust to luck and hope that if he fired sufficient rounds some of them might inflict casualties.

Slipping into an expert rhythm, the mortar team slid one round after another into the barrel. Hardly had one left the barrel than the next round was already being fed in. Squinting at the Khmer Rouge patrol through his binoculars, Colin opened his mouth to congratulate the mortar team on their accuracy and never saw the double-feed.

With their ears ringing from the constant pounding of the mortar's firing, the team's senses had become dulled, exhausted from the build-up of tension and the excitement of the battle. With the heavy firing, the inside of the mortar barrel had become coated with a fine layer of residue left behind by the bombs' propellant charge. Unnoticed by the crew, each round was taking fractionally longer to slide down and reach the firing pin at the base. Muddling his loading drills, the mortar number two fed one round and then, before it had detonated and left the barrel, began to load another one on top. For one split second time froze as he realized what he had done. Standing with the new bomb half inserted into the barrel, he heard the click of its predecessor hit the firing pin. He never even had time to register fear. Powering out of the barrel the bomb found its exit blocked. As it drove up into the fragile propellant explosives of the next bomb, both of them detonated simultaneously, the effect of the explosion amplified by confinement in the hard metal casing of the barrel, which fragmented in a thousand lethal splinters, adding its own deadly force to the two exploding rounds.

The mortar man never felt his arms being torn from his body for he was dead before the damage was complete. Kneeling close beside the barrel and squinting through the sight, the number one never heard the explosion that drove the shattered glass and metal directly into his brain. But across the small expanse of open grass, it was Colin who took the next greatest impact, as flying splinters accelerated away from the mortar in an orange and black ball of fire and smoke. He took two staggering steps, his binoculars still firmly to his eyes, then toppled over, his lifeblood pulsing from the head, chest, stomach and leg wounds that covered his body.

As he passed Terry, Tommy bent down to catch his orders.

'Once you're through Craig's platoon, exploit as far as the cookhouse if you can. When you get to the living quarters, I'll take stock and I might pass Craig through again. Right now he needs time to get his boys together.'

'Roger.'

'Watch out for those bunkers on the left. There's an ammunition and supply dump on the far side of the camp. Don't get stuck in there without combat engineer support. It's bound to be booby-trapped. Any questions?'

'No.'

'Go.'

With a slap on the back, Terry sent Tommy and his platoon on their way. Zigzagging through the breached wire, Tommy took a deep breath before entering the dense cloud of smoke. Craig's men had kept the screen thickened up, feeding it regularly with fresh grenades until Tommy's platoon had passed through. A passage of lines was always one of the most difficult operations of war as two separate units wove together momentarily, and the last thing they needed was interference from the enemy to complicate the difficulties of command and control.

Jogging through the acrid smoke, it was all too easy to imagine that you were impervious to incoming bullets, but Tommy remembered the screamed warnings of all his old instructors in the Hong Kong Military Service Corps: cover from view is not the same as cover from fire. Ducking low, he wove through the smoke until he came up beside Craig kneeling behind a low sandbag wall.

'You took your time,' Craig said, grinning. 'This is almost as much fun as the Golan Heights in '73.'

'Whatever you say, Grandad.'

'Cheeky bugger.' Craig pointed across the clearing. 'There's a bunker over there's been giving us some hassle. To the right, there's a communication trench. Some of the fuckers are bedded down there. They'll pop their heads up from time to time and have a crack.'

'Got it. And the left?'

'Not much. They've scarpered, but be careful. There are more positions in depth. They seem to hide their mutual support until you've committed yourself to attacking one particular bunker. Then, once you're in the open with your bum in the air, they open up from all sides.'

'Nice fire control.'

'Yeah, but it plays havoc with the bladder. I nearly wet myself the first time it happened.'

Checking for his men, Tommy saw that all eyes were on him and with a final signal he led them into the heat of the battle. Directing one section to take out the nearest bunker that Craig had pointed out, he held back the other two sections in reserve.

The fight was now at too close quarters for them to provide effective fire support but he wanted to keep them handy in case other bunkers opened up as Craig had warned.

Sure enough, his point section had hardly begun its assault on their objective when a stream of tracer fire from a flank stung the air above them.

'Got them?' he shouted to one of the reserve section commanders. The Cambodian corporal gave the thumbs up, and with a blood-curdling yell led his fire teams into the attack with fixed bayonets and hand-grenades. Reaching the communication trench, the corporal jumped into it, joined a moment later by the rest of his section. As he watched the savage hand-to-hand fight, Tommy was glad that the corporal was on his side. Properly trained, equipped and led, there was nothing those little men couldn't do.

From the bunker to his front came the dull, booming thud of a detonating grenade, and looking up, Tommy saw wisps of black smoke and earth drifting from the firing slits where the occupants had just been shredded with splinters of metal.

Sprinting across the open ground, he arrived at the scene as his men were completing the clearing operation and locating the next enemy position. In front of him Tommy now saw the heart of the enemy camp. Most of the buildings were on fire, set alight by the white-phosphorus rounds that Colin's mortars had aimed at the thatched *atap* huts on purpose. Nice work, he thought.

Smoke from the burning straw and *atap* drifted to and fro between the huts. This is my land, Tommy thought. The close-quarter fight. Terry had held him back for this very reason, matching each of his mercenary commanders to a particular task, making maximum use of their abilities.

Slinging his Colt Commando, Tommy drew his Glock 17, tightening his fists into the two-handed combat grip that had served him well in a score of similar engagements where speed of reaction, accuracy and fire-power were the keys to success. After splitting his sections to left and right, he began the slow methodical process of winkling the enemy from their bolt-holes in between the camp buildings. On the far side he would expect to see the supply dumps and beyond them the wire. But for now he steadied his breathing, and moving forward with the stealth and alertness of a stalking cat, Tommy prepared to do what he did best.

Back at the wire Manny was the first to notice that something was wrong. The fire support from the hillock had tailed off and then, to everyone's horror, another desultory bout of fire had started up, directed not at the enemy, but at the attacking troops themselves.

'What the fuck's going on?' Terry shouted. He reached for the radio and tried to raise Colin's headquarters, but no one answered his calls. Then, moments later, soldiers burst out of the jungle a hundred yards away, their eyes wide with terror.

'They're Colin's,' Manny shouted.

'Right, get them together, shake them out and put in a counter-attack,' Terry ordered calmly.

'But if the Khmer Rouge have taken the hilltop . . .'

'Then we'll just have to retake the fucker. Do it. Now!'

Manny looked for no more than a second into the

icy blue of Terry's stare. In his heart he knew that it was the only option. If the Khmer Rouge remained in control of the hill they would be able to pour accurate fire down on to the company just as Colin had done on the camp's defenders.

Without another word Manny got to his feet and raced back towards the edge of the jungle. Grabbing the nearest man from Colin's platoon, he slapped him in the face to bring him to his senses.

'Big disaster,' the terrified man jabbered. 'Commander is dead and the Khmer Rouge were too many.'

'How many?'

'Hundreds. Maybe a battalion.'

Manny slapped the man again. 'How many did you yourself see?' he barked, shaking the man.

'I myself didn't see any, but the others saw them. I promise.'

Cursing him, Manny swung the man round and kicked him back towards the hillock.

'Get back up there, you coward!'

Waving his M16 at the other soldiers who were standing around paralysed with fright, he drove them back into the jungle. He knew that speed was of the essence. If the Khmer Rouge had indeed taken the hill, the last thing they would be expecting would be a counter-attack. Whenever government troops had lost a position in the past, it had always taken days or weeks to reorganize and attack again. But after Terry's training, Manny knew exactly what he had to do. In any battle, and particularly in the jungle, where visibility was limited, enemy numbers could seem exaggerated out of all proportion. The hill had probably been attacked by little more than a handful of men. Well, if it had worked for the Khmer Rouge, it could work for him also.

Once in the cover of the jungle, Manny ordered his soldiers to fan out in an extended line while he moved in the centre, shepherding them forward and up the gentle slope. As they neared the crown where the ground started to level off, Manny heard voices ahead of him. Someone was laughing and he could hear weapons being cocked and reloaded. Hand-signalling to the men on either side of him, he drove his frightened command a little closer until he was convinced that the enemy were merely yards away.

'Fire!' he screamed at the top of his voice. A dozen M16s spat their vicious streams of bullets into the undergrowth, and as he and his men crashed through the trees Manny could hear the startled Khmer Rouge diving for cover.

'Charge!' he shouted, driving his men forward, their bayonets fixed and glinting in the dappled light of the jungle.

Bursting into the clearing that crowned the hillock, Manny almost fell over the dead body of Colin. The eyes were wide and staring, and seeing the dismembered mortar crew nearby, Manny understood in an instant what had happened. Without firm leadership the soldiers of Colin's platoon had been unable to face the Khmer Rouge counter-attack and had panicked and run. But there were other bodies on the hillock, their blood staining the flattened grass. Manny's surprise volley of fire had indeed caught the enemy unawares and a number of them had died in the first savage fusillade.

From farther down the hillside came the sound of

crashing and the snapping of branches as the Khmer Rouge fled in terror pursued by the men of Colin's platoon. Manny had seen such rapid changes in the morale of soldiers before. One act of courage, one firm stand by a leader, and the whole picture of a battle could change in an instant. He was also certain that any Khmer Rouge that were caught by his men would be shown little mercy; having been shamed in front of their captain, the soldiers would want to make amends for their earlier failure by an extreme show of aggression.

Sure enough, several minutes later, as Manny was reorganizing the defences of the hillock and redirecting the supporting fire on to the main Khmer Rouge positions in the camp, a couple of soldiers emerged from the bushes, flushed with the excitement of the pursuit. One of them saluted Manny smartly.

'They have gone, sir. At least the ones who managed to escape.'

He giggled like a naughty schoolboy and raised his arm. Swinging by the hair, the severed head of a man stared blindly into space. Manny looked away.

'Get back to your positions. Our men in the camp need your support. This isn't a bloody game.'

Sulking at the rebuke, the soldiers walked back to their firing positions, the one with the head tossing it away as they went. Bouncing on the grass like a discarded watermelon, it rolled into a small hollow, where it came to rest, emptied of the thoughts, loves, terrors and passions that had once animated its now waxen features.

Moving stealthily forward between two rows of accommodation huts, Tommy braced himself for contact with the unseen enemy. All around the fight raged among the narrow avenues that networked this section of the camp. This was now the close-quarter battle that would decide the outcome of the whole mission. If his platoon were driven off or if they failed to seize this heartland of the fortifications, then Terry would either have to commit Craig's platoon once they had regrouped or else withdraw altogether.

If he committed Craig's platoon then the company would be left without any reserve; a surprise counter-attack from the Khmer Rouge would find them unbalanced and would sweep them back into the jungle, where they could be hunted down and destroyed piecemeal. On the other hand, if he was forced to withdraw Tommy's men, then his only option would be to order a retreat in the hope that by maintaining the company intact they might be able to fight their way back to Battambang and thence to Phnom Penh.

Tommy gripped his Glock tightly. As far as he was concerned there would be no retreat. He was there to do a job and since his meeting with Sitha, the fight against the Khmer Rouge had become a personal one.

The face that appeared round the end of the thatched longhouse had hardly become visible when Tommy froze on the spot, steadied and put a single bullet clean through the temple. The man tottered into the open, staggering like a drunk. Tommy lowered his aim to centre chest but held his fire to conserve ammunition. Buckling at the knees, the man went down, dead from the moment the bullet entered the brain, only his reflexes keeping him upright. Sitting down heavily on crossed legs, he slowly toppled over backwards.

Sixteen rounds left, Tommy noted. Coming from the right, shouts and the sound of running feet alerted him to his next targets. Chased from one of the adjacent buildings by Tommy's men, a group of Khmer Rouge were crossing over to the left flank. Bolting from cover, they suddenly came into his field of fire, transiting the alleyway at full sprint. But Tommy was waiting for them. On one knee, his left elbow supported and the pistol hand cupped in the palm of the other, Tommy sighted along the barrel. As each man emerged into the open, running from right to left, Tommy fired a series of double taps. One by one the men went down, each one tumbling into the man in front as they were stopped in their tracks.

Waiting until the last of the bodies was still, Tommy rose from the ground and moved forward to the end of the building. Steadying his breath, he sprang across the open gap to the shelter of the next longhouse. As he did so, a burst of automatic fire snapped through the air behind him. Tommy cursed.

'Hold your fire, you stupid fuckers!' he screamed. 'Identify your targets first!'

From round the corner came the mumbled apologies from his flanking section. Jesus, Tommy thought, if the Rouge don't get me, my own blokes will.

With Tommy's platoon committed to the difficult fighting in among the longhouses, Terry doubled forward to Craig.

'Reorg your guys a.s.a.p., mate.'

'What's happened to the fire support?'

'Don't know. Manny's gone to sort it out. Move up behind me and be ready to pass through if ordered. Once Tommy's cleared the huts I want your combat engineers to get stuck into the supply dump area. Prepare the whole fucking place for demolition. We'll blow it back to Thailand.'

Craig grinned. 'Right.'

Terry was halfway across to the buildings when the air snapped at his ears.

'Sniper!'

He dived into a forward roll and threw himself behind a low parapet of sandbags.

'Got him!' Craig shouted.

'Where?'

'Bunker. Two o'clock. Seventy-five yards. Watch my tracer.'

Waiting for the crack of a rifle, Terry peered round just in time to see the 5.56mm orange tracer round from Craig's Colt Commando send a spurt of earth into the well-concealed firing slit of the hidden bunker.

'Seen!' Terry shouted. 'Cover me!'

Drawing his legs under him, Terry prepared to run. After tossing a smoke grenade into the open, he waited for the screen to take effect and then burst from cover towards the bunker. At the same time Craig pumped round after round into the firing slit.

'Suck on that, you bastards!'

Once he was out of the sniper's field of fire, Terry dived to the ground and crawled towards the slit, reaching for a grenade as he did so. Finding only a white-phosphorus grenade, he pulled the pin with his teeth, covered the final yard until he was side on to the slit, then popped the grenade through the hole.

'Special delivery from Postman Pat.'

A moment later there was a crump, and orange flame and fierce white smoke erupted from the firing slit as the Khmer Rouge sniper inside was incinerated.

On his feet again, Terry hurtled for the nearest building, the gutted cookhouse. Stepping over the dead guerrillas, he made his way to the far side just in time to see the green signal flare that indicated that Tommy had reached his limit of exploitation beyond the accommodation blocks.

'Good boy,' Terry muttered. Waving to Craig, he signalled him to close up and move on to the final objective: the supply dumps. On all sides the Khmer Rouge were falling back, throwing down their weapons and running for their lives.

With a shattering force that jarred his wrists, Terry's Colt Commando was smashed from his grip by the Kalashnikov bullet. Spinning on his heel, he found himself face to face with a guerrilla, his face a mask of hatred. Seeing the white mercenary unarmed, the man charged across the room, the bayonet shining on the end of his assault rifle. With a ferocious scream he lunged at Terry's stomach. But Terry was already moving, one hand deflecting the blade harmlessly aside with the *shotei* palm-heel, the block developing into a grip that pulled the attacker off balance. As the man went helplessly past, Terry's right foot spat out in a vicious *mae geri* kick, the ball of his booted foot driving in under his attacker's ribcage at the same time as a *kiai* shout rose up from deep in Terry's gut, serving to focus full power into the debilitating blow. With his wrists still sprained, Terry dropped on the fallen man with an *empi* elbow strike to the back of his neck, jarring the head backwards and breaking the spine.

Rubbing the feeling back into his aching wrists,

Terry retrieved the guerrilla's Kalashnikov, checked the rounds in the magazine and jogged after Craig's platoon, which had disappeared towards the far side of the camp. When at last he found them, Craig and Tommy were conferring together on the edge of the last open stretch of ground. Bullets stung the air as the Khmer Rouge put up a fierce rearguard defence.

'They're pulling out,' Tommy cried. 'The bulk of them have fucked off but there's a hard core holding us up.'

Terry glanced around, assessing the situation. With the battle so nearly won he didn't want to risk needless casualties, but at the same time it was essential to maintain the momentum in case the Khmer Rouge managed to regroup and put in a counter-attack. He hadn't come this far to have success plucked from his grasp now.

'Craig, get on the radio and tell Manny to move round from the airstrip side. Once the Rouge see they're being outflanked and that their escape route's about to be cut off, they might decide to call it a day and fuck off.'

'Right.'

As Craig ran back to his radio operator, Terry surveyed the devastated camp. 'No sign of Lon San, I suppose?'

'Hard to tell in all this shit,' Tommy replied. 'We'll get the guys to check the dead afterwards in the reorg phase. We might have struck it lucky.'

'Don't bank on it. He was probably one of the first ones out. I doubt we'll be seeing him again, but at least we've buggered his camp up. With luck he'll think twice about his plans for an offensive now.'

But Tommy wasn't listening. His head was tilted towards the northern sky.

'What's up?' Terry asked.

'Shh! Don't know.'

Shaking his head to clear the ringing in his ears, Terry listened. Slowly a look of extreme interest spread across his face.

'Well, well, well. An aeroplane.'

'Yes, and it's a big transport by the sound of it,' Tommy replied smiling.

'I knew I should have brushed up my Chinese.'

'Don't worry,' Tommy said. 'If we can coax the fucker on to the ground, I'll interpret for you.'

9

Colonel Kon had enjoyed the flight from Yunnan. With the plane crammed full of wooden packing cases, he had claimed a seat in the cockpit behind the pilot and co-pilot, peering over their shoulders as the passing landscape of barren desert plains gave way to rugged mountains and then to endless jungled hillscapes. After flying over southern China the lumbering transport plane crossed first into Burma and then Laos, before eventually banking west over Thailand and covering the final stretch towards the Cambodian border. On a normal run he would have set down at Paksaket, unloading his goods and enjoying a leisurely stopover in the company of General Sarit Chamonon and various female companions, but with Lon San's insistence that the arms be delivered direct to his Cambodian base, Colonel Kon expected nothing more than a brief reception marked by pious austerities.

He was feeling angry that he had allowed himself to be talked into it. Whereas the Chinese Communist Party had always diluted political purity with a healthy pragmatism, the Khmer Rouge, with all their claptrap of equality and proletarian rule, were considerably worse, blinkered in the extreme, as the Killing Fields bore silent witness. No, the stop would be no longer than absolutely necessary. He wondered if Lon San would even have arranged a cup of tea. No doubt he would be itching to unpack his new toys and set off on another murderous expedition.

'Fifteen minutes to Rurseng, sir.'

Colonel Kon acknowledged the pilot's shouted message. He liked the way that the old titles of 'Comrade' seemed to have been dropped. 'Sir' had a much more gratifying ring to it. He pushed himself back in his seat and stretched, turning round to watch the aircrew check that the loads were secure for landing. Deciding to stretch his legs, he went back to join them, sidling past the crates of small arms, mortars, anti-tank rockets, mines and ammunition. Lon San would certainly have enough here to start whatever offensive he had up his sleeve. The government troops were generally poorly equipped. For some reason the western powers of the UN seemed to imagine that it was enough simply to organize and administer an election. Both the US and Australia had been approached to supply weapons but so far both had refused; no doubt, Kon presumed, because the Cambodian government didn't have the cash to pay for them.

Perching on a crate at the rear of the aircraft, Kon squinted through one of the small side windows. The jungle below extended as far as the eye could see in one unbroken blanket of green foliage. Soon they would catch sight of a single brown tear, Rurseng appearing like a rip in the earth, the fortified camp of Lon San snugly squatting beside it.

A tap on the shoulder brought Kon back to the present.

'The captain needs a word with you, sir.'

Nodding to the aircrewman, Kon made his way

back to the cockpit, where the pilot was having an animated conversation with the co-pilot cum navigator.

'What's up?' Kon shouted above the noise of the four droning engines.

'Message from the Thai border authorities, Colonel. They say not to go near Rurseng. It's under attack or something.'

'What the hell do you mean?'

'That's all they said, sir. Apparently we're to divert to Paksaket and await further instructions.'

Kon thought quickly. The mention of Paksaket meant that the message was from Chamonon. That bloody idiot Lon San had fouled up again. The Khmer Rouge really must be in trouble if their bases so close to the border were within striking range of government forces. Perhaps the offensive wasn't going to happen after all. But that would mean that Kon wouldn't get his handsome pay-off of gems either.

'Where's Rurseng?' he asked angrily, leaning forward over the pilot's shoulder.

'Just behind that range of hills,' the pilot said, pointing.

'Take me over there.'

'But the message, sir . . .'

'I didn't say we were going to land, idiot.'

Banking the plane to the west, the pilot skirted the airstrip as far away as he could while still enabling his employer to see what was happening on the ground.

'Get me in closer,' Kon snapped.

Gritting his teeth, the pilot swung the plane back on line and headed straight for the strip. As the thin brown line appeared in the distance over the top of the last line of hills, a light trail of black smoke was just distinguishable creeping into the sky from Lon San's camp.

'Looks like they've been trying to douse a fire. No doubt hoping to lure us on to the ground and take the weapons and us intact.'

Kon chuckled. Good old Chamonon. He had no idea how the General had got word so quickly, but he was grateful for the warning.

'OK, that'll do. Don't fly any closer.'

With a sigh of relief the pilot banked away, setting a new course for the safety of the Paksaket airfield in Thailand. As Kon resumed his seat deep in thought, he mused that perhaps he would get his entertainment after all.

Deep in the bush, Lon San paused beside the narrow track, listening to the sound of the aircraft overhead and noting the surge of the engines as it banked away from the strip, accelerating towards Thailand, where he himself was headed. It was the only success story of the entire miserable day. Not having any communications with the plane itself, he had only managed a frantic last-minute call to General Sarit Chamonon's headquarters across the border. Coming on the radio himself, the General had listened patiently to Lon San's hurried account of the attack and his tactical withdrawal, before signing off and then using his superior radio equipment to locate the aircraft's frequency, retune and contact it with the warning. At least the arms would now be safe. Another rendezvous could be arranged in due course, perhaps at Paksaket itself, even though the General would then demand a higher pay-off. Lon San spat in the dirt. Everything seemed to be conspiring against him. Concerned only with regaining control of his country, he resented having to deal with such unscrupulous men.

But there was one other thing which had struck him a body blow. As soon as he had seen that the situation at the camp was hopeless, he had ordered its evacuation. The counter-attack on the hill had gone well and the rearguard action fought by the best of his men had delayed the mercenary-led company long enough for the main body of his fighters to make good their escape into the jungle. However, one of the last to leave, Lon San had been dodging his way through the camp perimeter on the other side of the supply dump, when he had stumbled and fallen beside the bodies of some of his comrades.

Getting heavily to his feet, dazed from the fall, he had suddenly found himself staring into the wide-open eyes of Comrade Mi Vi. She was curled in the dirt, her head twisted round at an unnatural angle, and it had only been when Lon San had tried to turn her over that the true extent of her injuries had become plain. She had been disembowelled by a mortar bomb. Detonating at her feet, the splinter fragments had exploded upwards, ripping through her stomach. As he flipped her over on to her back, Mi Vi's intestines had spilled from the ruptured sack of flesh in a purple cascade. Lon San had stared in horror at the sweet face, barely grazed, crowning a sight of such ugliness. Unable to stop himself vomiting, he had been pulled away by two of his soldiers just as the first of the government troops rounded a corner and opened fire. It had been a narrow escape, but all along the jungle track as Lon San fled from his devastated camp, Mi Vi's face was imprinted on his mind, staring at him in a mixture of mute bewilderment and accusation.

As the sound of the plane receded, Lon San was just settling back into his stride when further up the track, at the head of the column, a volley of automatic rifle and machine-gun fire crackled through the trees.

'Ambush!'

The cry echoed back down the lines of scurrying men, passed from mouth to mouth as soldiers dived for cover, waiting for orders from their tired commanders.

'On your feet, idiots!' Lon San screamed. 'It's just a cut-off force. Bypass and attack from the flank! Where's your training?'

Kicking and cursing the cowering men, he formed a handful into a rapid counter-attack force and drove them into the bushes on a wide hooking manoeuvre. He should have expected it, he thought. Damn him for allowing himself to become unbalanced by a woman! In the past this would never have happened. He had been renowned for having almost a sixth sense for impending trouble, yet now he had fallen prey to two surprise attacks in one day.

Thrashing through the dense undergrowth, he waited until he had reached a point at right angles to the ambushing force before shaking his men into an extended line and ordering them to sweep forward with weapons at the ready. If all went well they would be able to roll up the enemy position from the side.

Advancing in the middle of the line, Lon San crept forward with his Kalashnikov trained in the direction of the enemy. When they had gone little more than fifty yards, there was a shout from a man on the right end of the line and a flurry of shots announced that they had made contact with the government troops.

'Charge!'

Screaming at the top of his hoarse voice, Lon San sprang forwards, spraying the ground in front with bursts of fire. Taking courage from their leader, the other Khmer Rouge guerrillas followed hot on his heels and a moment later they found themselves among the startled cut-off ambush force.

Hacking and slashing with his bayonet, Lon San struck out at the prone figures on the ground, who didn't even have time to get to their feet before he was on them. Seeing only the pale, staring face of Mi Vi and remembering the burning devastation of his camp, he tore through the enemy in a frenzy of hatred, claiming with every stab and thrust the revenge that he had sworn would be his.

With the fire of the government ambush party halted, the main body of the Khmer Rouge swept forward to join their comrades in the massacre until none of their opponents remained alive. Venting their anger and frustration on the smaller group as they had been unable to do with the attacking platoons of Tommy and Craig, the guerrillas completed the slaughter and then stripped the dead of their weapons and equipment. Mad with blood lust, Lon San leapt on to one of the corpses and pulling back the neck, hacked the head from the body with several strokes of his jungle knife.

'All of them,' he shouted. 'Cut them all!'

Following his lead, the Khmer Rouge moved methodically from man to man, sawing and slashing until a dozen or more bodies had been decapitated and the heads wedged in the branches of the surrounding trees. Locating the beheaded torso of the sergeant who had been in command of the ambush, Lon San added one final touch of humiliation. Ripping open the dead man's combat trousers, he severed the penis and stuffed it, ragged and bleeding, in the man's mouth like a cigarette, then balanced the head on a branch facing down the track where Lon San knew that the company and the foreign mercenaries would eventually come looking for him.

With his rage abating, he stood with his blood-soaked arms hanging at his sides, surveying his handiwork. Around him his men, inured to horror, stared at the sight with blank eyes, bored now that the task was done and anxious to be gone. Heaving his Kalashnikov on to his shoulder, Lon San waved them away, waiting until the last of them had disappeared before himself following on behind. At least this part of the enemy's plan had failed.

As he strolled after his men, a grim smile spread across his face, for if all went according to plan he would get his revenge on his opponents in another way, a more personal form of revenge that would hit at the foreign mercenaries and the Cambodian government traitors themselves. For as well as asking General Chamonon to warn off the arms shipment, Lon San had given him a coded message to transmit to his agents in Phnom Penh.

Lon San felt his spirits rise as his lengthening stride bore him ever closer to the Thai border. If the government thought he could be destroyed so easily they were very much mistaken. It would take more than a bunch of westerners to put him out of action. The Chinese arms were safe, sufficient men had escaped to carry on the struggle from the safety of Thailand, where they could regroup under the protection of General Chamonon, and Lon San had arranged a surprise reception for the foreign mercenaries that would mar their triumphal return to Phnom Penh. The game was far from over.

As the plane banked away from the airstrip, veering off towards the north, Terry shrugged philosophically.

'I guess he got wind we were here.'

'It wouldn't have been too hard,' Tommy agreed, looking at the smoke from the cookhouse that his men had been unable to quench in time.

'They were warned off,' called a voice from behind.

Turning round, they saw Craig and Manny walking towards them.

'Manny found their frequency and picked up the message.'

Terry felt his blood rising. 'Who?'

'Who do you think? Chamonon. It was the man himself. He didn't even try to conceal his identity. He's completely his own boss and he does what the hell he likes.'

There was a moment's silence as the four men watched the plane become a speck and eventually disappear over the jungled horizon.

'There's one more thing,' Manny said. 'About Colin.'

Telling them of the mortar double-feed, Manny said how he had found their dead friend, adding: 'They're bringing his body down now.'

Terry looked around at the airstrip and the ruined camp. The soldiers had begun the task of demolishing every last trace of Lon San's presence. The bodies of the Khmer Rouge were being manhandled into the bunkers and the earthen and timber roofs collapsed on to them to form makeshift graves. Their own dead were being placed in a row to one side to await transport back to Phnom Penh, where they would be returned to their families and relatives for the traditional funeral rites.

'We'll take him back with us,' Terry said. 'Poor Colin. We couldn't have done it without his support.'

Having run up to the group of commanders, an ashen-faced soldier stood shaking at attention.

'Sir, you must see.'

'See what?' Terry asked.

'The ambush platoon. Come.'

Following the soldier quickly out of the camp perimeter, the four men retraced the route taken by Lon San and the retreating Khmer Rouge some time ago. They had heard the sound of firing, indicating that their plan for a depth ambush position had paid off, but none of them was prepared for the sight that met them when they reached the scene of the massacre and Lon San's revenge.

'Dear God in heaven,' Craig stammered, leaning on a tree for support. 'What kind of creatures are we fighting?'

'Now you see,' Manny replied coldly. 'The men who did this ruled my country. For five years these same men had power of life and death over all of us. Those they didn't kill, they tortured. Now you know why it is imperative that we destroy them.'

Stepping carefully among the corpses, Tommy Liu stared down in horror.

'I thought the Triad murder squads could be barbarous, but this beats the lot.'

Leading the way back to the camp, Terry issued orders for the demolition work, allocating areas to each of the three platoons. Taking command of Colin's platoon, Manny organized the collection of all the dead. Once that had been done, his men began dismantling the perimeter wire and booby-traps. Meanwhile Craig's platoon completed the destruction of all the bunkers and sangars, using demolition charges to cave in the roofs. After this, Craig turned his attention to the longhouses and administration buildings, stacking the bamboo furniture inside and setting each building ablaze by lobbing in a single white-phosphorus grenade.

At the supply dump, Tommy organized the placing of demolition charges on the stockpiles of weapons, ammunition, equipment and food that Lon San had carefully husbanded in preparation for his offensive. Using electrical detonators, the combat engineers laid a cable to a firing point on the far side of the airstrip.

'We'll blow it once everyone's clear,' Terry called across to Tommy. Searching through the camp as the destruction work continued, Terry located Lon San's personal quarters. Everything of intelligence value had been destroyed before the Khmer Rouge had left, but standing in the centre of the bare room, he could sense for the first time the man he was up against.

'Hello, Lon fucking San,' he said quietly in the empty room. 'We haven't met, but I'm Terry Williams.'

He went over to the upturned bed and idly kicked it. 'You tried to have me killed one evening, remember? Well, I hope you've enjoyed my return call.'

Stepping back to the doorway, he took in the feel of the room. 'I've got your fucking number, mate. Next time we meet, don't expect to get off so lightly.'

172

Turning back into the sun, he walked through the camp to the airstrip, and once everything was ready, gave a single long whistle, bringing the soldiers of the three platoons running in from all parts of the camp.

'OK, lads, let's get out of here. Your guys ready, Tommy?'

Tommy gave the thumbs up.

'Right. Move!'

Leading their men across the airstrip, Craig, Manny and Tommy grouped them under cover. To one side the bodies of the dead had been gathered, each carefully wrapped in a groundsheet. Manny had used the radio to call in an aircraft. With the attack completed, the need for secrecy had gone, and with a vacant airstrip on hand the return journey to Phnom Penh could be accomplished painlessly.

When the company had been formed into a defensive harbour, Terry walked back to the demolition firing point, where the combat engineers, Tommy and Craig lay behind a wall of sandbags.

'All set?'

The engineer sergeant grinned.

'Let them have it.'

After a final glance to check that all was clear, the sergeant waited until Terry was lying flat on the ground.

'Firing now!'

With a firm thumb press on the firing button, the sergeant shot the electric current along the cable to the clutch of detonators scattered throughout the Khmer Rouge supply area, each detonator buried in the heart of a bundle of explosives. Barely a second later, the whole camp heaved into the air as a series of violent detonations ruptured the earth, causing secondary explosions among the crates of ammunition until ripple upon ripple flashed through the camp, orange flame, debris and clouds of black smoke shooting high above the treetops.

Terry reached forward and slapped the combat engineer on the back.

'Nice work, mate. They won't be using Rurseng in a hurry.'

Several miles away on a Thai hilltop, General Sarit Chamonon paused in mid-sentence, his teacup halfway to his lips.

'What the fuck was that?' said the man opposite him. On the other side of the small camping table, Eddy Passenta stared hard into Cambodia like a Mongol commander searching for new lands to rape.

A sardonic grin twisted the General's mouth. 'That, I suspect, was Comrade Lon San's hearth and home.'

'Ha!'

'He called me shortly before you arrived, mumbling about being massively outnumbered. He was going to make a "tactical withdrawal", as he put it.'

Fat Eddy shifted his massive bulk in the straining canvas chair into which his buttocks were tightly wedged.

'The little fart,' he wheezed, suppressing one of his own.

Flying down from Chiang Mai on business, he had been invited by the General to tour his section of border. Whenever possible, the General liked to show off his domain to business partners, impressing them with his military muscle and rounding off the trip with tea overlooking Cambodia before a return to Paksaket and the delights of the whorehouse.

As the rumble of a second explosion rolled through the densely wooded valleys towards them, the General continued his tea, peering with satisfaction over the top of his cup at the plume of smoke smudging the horizon.

'Poor old Lon San. Things haven't been going his way lately. I expect he'll be joining us in a day or two.'

Fat Eddy picked his teeth, searching a corner of his mouth with one stubby, gold-ringed finger. 'I don't know why you do business with him. The Khmer Rouge is a spent force. Drugs, that's the business of the future.'

The General poured some more tea for his guest, adding a generous tot of whisky. 'There's no harm in diversifying one's business interests. So long as they can pay I'm happy to supply them.'

The drug baron shrugged. 'After this fiasco you'll be lucky if he can pay for a screw.'

'Don't underestimate the durability of a fanatic. You and I are businessmen. When one avenue closes, we'll find another one. But these guerrillas are different. Now Lon San's got his back to the wall he'll be at his most dangerous.'

'I'll remember that.'

'You would be wise to,' the General added, getting to his feet and signalling for his men to pack up and prepare to return to Paksaket. Coming out of the shadows, two of Fat Eddy's guards rushed to his side, one of them taking each plump elbow in an attempt to pop him out of the chair, which rose with him, refusing to part company with his buttocks.

By the time they arrived back at Paksaket, Colonel Kon's transport plane had landed and refuelled while Kon himself strode anxiously up and down, impatient at the delay. Hearing the noise of the approaching cars, he scarcely waited until the General's staff car had come to a stop before rushing up to the door.

'Did you hear the explosions? That bloody Khmer idiot almost got me killed.'

General Chamonon smiled warmly at the Chinaman, encircling his shoulders with a friendly arm.

'Come and have a drink to calm your nerves, Colonel. You're quite safe here, I assure you.'

'That's what Lon San said and look what happened to him. Where is he, by the way?'

The General pointed vaguely in the direction of the endless jungle. 'Out there somewhere. But he'll arrive in a day or two. He said so himself. If you can just wait until then we can complete the deal and you'll be off.'

Kon snorted. 'You must be joking. As far as I'm concerned the deal's off. How do you know Lon San will have the means to pay?'

The possibility that Lon San might have lost his stock of gems had already crossed the General's mind, but he did his best to hide his own anxiety. If the deal fell through he stood to lose his own considerable pay-off.

'Even if he has, the Khmer Rouge have plenty more.'

But Kon was not to be so easily appeased. 'Then you can fix up another rendezvous at some later date. I don't intend to wait around for that madman to turn up with the whole Cambodian army on his tail.'

'They'd never dare cross the border,' the General

continued more urgently, sensing the chance of big money starting to recede.

'Well, whoever was leading the government troops did a pretty thorough job at Rurseng. I flew over it. The whole place was a ruin.'

'I know,' the General added thoughtfully. 'We saw it ourselves.' With a sigh he allowed his resolve to slacken. 'When can we expect you back, then? I can tell Lon San when he arrives.'

'Paksaket? Never again. The next delivery must be somewhere completely safe.'

'But this is safe,' the General protested, verging on anger.

Seeing his opportunity, Fat Eddy shuffled forward. 'I think I may be able to help.'

He had a way of commanding instant attention whenever he spoke, and once both men were looking at him he continued.

'I've got an airstrip near Chiang Mai. Why not deliver the arms there? It's the other side of the country and there's no way any Cambodian army unit's going to march right across Thailand to interfere.'

The General beamed delightedly as Colonel Kon looked suspiciously at the vast drug baron and asked: 'What's the catch?'

Fat Eddy chuckled, making his whole body shake. 'There isn't one. At least not for you. Lon San can compensate us all for the extra inconvenience.'

A slow smile spread across Kon's face as he understood. 'It just might be possible. But what about Lon San? He's hardly going to take this lying down.'

'He doesn't have a choice,' Fat Eddy said simply.

'You leave him to me,' the General added. 'He'll

understand your concern. If you look at it one way, we're all simply trying to ensure the safety of his arms shipment. He'll just have to travel to Chiang Mai to take delivery, that's all.'

As the General led his guests towards his quarters he reflected that he could use this unexpected trip to look over Fat Eddy's latest stock of village girls for shipment to Bangkok. He couldn't wait to replace Lalin, who, seeing the threesome approach, was readying herself for their attentions.

It had been a hot, humid day in Phnom Penh. Sitha had met Suki at the market and the two of them had enjoyed the morning buying material for a new dress that Sitha was making. She was determined to look her very best for Tommy's return from the border zone. The cloth was an intricate pattern of flowers against a brightly coloured background and she could almost see the finished dress in her mind's eye. She would wear it at a celebration dinner that she and Suki were planning to welcome the men home.

Exhausted by the trip, the two girls had returned to the quiet villa for lunch, sitting on the veranda with bowls of noodles, glasses of lime juice and a tray of fresh fruit. When they had finished eating, Sitha made a pot of jasmine tea while Suki cleared away the empty dishes.

'You sit there and relax,' Suki insisted. 'It's my turn to wash up.'

Reluctantly, Sitha allowed herself to be pushed back into the wicker chair as Suki collected the dirty dishes and disappeared through the hall, heading for the kitchen at the back of the house. Suki was waiting for some water to boil when she became aware of voices on the veranda. Not having heard the bell and knowing that there was no one in the house besides her and Sitha, she moved quietly towards the door, being careful to keep out of sight.

Suddenly there was a scream. Rushing into the hall, she saw Sitha struggling on the veranda with two men. Flinging herself at them, Suki was able to take one of the men by surprise, catching him in the small of the back with a punch from her clenched fist. But never having hit anyone before, she was not prepared for the pain as the skin on her knuckles tore and the force of the blow jarred her wrist violently.

Spinning round, the man lashed out at her with a savage kick that sent her sprawling on the floor.

'Suki, get away! It's me they want,' Sitha screamed.

Struggling upright, Suki got to her feet just as the man swung with his fist, hitting her hard in the face. Turning to his companion, the man shouted something in Cambodian and clubbed Sitha on the back of the head, dropping her unconscious to the floor, but when he turned back to deal with Suki, she was already crawling through the door. He caught up with her as she reached the kitchen, pulled her roughly to her feet, grinned, and punched her again, spinning her across the room towards the stove. Then, grabbing a knife from the table, he came towards her.

Without thinking, Suki glanced dully at the knife, her senses dazed by the beating. But close beside her she could feel heat and fumbled for the pan, keeping it hidden from her attacker. Grasping the handle, she swung it with all her strength as she turned, sending a jet of scalding water over her attacker's face.

With a hideous scream, the man dropped the knife and clutched at his face and eyes where the water hissed as it seared his skin. Staggering blindly about the room, he walked straight into Suki's foot as she brought it up hard into his groin. As she scrabbled for the knife on the kitchen floor, Suki was suddenly alerted by the sound of a car engine in the drive at the front of the house and by voices of people running up the steps.

'Sitha!' she called.

But the only answer was a shout from the hall to which Suki's blinded attacker screamed a reply. Suki darted towards the back door and tore it open as another man burst into the kitchen from the hall, waving a pistol. Flinging herself down the steps, she ducked as a shot cracked in the air above her, another smashing into the rough stone pavement that led away from the house.

Pushing her way through a garden gate, she found herself in a side alley. It was the hottest part of the day and the streets of the quiet residential district were deserted. Shouting at the top of her voice, Suki ran and stumbled along the alleyway until she emerged on to the main road, fifty yards from the front of the villa. Still shouting for help, she ran across the street. From somewhere in a neighbouring garden a dog began to bark. A man leaned out of an upstairs window and called angrily for her to be quiet. When she screamed at him to go for help, he slammed his shutters, returning to his siesta like the rest of the neighbourhood.

In a spurt of gravel, a car burst from the driveway of the Trons' villa, turned towards Suki and accelerated. Flinging herself out of its path, she landed badly, cutting both knees and hitting her head against the kerb. As she stared after the retreating car, she saw the slumped figure of Sitha in the back seat, framed between her abductors, her head and face masked with the bright cloth that they had bought from the market.

10

During a short stopover in Battambang, Captain Tron took Terry to report to the regional military commander on the success of the operation against Rurseng. Received like heroes, they briefed the headquarters staff and answered a tirade of eager questions about the strength and capabilities of the Khmer Rouge and the fate of Lon San himself.

'I am sure you will all agree,' the brigadier concluded, addressing his officers at the end of Terry's briefing, 'that we owe an enormous debt of gratitude to Mr Williams, Captain Tron and their men. With luck, it may be that they have thwarted the offensive that we know Lon San was planning.'

Looking down at his boots, Terry felt himself blushing, not so much from the barrage of praise, but more from a nasty feeling that the offensive, rather than having been thwarted, had merely been delayed. Catching his eye, Manny shrugged and leaned across to whisper: 'We have a saying. Enjoy the sunshine while it lasts. Tomorrow it might rain.'

'As regards Comrade Lon San,' the brigadier continued, 'although he was not found among the dead, let us hope that he has been sufficiently discredited among his own men that they dispose of him in some worthy ditch along the way to Thailand.'

Acknowledging the ripple of laughter, the regional

commander led Terry and Manny from the hall as everyone stood to applaud them.

They were crossing the parade square of the army barracks, heading for the Officers' Mess for a celebratory drink, when Craig and Tommy strode briskly towards them, waving urgently to attract their attention. Even before they spoke Terry could see from the expression on Tommy's face that something was terribly wrong.

Making their apologies to the brigadier, they drew Terry and Manny aside, Craig gripping Manny firmly by the shoulders. Staring back at him, Manny's face blanched.

'It's Sitha, isn't it?'

'She's alive, Manny. That's the most important thing,' Craig tried to reassure him.

'What happened? Tell me!'

Bursting like a dam, Tommy poured out the story that they had heard only minutes before over the telephone from Minister Yon Rin's office.

'How's Suki?' Terry cut in.

'She's OK,' Craig said. 'A swollen eye, cut lip and a few bruises. Apparently she almost killed one of the bastards. She did all she could to stop them. They nearly shot her in the process.'

Overhearing the conversation, the brigadier offered his personal staff car to drive them immediately to the airfield where the rest of the company was waiting for the return flight to the capital, and two hours later they were circling Phnom Penh preparing to land.

As the plane taxied to a standstill, Terry could make out two figures standing outside the arrival hall. Even from that distance he could see the toll that the ordeal had taken on Suki. Her shoulders were stooped and she leaned on the slight figure of Yon Rin.

The aircraft doors were barely open before the four men were out and racing across the tarmac. First to reach the waiting figures was Tommy, overwhelmed by the frustration of powerlessness. As Minister Yon Rin tried to calm him, telling him and Manny such facts as his intelligence network had been able to ascertain, Terry wrapped his arms around Suki in a tight hug. Feeling safe at last, she broke down, sobbing in the hollow of his neck as he tenderly stroked her hair, soothing her like a frightened child.

Yon Rin ushered the little party into the waiting cars and drove them back to Manny's villa, where armed guards had been posted on the front and side gates. The police had scoured the house and grounds for clues and Yon Rin assured them that everything possible was being done to track down the kidnappers. Sitting in a stunned silence on the veranda from which Sitha had so recently been snatched, the mercenaries listened to Suki's account of the abduction, shocked to the core by the assault on an innocent woman who had already suffered so much at the hands of the Khmer Rouge.

Feeling the anger grow inside him like a raging forest fire, Terry heard Suki tell how she had been beaten to the ground.

'Some bastard's going to pay for this,' Craig muttered.

'I agree,' Yon Rin said, keeping a firm hold on his emotions. 'The question is, who?'

'Isn't it obvious?' Tommy burst out.

'Probably,' Yon Rin nodded thoughtfully. 'But the

Khmer Rouge have friends in many places. They could have taken Sitha anywhere. Until my men can locate her it is best that you wait and fill your time as best you can.'

Tommy leapt to his feet and strode back and forth across the veranda like a caged tiger.

'The Minister's right,' Terry said with resignation. 'Until we know exactly who's holding her and where, we'd just be flailing about in the dark.'

Throughout the talk Manny had sat stiffly, his hands heavy in his lap, the three mercenaries hardly daring to look at him. Now, with all words expended, Terry reached across and put a hand on his shoulder.

'We'll stay here with you if you like.'

Manny smiled bravely, his face ashen. 'No. Go back to the hotel. I think I need to be alone right now.'

'Whatever you say, mate. But you know where to find us.'

The three men and Suki rose and made for the door.

'Let us know the moment you hear anything,' Terry said to Yon Rin.

They drove back to the hotel in silence, and when they got there Craig and Tommy unloaded the gear while Terry helped Suki from the car. Before disappearing into the lobby, Craig whispered: 'Don't worry, Dojo. I'll keep an eye on Tommy.'

'Do. He loved the girl.'

Craig smiled. 'You've only got to look at him to see that.'

Shouldering his bergen, Terry climbed up to his room, one arm round Suki, who clung to him as if he too was about to be snatched away. When they reached his door she opened it for him, following behind without question.

'Do you mind if I stay for a while?'

Terry dropped his pack on the floor and eased out of his combat jacket. 'I was hoping you would. I wasn't sure how to ask you. I guess I'm a little out of practice.'

He started to unlace his boots. 'I think I'd better do this in the bathroom. A few days in the jungle doesn't do much for a guy's appeal.'

He hobbled with half-opened boots into the bathroom, ran the shower until the gushing water was hot enough to steam the mirrors, and undressed. He gasped as he stepped under the shower, the jets of water stinging his skin. Having soaped himself all over, he leaned back against the tiled wall, letting the suds run themselves down his body and into the drain, feeling his muscles relax for the first time since the start of the mission.

When at last he'd had enough, he rubbed himself down with a clean towel, combing back his damp hair and slipping into jeans and a clean T-shirt. Back in the bedroom he found Suki lying fast asleep on the mattress, curled up like a baby, her sides gently rising and falling. He eased himself on to the bed beside her, draping an arm over her shoulder and feeling her move unconsciously against him, moulding her body into his.

Almost asleep himself, Terry suddenly felt soft lips on his cheek and opened his eyes to look at Suki, inches away. Reaching up to stroke his hair, she covered his face with kisses, brushing his mouth with hers. Pulling her against him, Terry ran his hand the length of her spine, feeling a shudder travel through her body like the vibration of a string.

'Suki.'

The word escaped him without thought, an expression of want and need, answered by the tears of relief that filled her eyes.

'I was so frightened for you,' she said between kisses. 'I longed for you to come back.'

Terry felt his heart race with emotions he had almost forgotten, and as Suki ran her hands under his shirt he remembered that a man could only travel the road of love unarmed. He had seen it that very afternoon, watching Tommy Liu being pulled apart, piece by merciless piece. Yet even though he heard the warning, he knew that he loved Suki Yamato, even if doing so might destroy him as no enemy had ever managed to do.

In the darkened room Sitha could tell it was still day from the distant sounds of heavy traffic. Lying on a bare mattress, her hands and feet securely bound, she had tried to keep track of time but with the passing days and the constant moves during which she was blindfolded, it had become increasingly difficult. But now the travelling had stopped, at least for the time being.

Hearing someone approach, she swung her legs off the bed and forced herself upright into a sitting position. There was the sound of a key in the lock, a bolt was slid back and the next moment she was clenching her eyes against the glare of an overhead bulb.

'Who is it?' she asked, squinting into the doorway.

'Who do you think?'

'Oh, it's you.'

Recognizing the voice of the girl who brought in her meals, Sitha waited until her eyes had adjusted to the dazzling light before looking at her. In sharp contrast to her own face, the girl's was so heavily made up it was impossible to tell her age beneath the crude mask of lipstick, powder and cream.

'You should eat,' the girl said sullenly, sliding the tray across the floor towards the bed.

'It's not easy with my hands tied.'

'I managed.'

Sensing a chink in the girl's usual reticence, and anxious to take advantage of every possible opening that might enable her to escape, Sitha tried to prolong the conversation.

'Did you come here as a prisoner too?'

'We all do at first,' the girl replied, leaning back against the wall and inspecting her long scarlet nails.

'Now you're free why don't you run away?'

The girl laughed cruelly, shaking her head at Sitha's innocence.

'Run where? They'd catch you before you even got out of Bangkok.'

Bangkok! The name resounded in Sitha's mind like a warning bell. So that's where they had brought her. Noting that the girl didn't realize she was giving away information valuable to the captive, Sitha kept her face expressionless, scanning the tray of food while her mind raced for new ploys to extract more information.

'What's that?'

'Pork.'

'Did you cook it yourself?'

For the first time the girl smiled, albeit self-consciously. 'What if I did?'

'It smells good. Who taught you to cook?'

'Who do you think? My mother.'

Reaching down to the tray with difficulty, Sitha picked up the bowl with her bound hands and started to eat.

'Mm! Not bad. Where's your mother now?'

'Home.'

'You're Burmese, aren't you?'

'You ask a lot of questions for a whore.'

'I'm not a whore,' Sitha replied, keeping her voice level lest she offend the girl and lose her attention.

'Not yet perhaps,' the girl sniggered.

'Oh?'

Becoming conspiratorial, the girl drew closer, checked to see no one could overhear, then sat on the bed beside Sitha.

'Don't think I'm a whore,' she said, gathering her tattered pride about her like a worn cloak against heavy rain.

'I didn't think you were,' Sitha replied quickly. 'I can see you're too clever for that.'

'You can?' The girl grinned.

'Of course. I'd say you're someone pretty important in the organization.'

'Don't be silly. Me?'

'Sure. The moment I saw you I could tell there was something special about you. I think we'll become good friends, you and I,' Sitha said, smiling warmly at the girl.

'Yes. I think you're right. It's good to have someone to talk to. No one ever talks to me here. All the General wants is fuck, fuck, fuck. I'm sick of it.'

'I can imagine,' Sitha replied, latching on to this new titbit. 'The Thais are all the same. We Cambodians are like the Burmese in that respect. We've been exploited just the same. Look at us, you and me. Both of us prisoners while General . . .'

'Chamonon,' the girl supplied eagerly.

'Yes, while General Chamonon does what he likes and gets away with it.'

Giving the seed time to take root in the girl's simple mind, Sitha thought frantically of her next step. She had to make the most of this opportunity to get word of her whereabouts to Phnom Penh, but if she asked too many questions the girl would take fright and leave. Then in a flash it came to her.

With a heavy sigh of resignation, she pushed her bowl aside. 'I never thought I'd end up in a place like this.'

The girl looked at her sympathetically, patting her hand. 'It's not as bad as all that. We get enough to eat.'

But the sudden look of misery on the girl's face told of her true feelings beneath the brave mask. Sitha gauged the moment, weighing her chances. The girl was obviously scared. There was even a chance she would warn the General if this new prisoner attempted to subvert her. Instead Sitha decided to rely on her cunning. During her years under the Khmer Rouge tyranny she had honed it to perfection.

'Well, if I've got to become a whore,' she said as merrily as she could, 'I know of a man who'd like to be my first customer!'

The girl elbowed her playfully. 'Go on! You're not serious?' she giggled.

'Of course I am. I also bet he'd pay well to know I'm here.'

Instantly the girl was on her guard and Sitha

felt her stomach tighten, fearing she had gone too far.

'What do you mean?'

'Nothing. Just that he could give the General his custom. He's a complete bastard in all other respects.'

The girl was silent. Toying with the remains of the rice, Sitha forced herself to appear completely unconcerned.

'His name's Sy Tron,' she said after a while, wiping her mouth with her sleeve. 'The biggest crook in Bangkok. He lives in one of those big houses in Vijdami Road. I expect the General knows him.' She laughed. 'I wouldn't be surprised if they're even friends.'

'I'd better be going.'

'Just a minute,' Sitha said quickly. 'What's your name?'

The girl paused by the door, the tray with its empty bowl in her hands.

'Lalin.'

Arriving back in Bangkok from his border headquarters, General Chamonon went straight to the Black Lotus. He always found it the best place to relax after a hard tour of duty up on the Cambodian frontier. True to his expectations, Lon San had been livid to arrive at Paksaket after a difficult march through the jungle, only to discover that Colonel Kon and the arms shipment had already gone. But in the end his only option had been to accept the terms of the new deal which Eddy Passenta had put to him with obvious glee.

It seemed that they were all to convene again at

Chiang Mai as guests of Fat Eddy. It would be a bit like a holiday, the General reflected as he slipped out of his uniform and put on a white embroidered silk shirt, the tail hanging loose outside a pair of light-grey slacks. He liked the unscrupulous drug baron and secretly enjoyed watching him humiliate Lon San.

There was a knock at the door and Lalin came in. The General ignored her welcoming smile.

'What do you want?' he asked coldly.

She walked up beside him and stroked his arm. Shrugging her off, the General strode to the mirror and combed back his hair, rubbing in liberal amounts of strongly scented oil.

'I am happy to see you,' Lalin tried.

'Don't lie, you ignorant slut. Why are you still here anyway?'

'What do you mean, General?'

'I told the boys to send you to the Clouds of Heaven.'

Watching her face in the mirror, Sarit Chamonon thrilled to see the shock and alarm registering on her face.

'Yes, you've had your last decent fuck, my Burmese chicken. From now on it's the great Proletariat for you. I wish you well of them.'

'What have I done to upset you?' Lalin asked, fighting back her tears.

'What have you done? Nothing. It's what you are, my dear. A simple-minded village idiot. All your thick perfumes and powders can't hide the smell of the peasant. Putting it simply, I despise you. No,' the General continued absently, 'that's too harsh. I don't think of you often enough to despise you.'

Reaching to the back of a chair for support,

Lalin felt a great sob break from deep in her throat.

'Oh, get out of my sight,' the General suddenly bawled. 'I don't want to see you again. Enjoy the Clouds of Heaven.'

Feeling her way out, Lalin closed the door behind her. Blind with tears, she stumbled to her room and shut herself in, sinking on to the bed and giving way to the tears that poured from her in an unstoppable tide. The Clouds of Heaven. She had been there once with the General when he went on a visit. She had seen the worn, diseased hags that were still only in their twenties. She had seen the customers who went there, not even rich foreigners or businessmen, but Bangkok taxi drivers, boatmen and labourers. No one escaped from the Clouds of Heaven, and death was a long time coming.

Forcing herself upright, she suddenly found herself thinking of the strange girl locked in the basement room. Lalin laughed bitterly at such stupidity; how could anyone be so unconcerned about such a fate as that Cambodian?

Drying her eyes, she looked at herself in a small mirror. Her make-up had smudged and she looked more like a clown than the girl who, until moments ago, had been the personal companion of General Sarit Chamonon. At Paksaket, when he had forced her to do things with the Chinaman and the appalling Eddy Passenta while he himself had looked on, she had already suspected that her time of privileged treatment was coming to an end. Now that moment had come. She could expect little sympathy from the other girls or the guards; her position as the General's own whore had won her nothing but envy and resentment. They would all take pleasure in her downfall. She was alone in a hostile world, without a single ally to help her and not a soul to whom she could turn for help.

As they strolled through the crowded market, Terry glanced at Suki, feeling her hand warm and tight in his and hardly believing the emotions pounding through him. Despite Sitha's abduction he had been unable to stop a deep joy from welling up inside him and knew that for Suki it was the same.

'I just can't stop myself,' he said as they approached the edge of the market-place. 'Why the hell do we have to fall in love at a time like this?'

Suki smiled at him. 'No one ever chooses the time, do they? It just happens.'

'Well, I'm bloody glad that it's happened to us.'

Terry slipped his arm round her waist and led her to a scattering of chairs on the pavement outside a café.

'This must have been a beautiful city once,' he said when they were sitting in the sun and two cups of coffee steamed invitingly on the table between them. 'The UN must have sent you to some interesting places in your time.'

Suki held her coffee cup in both hands, feeling the comforting heat penetrate her skin.

'It has. What about you?'

'Oh, I've been around.'

'How do you justify it, though? Don't get me wrong,' she added quickly, 'I'm not getting at you. I think I agree with you now that force is the only language some people understand.'

'There's no need to be kind,' Terry said with a sigh, leaning back in his chair. 'I've always been a bit of a misfit. I don't know why but I could never stomach the thought of a life selling insurance or cars.'

'There are other alternatives.'

'Perhaps. But I haven't found them yet. I'm a soldier, Suki. I don't apologize for that.'

'I'm not asking you to.' She reached across the table and took his hand. 'Right now I love you just the way you are.'

Terry smiled. 'Do you think you'd like Swansea?'

'Not from what you've told me about it.'

'Oh. It doesn't always rain, you know. Well . . . not heavy rain.'

'That's not much of a consolation,' she said, laughing, then thought for a moment. 'You've been in Japan. Do you think you could ever settle there?'

'Sure I could. Bit expensive, though. I suppose I could teach karate. Coals to Newcastle and all that.'

'I don't want to disappoint you but hardly anyone practises the martial arts nowadays. It's all a bit of a myth from the movies. Baseball's a far bigger craze. Karate's looked on as the sport of the poor. It hurts your hands. Nowadays Japanese kids would rather save up for a motorbike and listen to rock music.'

'The Senseis are a dying breed, eh?'

'I'm afraid so.'

Terry shook his head. 'Isn't that just the story of my life. Too late for everything. A fish out of bloody water.' He smiled. 'Perhaps I'd better look around for a decent job, then. Would the UN have me?'

'I don't think you'd have them.' Suki laughed. 'Too much diplomacy and self-restraint.'

'What about a bodyguard? Surely the Secretary-General needs one?'

'You certainly believe in aiming high, don't you?'

'There's plenty of time to drop your aim later. Best to go for a head shot first, when it comes to jobs.'

'I'll remember that the next time my postings branch asks me for my preferences.'

'So what about Swansea, then?'

'I didn't know there was a UN mission there.'

'There bloody should be. It's a proper war zone on a Saturday night.'

'I don't think it's for me.'

'Even if I asked you nicely?'

Suki looked around at the crowds, people hurrying between the stalls with shopping baskets laden with vegetables. The babble of voices haggling over prices, laughing and calling, the cries of children, the sheer bustle of life.

'I think perhaps we're too similar, you and I, Terry. It feels good to travel, to come to places like this. Could you give up your life to stay in one place for ever?'

'I never said anything about for ever. That's a bit beyond my control.'

Suki smiled. 'In that case I think I'd need to think about it.'

Terry breathed in the smells and sounds of the city. He could understand exactly what Suki meant. They were similar, but that was just why he felt that he couldn't leave here unless she was with him. But the UK? It was stupid of him to expect her to leap at the chance.

He was just about to ask for another coffee when Tommy Liu burst through the crowd with the eyes of a man possessed. Spotting them, he dashed across, narrowly avoiding a collision with a heavily laden bicycle.

'There you are. We've been looking all over for you. They've found her!'

'What?' Terry was on his feet immediately. 'Where?'

'She's in Bangkok. That fucker Chamonon's got her.' Tommy's eyes narrowed. 'The bastard's as good as dead.'

'Does Manny know?' Suki asked urgently.

'It was him who got the message,' Tommy replied. 'Come on. Yon Rin's at the villa. He wants us all there to talk it over.'

Terry paid the waiter, took Suki by the hand and followed Tommy back through the crowd to the parked jeep on the far side. As they hurried back to the villa through the busy streets, Terry's mind raced with the possibilities. In no time at all the jeep skated to a halt on the gravel of the driveway and Manny greeted them at the top of the stairs, ushering them into the house where Minister Yon Rin and Craig were poring over maps.

'It's Chamonon,' Yon Rin said. 'It was Lon San's men who snatched her but for some reason he's handed her over to his Thai friend.'

'Why'd he do that? If he wanted revenge for what we did to his camp, why not just kill her?'

'Because to Lon San, killing means nothing,' Manny replied.

'He's butchered so many people the process has lost all significance for him. He murdered my whole family, so how would one more death add anything to the harm he's done me?'

'What, then?'

'She's being held at a place called the Black Lotus,' Manny continued. 'It's one of Chamonon's brothels.'

'Jesus Christ.'

'If that fucker harms her in any way . . .' Tommy said softly.

'Cool it, Tommy. This is going to be a military operation, Terry said. 'I know it's fucking hard, but we've got to detach our personal feelings if we're going to get Sitha back alive. If we're going into the heart of Bangkok . . .'

'You're not going to Bangkok.' With his back turned to them, Manny's words cut them dead. 'This isn't your fight.'

'The fuck it isn't!' Tommy shouted.

'Shut it, Tommy,' Terry snapped. 'Why not?'

'I've already talked it through with the Minister. It's too risky. If foreign mercenaries in the pay of the Cambodian government were caught on a covert operation in Bangkok, the Thai government would break off all relations with us. Right now we need every ally we've got.'

'But she's your own sister, damn it!' Tommy raged.

'That's why I'll go in myself and get her,' Manny continued calmly. 'If I am caught, it'll be obvious it's just a simple matter of personal honour.'

'And if you go by yourself, you stand every chance of getting caught,' Terry said, folding his arms across his chest. 'I don't mean to be rude, Manny, but what the fuck are you thinking of? You're not up to it. Not by yourself, you're not.'

A polite cough reminded everyone of Yon Rin's presence in the room.

'Forgive me, gentlemen, but the option of going with Captain Tron is no longer open to you. He was right when he said that the Cambodian government cannot risk a split with Bangkok.'

'But they support the Khmer Rouge!' Terry exploded.

'Wrong. The Thai government is doing its best to help us, but they are afraid of their army generals, especially the renegades like Chamonon. Such men would seize any opportunity to embarrass their own democrats and get back into power. I'm afraid that if the rescue is to be attempted, Captain Tron must do it alone. And anyway, he won't be alone.'

Puzzled, Terry looked to Manny for an explanation.

'The Minister's right. We received the message from my brother, Sy.'

'But I thought you said the family had disowned him.'

'We did, but in a situation like this I'd ally myself with the devil himself.' A sarcastic smile twisted the corners of his mouth. 'In fact, I think I'd rather trust the devil than my own brother.'

Terry sank into a chair. 'You're mad. Absolutely fucking barmy.'

Yon Rin smiled kindly at the three mercenaries. 'You have already helped us immeasurably in our fight. But this is one battle that we must face alone.'

From his briefcase he pulled out three envelopes and handed them round. 'I think you'll find that the amounts are correct. Colin's has been forwarded to his next of kin. On behalf of the government of Cambodia it only remains for me to thank you all for your sterling service.'

Seeing the tell-tale move from Tommy, Craig gripped him firmly, pinning his arms at his sides. 'Easy, lad.'

'Say something, Terry,' Suki urged. 'Do something, for God's sake!'

Steepling his fingers, Terry sat back, appraising the diminutive Yon Rin, their eyes locked in silent communion.

'Terry?' Suki repeated.

'Be quiet, love,' Terry said slowly. 'The Minister's right.'

'What? Have you gone mad too?' she asked incredulously.

'Good,' Yon Rin continued, making for the door. 'I knew you'd see it my way. I'll inform the Prime Minister that your engagement with us has been successfully completed and all agreements are hereby terminated.'

A slow, dangerous smile played across Terry's face.

'Please express our thanks to your Prime Minister and tell him that we enjoyed our time in your country.'

'I will indeed.'

Opening the door, Yon Rin paused to sniff the warm air like an old badger venturing from his sett.

'You will find that I've included a modest bonus in your pay packets. It would be a shame if you returned to your homes not having enjoyed some R & R in the region.'

Turning to the group, he smiled shyly. 'There are so many wonderful places to visit. Don't you agree?'

11

'I'm not angry. I just don't think you should have come, that's all.'

Staring out of the aircraft window, Terry watched the jungle sweep past below, the same stretch that only days before he had crossed on foot with a full company under his command. Now, on the short hop to Bangkok, he felt distinctly uneasy, not so much because he was accompanied only by Manny, Craig and Tommy, but because Suki Yamato had insisted on joining the expedition.

'I mean, it's not going to be a sightseeing trip, you know.'

Sulking on the other side of Manny, who had tactfully placed himself between the two of them, Suki glared back.

'That wasn't what you told the Thai embassy officials when you went for the visas.'

'You know damn well what we've come for.'

'Of course I do, and there's no way I was going to let you leave me behind. I feel partly responsible.'

'Don't be bloody daft, woman,' Terry snapped. 'How could you have stopped those blokes from taking Sitha?'

Holding up his hands, Manny pleaded for peace. 'If you two are going to kill each other before we even arrive in Bangkok, let me know and I'll get out of the way.'

Terry blushed. 'I'm sorry, mate. I guess we all feel partly to blame.'

'Well, I'm her brother, so take it from me. The blame lies with Lon San and Chamonon. If Suki wanted to join us, that's her affair.'

'Thank you, Manny,' Suki said triumphantly.

'However, if there's going to be any shooting, I'd be grateful if you'd stay out of the way,' Manny added.

'Don't worry about me. I can take care of myself.'

Judging it high time to change the subject, Suki asked Manny about his brother.

'The break happened a long time ago. We were all pretty young and innocent in those days. My brother was sent to study at Bangkok university in the early seventies, just before the US expanded the Vietnam war into Cambodia. My father, seeing that things could only get worse, decided that it would be safer for Sy to stay there. Hedging his bets, Father moved a considerable amount of his wealth to Bangkok, where he entrusted it to Sy to invest and look after so that if the family ever had to flee the country we would all have somewhere to go.'

'But the prodigal son had other ideas?' Terry offered.

'I'm afraid so. Shortly before the Khmer Rouge seized power we discovered that, far from investing our parents' money, Sy had squandered the lot on women and drugs. He had become a useless playboy. With nowhere else to go, my family remained in Phnom Penh. The rest you know.'

Suki reached across and took his hand. 'I'm so sorry.'

She looked at Terry, both of them stung by guilt for their petty argument.

'But why should he suddenly try to help Sitha?' Terry asked.

'Who knows?' Manny shrugged. 'Perhaps as he gets older he feels the need to make amends?'

Terry looked thoughtfully out of the window. 'Perhaps.'

And perhaps he's got other motives altogether, he thought to himself. Perhaps, if he's the kind of character you say he is, he's trying to ingratiate himself with Chamonon. The General's probably an influential guy in Thailand and what better way to become his friend than by delivering to him a whole plateful of opponents like us? The more Terry thought about it the more uncomfortable he became.

'You think we might be walking into a trap?' Manny said, reading his thoughts.

'It's worth considering.'

'I've had the same idea myself.'

'But what choice do we have?' Suki asked.

'None.'

'Right,' Manny said. 'I came to the same conclusion. My brother's the only one who knows where Sitha's being held.'

'So what do we do?'

'Nothing,' Terry said. 'We proceed as planned but we keep our guard up. Even more than usual.'

As they came in to land at Bangkok's Don Muang airport, Terry stared out across the flat landscape, the golden tips of pagodas punctuating the anonymous spread of suburban bungalow gardens, regretting that he wasn't arriving for a spot of genuine leave instead of a high-risk rescue mission that could prove even more perilous than the hit on the Khmer Rouge camp at Rurseng.

The plane touched down with a bump and its engines roared as it slowed to taxiing speed and swung in a wide arc towards the terminal buildings. When it had come to a halt and the engines sighed into a low hum, Terry got up and reached for his bag in the overhead locker, winking at Suki, who nervously bit her lip.

'Party time, sweetheart.'

The five of them squeezed into a taxi and Manny ordered the driver to take them to a mid-price hotel. As soon as they had checked into their rooms they gathered in a corner of the lobby, sitting in soft low armchairs round a glass-topped table as Terry and Manny outlined the next step.

'There's no point all of us trooping in to meet Manny's brother,' Terry said. 'Until we know exactly where he stands we won't risk more than we have to.'

'Dojo, if I don't do something I'm going to explode,' Tommy interrupted.

'You'll explode when I tell you and not a moment earlier.'

'Don't worry about him,' Craig smiled. 'Tommy and I will sort out the hardware. I know this guy who's fixed me up before.'

'Good. Suki, I want you to stay here at the hotel, and before you give me any hassle we're going to need someone here to act as anchor for the moment. I have to be able to find out where everyone is at all times, OK?'

'OK,' she said miserably.

'Good girl. We'll all meet up in my room this

evening before dinner. Any questions? Right, then.
Go to it.'

Turning out of the hotel driveway, Manny and
Terry slid into place in the stifling humidity of a
Bangkok traffic jam.

'Haven't you got air-con, mate?'

Shaking his head merrily, the taxi driver turned
up the fan, increasing the stream of scorching air
to a jet.

'Jesus, it's like a furnace,' Terry said, winding down
his window and staring at the slow-moving stream
of cars, edging nose to tail along Chakrapong Road.
'Have you been here before?'

Manny shook his head. 'I haven't seen my brother
since he left to go to university. I'm not sure I even
want to see him now.'

'I can imagine how you feel.'

'Can you?'

Terry smiled kindly. 'Yes, I think I can.'

'I'm sorry. I didn't mean to be rude,' Manny said
quickly. 'It's just that I feel like a traitor to my family,
coming here like this to visit my brother.'

'Well, right now we need him, so try to keep your
cool.' Terry mopped his brow. 'In this heat that'll
take some doing.'

The driver turned into Larnluang Road and sped
east, heading towards the suburbs. The farther they
got from the centre of town the more the traffic eased,
until they were at last able to cruise at a steady speed,
the windows open and a cooling rush of air swirling
pleasantly through the car. Half an hour later the
driver slowed for a right-hand turn and announced
that they had arrived at Vijdami Road.

'What number, sir?'

'Twenty-six.'

Glancing at Manny, Terry noticed that his lips were tightly set, beads of perspiration standing out on his forehead.

'You OK?'

'Yes. But stop me if I try to kill him.'

As the taxi drove away, they stood for a moment looking up at the building. It had once been an impressive house but at some stage the owner had divided it into apartments and it now housed half a dozen families. Checking the line of bells, Manny read his brother's name with distaste. A voice crackled over the entryphone, a buzzer sounded and a moment later they were standing in the hallway. A broad staircase led up past the doors to the other flats and as they made their way to the third floor, Terry absorbed the feel of the place, noting carefully the fire escape, corridors, windows and exits. Feeling naked without a gun, he thought longingly of the hardware that Craig was going to procure from his source, wishing that they had been able to delay the meeting until they had all been armed. But with Sitha's life at stake the clock was ticking and every hour counted.

Clenching his fists, he steadied his breathing for instant combat, but as they approached the front door it opened and they found themselves facing only a thin, hollow-chested man in a crumpled white linen suit. Despite the differences Terry could see that he was related to Manny like a pale shadow image, a dark flip-side to Manny's athletic, healthy demeanour.

'So,' the man said pleasantly. 'My brother.'

He began to hold out his arms but thought better of it and let them drop to his sides, where they hung as useless as if the nerves had been cut.

Manny stared at him evenly. 'This is a friend of mine. Terry Williams.'

For the first time Sy Tron's eyes shifted reluctantly from his brother to focus on Terry. Watching the movement, Terry noticed the immense effort that he put into the smile. It was not in any way artificial, but simply that Sy had become a man with little to smile about. He had forgotten how to and the sudden and unexpected need for civility required a painful rediscovery that creased his sallow face into a loose impression of happiness.

'I'm pleased to meet you,' he said, and Terry, taking the offered hand of friendship, believed that he was.

'Won't you both come in? I've got some fresh lime juice ready. I was expecting you.'

Terry was about to admire the tastefully decorated interior of the apartment when he recalled that it had probably been furnished with the dead Tron family's wealth. Instead he accepted the glass of iced lime juice with a polite smile and moved aside to leave the greeting of the two brothers room to mature.

'I'm afraid I can't offer you anything stronger,' Sy continued apologetically. 'I, er . . .' And although the explanation petered out, Terry guessed the ending, for he had seen reformed drug addicts and drunkards before, on their long, painful road to recovery.

'I'm only here for one reason,' Manny said formally. 'Where's our sister and how did you come by the information?'

Noticing Sy waver unsteadily on his feet, Terry suggested that they all sit down. Reluctantly Manny moved across to a sofa keeping as far from his brother as he could, as if fearing that physical contact might pass on some contagious disease.

'I had no idea that she was here in Bangkok. I returned home one evening from work . . .'

'Work?' Manny asked bitterly, the disbelief evident in his harsh tone.

In response, Sy simply smiled sadly. 'It's not much of a job but I do some translation and write some articles for a journal in town. I dignify it with the term "freelance" but they rarely publish what I write. Anyway, I came home to find this woman, a girl really, waiting for me outside. Her name was Lalin, a Burmese . . . well, she's a prostitute, I suppose. She told me that Sitha was being held at the Black Lotus of General Chamonon. He's . . .'

'Yes, we know all about him,' Manny said impatiently.

'Manny, let the guy finish,' Terry cut in. He could see that the whole effort of the meeting with his brother was proving painful for Sy, and Manny's offhand manner, however understandable, was not going to make things any easier.

'Thank you, Mr Williams, but my brother has every right to speak to me as he pleases. Anyway, this Lalin gave me some garbled account of Sitha having told her that I was an old boyfriend of hers and that I would pay well to know she was here in Bangkok. Of course, I realized that something was desperately wrong, so I did some checking through a few journalist contacts, put two and two together, and then rang you.'

Running the account through his mind, Manny looked round the room, gauging the truth of his brother's story.

'This Lalin, why should she risk her neck to tell you all this?'

'I think she and Sitha had become friends. And I

think she was also, well, too stupid to realize exactly what Sitha was using her for. She also said several things that make me believe that she has grievances of her own against General Chamonon.'

'This Black Lotus, where is it?' Terry asked, unfolding a street map of Bangkok on the table.

'Near the floating market. But you won't find it on there. It's not the sort of place the Tourist Information Centre likes foreign visitors to know about. It's a brothel and an illegal boxing den.'

'Thai boxing?'

'You know about it?'

'Terry is a karate expert himself,' Manny added proudly. 'One of the best.'

'That's interesting, but this is no sport. They fight for big money and it's well known that many of the fights are to the death.'

'Sounds like a proper little amusement arcade,' Terry said.

'Can you take us there?' Manny asked abruptly.

'Of course, but you won't be able simply to walk in and take her.'

'We didn't think we could.'

'No, you don't understand. It's not just the guards, although Chamonon's got plenty of those. The General's an influential man. If you went in there by force you'd bring the entire Bangkok police force down on you. You'd never get out of the country.'

'Well, we're not going to sit around and do nothing. I'll leave the role of traitor to you!'

Terry got to his feet. 'Steady on, mate. I've heard what you say your brother did in the past but right now the problem is how to get Sitha out of here. Sy didn't have to call us, and sure, the whole thing could be a trap, but let's at least hear what he has to say. Once we're in the clear you can tear each other apart with recriminations if you want to.'

Turning to Sy, Terry tried a smile. 'Now, I hear what you say but what's your suggestion? You seem to know the layout.'

Sy was silent for a long time, staring darkly into his glass of lime juice, where the ice cubes had melted into thin transparent slithers.

'Manny said you were a karate expert. Exactly how good are you?'

'Fourth Dan,' said Terry, puzzled.

'That means nothing to me. Put it this way, could you take on a top-class opponent? We're talking about the top Thai boxer in the country.'

Terry whistled softly, weighing his answer. 'I could take him on. Of course I might get the shit knocked out of me in the process.'

'What are you thinking of?' Manny asked irritably.

'The idea only just came to me. The General's boxing operation relies on keeping the crowd happy. A good fight means lots of money and then everybody's happy. I've already said that you can't shoot your way in there, but perhaps a little guile might work instead.'

'In what way?'

'Suppose we were to represent Terry as a professional fighter, someone prepared to take on the General's best? Such a fight could have a huge appeal to the crowd, the novelty value of a westerner taking on their champion. The General would never allow such a fight to go to the death. He wouldn't have to. The crowd would get enough thrills from the spectacle itself.'

'Where would that get us?'

'From what I understand, the General doesn't have any personal interest in Sitha. Lon San simply gave her to him to humiliate you. Forcing the sole surviving female member of the Tron family into prostitution is far better than killing her.'

'So?'

'So I ask for her as my prize for winning,' Terry said, a smile spreading across his face as he looked at Sy with a new admiration.

'And what if he doesn't win?'

'Leave that to me,' Terry said. 'But will the General agree to our terms? Won't he be suspicious?'

'Why should he be? He's never seen you, has he?' Sy answered.

'No.'

'Well, then, we'll call you something else and say that your particular taste is for Cambodian girls, and has the General got any he would be prepared to put up as a wager? As far as Chamonon will know, giving Sitha to you will be as bad as forcing her to sleep with some Bangkok labourer.'

'Thanks a bunch!'

'The General's no fool,' Manny said. 'He'll smell a rat.'

Leaning forward in his chair, Sy spoke with conviction. 'He'll smell money, nothing else. Listen, brother, I've lived in the hell that these people have created. I don't ask you for any forgiveness for what I've done. I live with the guilt of it every day of my life. When Lalin came to me I saw for the first time a chance to . . .'

'Make amends? Is that it? An easy penance for the deaths you caused?'

Sy looked at his brother sadly. 'No. I long ago

211

accepted that there will never be any salvation for me. I am damned. But our sister might not be. To Chamonon Sitha's just another whore. If he smells a good fight and lots of money, why shouldn't he give Sitha to some westerner as a prize?'

A heavy silence fell over the room as the three men weighed the options. Looking at Terry standing beside the window, Manny suddenly shook his head.

'No. I can't allow Terry to do it. This is my fight. I'll be the challenger.'

'You wouldn't have a chance,' Sy said. 'Besides, the General has plenty of Asian boxers he can use. The lure of Mr Williams will be that he's a westerner.'

'I don't care. He won't do it.'

'Hang on a minute,' Terry said, turning slowly from the window. 'That's for me to say.'

'But you can't be serious?'

'What other option is there?'

Manny started to speak but fell silent.

'Exactly.' Terry moved across to the sofa and smiled down at him. 'Besides, I could use the practice.'

After arranging to visit the Black Lotus that evening with Sy as guide, Terry and Manny prepared to leave.

'By the way, this champion I'm supposed to take on, what's his name?'

'Promarik. Than Promarik.'

'You must be crazy! Absolutely screaming mad! Tell him, Craig.'

As Suki stamped across to the hotel window, glaring out at the traffic jam in the street below, Craig frowned at Terry perching on the side of the bed, his iron determination evident. Staring miserably at the rising clouds of smog outside, Manny put his arm round Suki's shoulder.

'It's no good. I've already tried to talk him out of it. This is my problem and I wish you'd all let me solve it in my own way. I'm grateful for your help, but . . .'

'Let's cut the crap. Dojo's a big boy,' Tommy said, slamming home the magazine into the butt of the Glock that he had added to Craig's shopping list. 'And anyway, I agree with him that it's our best option.'

Suki turned on him. 'It's not your lover that's going to get their head kicked in.' Instantly realizing what she had said, she felt her face turn scarlet. 'I'm sorry, Tommy. I didn't mean it to sound like that. I know what you've been suffering since Sitha was taken.'

Forcing a smile, Tommy waved her apology aside. 'Forget it. We're all uptight.'

There was a knock at the door and Craig opened it to reveal the slim figure and crumpled linen suit of Sy Tron. Terry had talked it through with the others and they had decided it would be best for their initial visit to the Black Lotus if Sy, Craig and he went by themselves to set up the fight. With such close personal involvement, there was no telling how Manny or the volatile Tommy would behave when they came face to face with General Sarit Chamonon. Terry and Craig, however, would be better able to maintain a detached calm.

Leaving the others at the hotel, Terry, Craig and Sy got into the waiting taxi and set off for the River Chaophraya, where they transferred to a small boat and ordered the boatman to take them to the floating market and the Black Lotus. With their story already worked out, they completed the journey in silence, watching the multicoloured sights of the floating market and listening to the cries from the passing stalls.

At last the boatman swung his slim craft towards the bank, where a long wooden jetty protruded into the murky green water, the waves lapping and foaming against its rotting wooden legs.

'You know the way?' the boatman asked with a leering grin.

Sy thanked him for his concern and silenced him with a tip. Leading the other two, he made his way down the jetty and through the cluster of ramshackle dwellings until, on firm land again, they approached the entrance to the Black Lotus. As they neared the doorway two large men got to their feet and barred their path.

'What do you want? The fight's not till tonight.'

Sy smiled. 'Do you only serve those with an appetite for fighting?'

The smaller of the two men grinned. 'Perhaps not.'

'Good. I have a business proposition to put to General Chamonon.'

Instantly the man's grin disappeared, replaced by a far less pleasant scowl. 'Never heard of him. Now fuck off.'

'Oh come, come,' Sy urged smoothly. 'He won't be very pleased if he discovers you've prevented him from making a considerable amount of money.'

'How's that?' the man asked suspiciously.

Terry pushed to the front. 'Do you want me to shove his teeth down his arse, boss?'

Waving him aside, Sy smiled at the man. 'Please forgive my client. Professional fighters are so aggressive,

214

aren't they? But that's what made him a champion in his own country.'

A light dawned on the man's face as the thought process worked its way painfully through his brain. He stabbed a finger in Sy's hollow chest.

'Come with me. But don't speak until you're spoken to.'

Frisking the visitors and finding them unarmed, the guard led the three men into the club, walking down a long passageway until he entered the main warehouse, with the roped-off arena raised in the centre. On the far side a door led into a small suite of offices, outside one of which the guard paused, knocked and went in, returning a moment later to fetch the visitors.

The door opened into a large, windowless room. Four other men slouched in armchairs around the side walls, their hands involuntarily moving to concealed shoulder holsters at the appearance of three strangers in their midst. Behind a large desk, leafing through papers, sat a small plump man in an embroidered white cotton shirt. His well-oiled hair had been combed neatly into place, the traces of grey poorly disguised, and looking up from his work he revealed the makings of a double chin that, given time, would become substantial. Without smiling he appraised the visitors, leaving it to Sy to make the first move.

'My name is Sy,' he said, judging it best to leave the rest of his name unspoken. 'We haven't met before.'

Without getting up, the General stuck out his hand, which Sy took, bowing from the waist.

'Thank you for seeing me, General Chamonon. You will not regret it.'

With a simple gesture of impatience the General

indicated that he was a busy man who was not to be bothered lightly.

'I have come to you with a proposition,' Sy continued undaunted, getting straight to the point. 'The Black Lotus has a reputation as the best venue in Bangkok for fighting tournaments that are, shall we say, unorthodox.'

'Go on,' the General said evenly, weighing the frail-looking man's words carefully.

'This gentleman has come to me as a visitor to our city, asking me to set him up with a bout or two.'

The General guffawed. 'A bout or two? What does he think this is? A ballet school?'

At the side of the room the guards sniggered on cue. Staring at the General, his face expressionless, Terry sighed heavily, making his boredom evident. 'I told you this arsehole would be a waste of time, Sy. Let's get out of here and find a proper venue.'

From the depths of their armchairs the four guards shifted forward into the intense silence.

'Easy, Dojo, easy. We'll give him one more chance,' said Sy.

With a snort of derision the General waved to his guards. 'Get these idiots out of here.'

The first man never even made it out of his chair, rising straight into the edge of Terry's foot as it shot out in a *yoko geri* mid-level side kick, and although the next guard managed it all the way up, barely a second later he was flying backwards, propelled clean through the glass door as Terry swivelled on his supporting leg, lashing out with an *ushiro geri* back kick.

Seeing the turn of events, the other two guards had both pulled their guns.

'I told you this guy was an arsehole,' Terry said, staring at them unimpressed, his hands moving into an open *kamae* fighting posture.

'One minute!'

Standing behind his desk, General Sarit Chamonon ordered his men to holster their weapons. In his eyes, a new light of respect had replaced the previous disinterest.

'You handle yourself competently, Mr . . .?'

'Just Dojo,' Terry replied.

'Dojo, then.' The General looked at the two fallen men, spread-eagled on the office floor. 'Perhaps we can come to some kind of arrangement after all.'

Turning to Sy, he ushered the visitors into the vacated armchairs. 'Tell me what sort of contest you had in mind?'

Sinking into his new role as fight promoter, Sy examined his nails as he spoke. 'Well, we certainly wouldn't want it to go, how shall I say it . . .?'

'Directly.'

'To the death.'

The General smiled amiably. 'Please, my dear friend! Bouts at the Black Lotus never go that far. We are a civilized people. Although of course, as in all dangerous sports, accidents do occur from time to time.'

'Of course,' Sy agreed sagely.

'And what sort of percentage winnings were you thinking of?'

'Well, here's the funny part,' Sy said, leaning back in his chair. 'As a martial artist dedicated to his skill, all my western friend requires is the honour of taking on the great Than Promarik. As a promoter myself, all I ask is that if you are happy with the contest, you might be willing to do business with me in future on more orthodox commercial lines, but for now, as a sign of goodwill, we are willing to waive any fee or winnings.'

The General stared at him agog. 'You're willing to fight for nothing?'

Sy leant across to Terry as if discussing with him some secret matter of confidence. He smiled slowly at Terry's reply.

'I must qualify that. Dojo is also in Bangkok for a good time.'

The General grinned. 'Which foreigner isn't? Go on.'

'Travelling is a lonely business. If he provides you with a satisfactory service, perhaps one of your employees might . . .'

'Do the same? I think I get the drift. That won't be a problem. If he can give Promarik a run for his money – and I must say that I don't think he will – he can have the choice of the house's best.'

'Excellent.'

'All that remains now, then, is for us to arrange the date of the fight,' the General said.

Sy frowned in surprise. 'I'm sorry, I thought I had made that clear. I thought we were talking about tomorrow night?'

After a moment's reflection the General answered slowly. 'Perhaps. Yes, why not? I'll stand down the opponent I'd programmed. We'll substitute Dojo instead. I'll put the word out to ensure a healthy attendance.'

Getting to their feet Sy, Terry and Craig made to leave.

'If Dojo wins, I take it he'll be able to select his reward there and then?'

'Of course.'

'Perhaps if we make the announcement in front of the crowd it will add to the spice,' Sy suggested innocently.

The General chuckled. 'You have the mind of a true showman. The crowd will love it.'

'I'm sure they will,' Sy said as he led the way out of the office.

When the three men had gone General Chamonon sat alone at his desk for a while, planning the next day's entertainment. It had come as an unexpected windfall just as the popularity of the fights at the Black Lotus had been starting to flag. A contest between Than Promarik and the westerner would indeed exercise a novel pull that should appeal to the many compulsive gamblers whose money the General was happy to take. The westerner certainly looked fit, although Chamonon was in no doubt that in the end Promarik would grind him into the dust. The absence of any demand for payment had come as no great surprise. New promoters would often try to break their way into the business with a dramatic show fight. And as for that ridiculous request for a whore, the man could have whichever one he chose.

Of course, there was also the business about how far the fight should go. The crowd had come to expect a certain thrill at the Black Lotus. To deny it to them would detract from the novelty value of having the westerner participate.

But then, as the General himself had admitted, accidents were common in the ring.

12

Waking before first light the next morning, Terry slipped out of Suki's arms and went quietly out on to the balcony. They had spent the night together in Suki's room at the back of the hotel, where the broad sweep of the windows looked out on to a beautiful garden. Their lovemaking had been tender as if compensating for the harsh brutality to come, and as Terry slid the glass door closed behind him and stepped on to the cool tiles of the balcony, he looked at Suki asleep in the tousled bed. Curled on one side, she was still fast in her dreams, a frown creasing her brow over some conundrum hidden from all sight but her own inner mind.

Leaning on the sill, Terry gazed down at the spreading profusion of tropical flowers and trees. Overhead, great palm boughs creaked in the early-morning silence and a silver film of moisture clung to every natural surface, resisting the pull of the growing heat that would eventually burn it off, leaving the greens and myriad brilliant colours harsh and almost violent with intensity.

The air too was moist, but lacking the humidity that the sunrise would bring. Standing in the natural *heiko dachi* stance, Terry steadied his breathing, gently shaking his limbs to loosen them of sleep. Working from the feet up, he focused his attention on each set of joints in turn, rotating the ankles, knees, hips, waist, arms, shoulders and neck. Then, dropping into the *zenkutsu dachi* stance, he stretched his legs, allowing himself to sink ever lower until almost touching the floor, shifting to the other leg to repeat the process several times, both left and right.

Having worked at the warm-up exercises, he next began a simple series of basic punches and blocks, moving into a *sanchin* hourglass stance, the centre of gravity low and stable, the knees and thighs tightly locked, his feet gripping for purchase on the smooth tiles. Straight punches at lower, middle, and upper levels were followed by open-hand *shuto* blows, the roundhouse *shuto uchi* and the direct *sakotsu uchikomi* thrust to the imaginary opponent's collar bone or sternum.

When he had completed the full range of hand strikes and blocks, Terry worked through the catalogue of kicking techniques, from the simple but effective *kin geri* instep strike, delivered to an opponent's groin, to the powerful *ushiro geri* back kick and the *jodan mawashi geri* roundhouse kick to the head.

Lastly, he went through his *kata*, the set forms that exercised timing and distancing, from the basic functional *Sanchin* and *Gekisai* katas, to the beautiful fluid motions of the complex *Sanseru* and *Suparinpei*, accuracy, power and speed combining with the focused will and strength of spirit in a potentially devastating display of technical mastery.

Sinking to his knees Terry inhaled the sweet perfume of the emerging day, calm in the face of the approaching danger. Confident of his own abilities, he would submit himself to the trial of skills with a focused mind. Clearing it of all abstraction, he made it a still pool, his unconscious reflexes close beneath the surface like a predatory fish, passive until the stimulus of the fly.

Than Promarik felt little more than mild interest as he pranced towards the ring through the roars of the worshipping crowd. He had received the news of his new opponent some hours before but had stuck to his usual warm-up routine. Now, as he saw for the first time the westerner, his back turned to Than's approach, Than wondered what had brought such a man to the boxing ring of the Black Lotus. He had fought westerners before and found them slow and ungainly. They seemed to be able to take the punishment but the end had always been the same: his own speed and accuracy beat their ponderous techniques every time.

He swung up into the ring between the ropes, raised his gloved hands above his head, shrugged off his red silk cloak and acknowledged the adulation and applause. The General had obviously pulled off a real coup. The warehouse was packed and on the neighbouring tables where the bets were made, Than could see heaped piles of banknotes. Starting his usual dance round the ring, he glanced at his opponent, still standing with his face turned away. He seemed to be talking to someone, mumbling something, but when Than looked down to the side of the ring he could see no one there, only an odd collection of foreigners who must have been out of earshot. The man was obviously saying his prayers! Than grinned. There was only one other westerner in the man's group of supporters, but none of the others was Thai. There was a girl whose eye Than caught but who scowled severely when he winked at her. Then there was a Chinese man, probably Cantonese, judging by the sallow complexion. Lastly there was an ill-matched pair of Cambodians, brothers by the look of them, although their dress, build and general appearance couldn't have been more dissimilar.

The referee stepped into the ring and started to make the usual announcements but still Than's opponent remained in his own private world. Behind his table on the raised dais Than could see General Chamonon. The General was by himself tonight, although as Than watched, the Burmese girl Lalin moved towards him, approaching with the miserable mix of caution and optimism of a dog that has been beaten yet can't overcome its dependence on the hand that feeds it. All the signs were present that the General was tiring of her and Than wondered if he himself might make use of her for a while when she eventually slid from her position of eminence astride the General's thighs.

Jogging back to his own corner in readiness for the start of the bout, Than looked again at his opponent. The man had broad shoulders and a lean back, trimming towards a firm waist. He was not tall for a westerner, but his body was in perfect proportion, the legs solid and muscular and balanced by arms that spoke of strength. Wearing dark-blue shorts and with feet bound like Than's own, the man was gently flexing his tendons, dipping on the ropes and springing to his feet again. There would undoubtedly be a certain agility in him. It would be wise to get proper measure of this one before committing to an attack, Than thought.

But the wariness that had started to creep over Than Promarik when faced by his opponent's apparent disregard for his presence turned suddenly to alarm when the referee at last sounded the bell and stepped aside, leaving the ring to the two fighters. For at that moment the man turned and Than Promarik knew that he was about to face the fight of his life.

Somehow, in a way that Than couldn't quite understand, the man saw him without looking at him. But it was more than that. His steady, untroubled gaze stripped Than to the core, penetrating his very being and gauging his most hidden weaknesses. Than felt as though he had been stripped, bound and laid at the feet of this extraordinary opponent.

Shaking off the torrent of self-doubt and panic that threatened to flood his mind, Than danced out into the centre of the ring, relying on the tried-and-tested experience of countless fights to get him through the opening moves. Thereafter it might become easier, once the man had also revealed his style and capabilities. The westerner was wearing gloves, but they were trim and solid, as though his fists barely fitted into them, waiting behind the leather like sheathed knives.

Trying a couple of high kicks, Than noted how the westerner hardly bothered to block, shifting his body sideways at each exploratory attacking move so that Than's feet met nothing but the stifling, humid air of the ring. Switching in mid-kick, he next tried a dummy feint, followed by a jumping turning kick, but once again his opponent moved without even seeming to, his speed of reaction masked by a smooth grace that glided with the motion of a snake.

Becoming desperate, Than closed in, lashing out

with a flurry of hand blows, all of which were deflected with almost casual disdain, the hardest being knocked aside as if little more than a troublesome branch. But with a sudden shock, Than realized that his opponent had been waiting for exactly this moment of close-quarter contact, and before his legs could obey the command from his brain, whipping him back out of reach, Than watched with slow-motion horror as the westerner exploded into life and struck.

Watching from his table, General Chamonon was the first to notice the change in the crowd, sensing their shift of mood as the latest of his man's attacks foundered on the unbelievably simple defences of the foreigner. With an effortlessness that was positively insulting, the westerner brushed aside another spectacular kick, making it obvious to even the most drunken observer that there was little the Thai champion would be able to do about it. As the roars subsided, stilling into an oppressive hush, the General looked around the audience with mounting alarm, watching the agog expressions form on the sweating faces, teeth bared in gaping mouths except where a cigarette dangled with its long, delicate train of ash.

'Do something, you useless bastard!' the General hissed under his breath, cursing his erstwhile champion, who tomorrow would be the laughing stock of Bangkok unless saved by a miracle. But the General no longer believed in miracles, only money, and with the betting almost totally on Promarik, there was a considerable amount of cash at stake. The warehouse was full to bursting, the scum of the city had thrown down their hard-earned wages on the outcome of a fight that now appeared to be so one-sided as to seem rigged. From somewhere in the crowd a man shouted out that Than had been drugged, then another called that the whole thing was a fix and that they had all been cheated. From an initial outburst or two, the chorus of disapproval built into a roar, different from the one that had greeted the Thai's arrival, for now it was a roar of protest. But as the General's guards closed swiftly about him, the situation was prevented from growing uglier by the least likely of saviours. For suddenly the glares of the audience were snatched back from the General's table, where a clutch of nervous guards fingered conspicuous guns, and returned to the ring itself, where the westerner had gone into action.

Like Terry himself, the crowd had seen what Than Promarik had missed, mesmerized by the calm, cobra intensity of Terry's glare. With fascinated horror they saw their hero and champion close within range of the westerner's powerful fists, like a lamb meekly entering the abattoir. Launching himself with the drive of an Olympic sprinter, Terry shot forward into his opponent, his fists executing a barrage of punches, every one of which found its mark. Even shielded from the full intensity of the lethal knuckles by the padding of the leather gloves, Than felt the impacting blows like the touch of death itself.

Reeling backwards across the ring, he desperately sought some respite from the attacks, but the westerner seemed stuck to him by some perverse gravitational link. Impossibly, the man's unshakeable stance both rooted him to the floor and yet at the same time carried him wherever Than attempted to flee, the distance between the two fighters always sufficiently exact for the westerner's every punch to reach its mark with maximum effect.

Staggering beside the ropes, Than could hear a roar in some distant part of his brain, like a name being chanted. He was puzzled because the sound of it was unfamiliar to him. His own was Than Promarik, the Thai champion, the best fighter in the entire stable of General Sarit Chamonon. He had lost count of the men he had killed in the service of the General, the same General whom he could now glimpse above the screaming crowd. But Chamonon's expression was a mixture of contempt and fear. Nothing added up any more, for the name that suddenly clarified in Than's head was 'Dojo'.

Hugging the ropes, the referee glanced nervously across at General Chamonon, but receiving nothing more than a blank shrug, he left the westerner to finish the business of execution. Then Terry himself halted his relentless assault and stood looking down at the bleeding wreckage of his opponent, suddenly frail and pathetic on the canvas, the towering arrogance shrunk into a panting, gasping ball.

Waiting for the referee to stop the fight, Terry was surprised to see the man grin like an idiot, gesturing for him to continue the slaughter. Instead, he withdrew to his corner, where Craig was waiting to meet him.

'Nice going, Dojo.'

But Terry was still watching Promarik. 'Isn't anyone going to help the poor little fucker?'

'He's beyond help now,' Sy called up from the foot of the ring. 'This defeat will have finished his career. In fact, he's stirred up so many blood feuds with the friends and families of opponents he's killed that he'll be lucky to live more than a week once he's out of the General's protection.'

'My heart bleeds for him,' Craig said bitterly.

As Than Promarik was carried out of the ring to be spat on by those in the crowd nearest to him, the referee led Terry back to the centre of the stage, raising his right arm aloft and pronouncing him the victor. Surging between excitement at the thrill of the fight and anger at the loss of their money, the crowd were becoming ugly.

'Now!' Terry called out to Sy above the noise of the mob.

Clambering into the ring, Sy strode up to the referee and snatched the microphone out of his hand, waving and shouting for silence.

'Brothers! Friends! Quiet, please.' When the noise had abated sufficiently for him to be heard, Sy turned to where the General now stood, eyeing this new development with suspicion.

'As Dojo's manager I would like to thank General Sarit Chamonon for his foresight in allowing Dojo this wonderful opportunity to demonstrate his skills for you tonight.'

Hesitant at first, the crowd started a low murmur of approval.

'But more particularly, I am sure you will all want to thank him for his generosity because he has asked me to announce that, owing to the unforeseen imbalance in the contest, you have not only enjoyed a spectacular display of martial arts, but you are all to have your money back as well!'

A moment's stunned silence was followed by a cheer that lifted the roof as the crowd leapt to their feet, showering the General with further banknotes

228

and cries of praise. Smothering his pallor with a sickly smile, the General graciously acknowledged the rapturous applause. Momentarily his eyes locked with those of Sy Tron, sending a very different message of warning that was noticed only by Sy, Terry and their friends at the ringside.

'Give it to him!' Suki called.

'Quiet, please,' Sy continued. 'I am sure you will all agree that Dojo himself deserves something special for his effort. Well, he has also waived any financial reward so that there will be more money to return to yourselves. All he has requested is the company of a young lady.'

Again the crowd leapt to their feet with cheers and applause.

'General, as agreed, could you please reward the victor with his prize. His choice is Sitha Tron.'

As the crowd roared their approval, jostling towards the betting tables, where the General's men stared frantically at their boss for guidance, General Chamonon pushed his way towards the ring with his phalanx of bodyguards. Climbing through the ropes, he went up to Sy and for the benefit of the crowd embraced him like an old friend, whispering in his ear as he did so.

'I don't know what you're up to but I want you out of here. Now. Think yourselves lucky I don't have you shot.'

'In front of such an appreciative audience?'

Taking the microphone from Sy, the General called for silence, reassuring every member of the audience that he had indeed spoken the truth and that they would all get their money back.

'Tell me one thing, though,' he said quietly, switching off the microphone once the crowd's attention had turned from the spectacle in the ring to the betting tables, where the first arrivals were already reclaiming their bets. 'What's your interest in this Tron girl?'

'Nothing in particular,' Sy shrugged innocently. 'My client has a taste for Cambodian ladies, that's all. We asked one of your men if you had any and he gave us her name.'

'Indeed? Well, that's a pity. Any other and I would have been happy to oblige.'

'You're not still angry about the refund, are you, General? Look what it's done for your popularity. Of course, that mood could change. Crowds are unpredictable creatures.'

'I'm sure you're right. But the problem's more fundamental than that. You see, Sitha Tron's no longer here.'

For a fraction of a second the smile faltered on Sy's face.

'You don't expect me to believe that, do you?'

'Believe it or not, it's the truth. She left early this morning. I've sent her north to Chiang Mai to a friend of mine.'

While the crowd were contentedly receiving their money, the General's guards had discreetly moved to surround Terry's supporters at the ringside. Having known that they would be frisked before being allowed to enter the Black Lotus, they had come unarmed, relying on guile to see them safely through. Tommy's hand moved involuntarily for his Glock but finding nothing there, clenched in frustration.

Detecting the shift in advantage to Chamonon, Sy thought furiously. Each of his friends was now covered by at least two armed guards. At the moment, there was no reason to suppose that the General suspected their real identity; the name of Sitha Tron seemed to mean little to him, but to press for her further might arouse his suspicion and put them all at risk. Nor was there any reason to suppose that the General was lying about Sitha having been sent to Chiang Mai – not that they had any way of checking. He was hardly going to allow them to search the premises for her. There was only one way out.

Breaking into a broad grin, he shook the General by the hand like an old friend.

'No hard feelings, then. One girl's as good as another, I suppose.'

Then, in a burst of inspiration, he pointed across to the General's table. 'What about her? She'll do.'

Turning round, the General found himself looking at Lalin.

'She's Burmese, isn't she? I'm sure I can persuade Dojo to make do.'

With unexpected good humour the General chuckled as he beckoned Lalin over to the ringside.

'Congratulations, Dojo,' he said, shaking Terry by the hand, aware of the many eyes still on him. 'Don't expect me to offer you a job. I think you should take your whore and your other friends and get the fuck out of here. If I ever see any of you again I'll kill you.'

Taking a step towards Chamonon, Terry ignored the barrels of two pistols glinting at him from beneath the jackets of the General's flanking bodyguards.

'You want to be careful with threats like that, boyo. They might rebound on you one day.'

'Get out.'

Vaulting over the ropes, Terry joined the others and made for the exit, seeking the anonymity of the crowd as protection against Chamonon's guards.

'What's your cut?' Manny screamed at his brother when they were back at the hotel. 'I bet you lied about Sitha being there in the first place. The whole thing was a set-up. The crowd was given a great spectacle, the great Promarik knocked out by a foreigner, the General's more popular than ever, and we've been well and truly screwed.'

Slumped on the sofa with his head in his hands, Sy shook his head, hardly able to find the energy to protest. The evening had sapped his strength and all he could manage was a muttered: 'You're wrong. You think I could do that to my own sister?'

'You did it to our whole family, so why not to Sitha?'

'That was a long time ago. I've changed, Manny. Really I have.'

'He's telling the truth.'

As she stood on the edge of the maelstrom that had erupted in Sy's apartment, Lalin's quiet voice went barely noticed.

'Listen to her for yourselves,' Sy said wearily. 'That's why I brought her here.'

'Sitha was at the Black Lotus,' Lalin said. 'It was I who told Mr Tron about her.'

'Then why has she been moved?' Tommy asked.

Lalin looked at the faces surrounding her. 'General Chamonon has sent her to a friend of his, Eddy Passenta. As a gift.'

'Dear God.'

Sinking into a chair, Manny stared at the floor.

'Dear God. That bastard, using human beings like trinkets.'

'Worse than trinkets,' Lalin said, and told them how she had been used by the General to entertain Fat Eddy and his other Chinese guest at Paksaket.

'Your sister has a strong spirit, but if they treat her as they treated me it will break.'

'We can't just leave her to them,' Tommy protested.

'I don't intend to,' Terry said. 'Manny, have you got a map of the Chiang Mai area?'

Manny threw up his arms in desperation. 'You're talking about the Golden Triangle. This Passenta character will be safer there than Lon San was at Rurseng. It's drug-baron country.'

'Who was that you mentioned?' Lalin asked.

'Lon San.'

'That's the man they were talking about!' she burst out. 'They're going to have some kind of big meeting there. I heard them talking about it. I remember now. Colonel Kon, the Chinese man, said he wouldn't fly to Paksaket again. He was frightened of something. Then Fat Eddy offered them the use of his own airstrip, so the General said that he would tell Lon San that he could meet them there to collect his stuff, whatever that was.'

'The arms,' Craig said quietly. 'So his offensive will go ahead after all. Lon San gets his weapons, Chamonon gets his money, and this Fat Eddy character doubtless gets a rake-off of both. Nice.'

'Do you know when Colonel Kon's returning, Lalin?' Terry asked, smelling the scent of a new trail.

'Yes. I think it's in three days' time.'

'Three days? Then we're lost,' Manny said. 'We could never get all the way to Chiang Mai, locate Passenta's hide-out and infiltrate it in three days.'

Sy had sat up straight, his features alive for the first time since leaving the Black Lotus. 'Yes we could.'

'I'm not trusting you again.'

'Give the guy a break, Manny,' Terry said. 'How could we?'

'I know this Eddy Passenta. I've been to his ranch,' Sy continued. 'It was some years ago when I got involved in . . . well, the drugs trade. I wasn't at my sharpest in those days but I'm sure I can remember the place. He used the airstrip to fly his drugs all over the country and even into Burma and southern China.'

'And a big transport plane could land there?'

'Sure. It'd be far easier than Paksaket. It's not ideal for this Lon San guy but Fat Eddy would probably help him shuttle his arms down south for a fee.'

Terry was silent, a plan forming in his mind. 'What's the quickest way to Chiang Mai?'

'Plane. I can check for vacancies right away,' Sy answered getting to his feet.

'No. We're going to be taking a lot of hardware. What's the security like?'

'Pretty tight. Even the internal flights are thoroughly screened.'

'I thought so. What about the trains?'

'There'd be no security problem. There's an overnight express that leaves Bangkok at six every evening. Gets into Chiang Mai just before eight the following morning.'

Terry thought for a moment. 'That means we kick our heels here for another day. Craig, if we go for the express train at 1800 hours tomorrow, would that give you enough time to get the kit?'

'Such as?'

'We'll need a lot more than just the stuff we've got now. Can you get your hands on assault rifles, grenades and explosives?'

Craig sucked his teeth. 'Between now and tomorrow evening? It won't be easy. It'll cost us.'

'Do it. Suki, go to the station and book the tickets.'

'I'd better go with her,' Sy said. 'We're too late to reserve seats for tomorrow's train but I've got a friend there who owes me a favour.'

'OK then, but don't do anything to draw attention to us.' Terry smiled. 'Minister Yon Rin suggested we take a look at the sights, and everyone who comes to Thailand has to visit Chiang Mai. We'll be just another happy band of tourists.'

Sharing a taxi with Sy and Suki on their way to the station, Craig dropped off near the centre of town and went to organize the weaponry. Leaving Lalin to stay at his brother's house, Manny accompanied Tommy and Terry back to the hotel, where they gathered in the bar to study a map of the area that Sy had indicated.

'It doesn't look far from Chiang Mai,' Tommy said.

'Yes, but we'd better hope that there's more than that single road leading to it. It's hard to tell, but I'd say that anyone approaching would be detected a mile away.'

'My brother says he knows of another track,' Manny said. 'He told me that they used it for transporting drug traffic into the city when they wanted to avoid police patrols. Mind you, Sy was probably stoned out of his brain at the time. We'd be stupid to rely on him.'

'I'm afraid we've no choice. He's the best bet we've got. And Manny,' Terry added, 'I understand how you feel but try to get off his back. He risked his neck taking us into the Black Lotus. If it didn't work it wasn't his fault. Lalin confirmed the story about Sitha and I reckon she's too stupid to lie.'

'That's a fact,' Tommy said.

'Yeah, but remember the kind of life the poor kid's had. It's a bloody miracle she's survived this far.'

Terry downed his whisky and got up to go to his room. 'Chamonon and Passenta have both got a lot to answer for.'

'And you're going to be asking the questions, right?' Manny smiled.

'Not if I get to the fuckers first,' Tommy said coldly.

'I hope I'm there to see it,' Manny replied. 'I'll ask only one thing once Sitha's safe. Leave Lon San to me. He's mine.'

Sitha waited until the car stopped for fuel before making her move. She had noted when they left Bangkok that morning that the tank was full. She could see the petrol gauge from her seat in the back, squeezed between Chamonon's two henchmen. Painfully slowly, she watched the needle drop until at last, towards nightfall, the driver mumbled casually to his companions that he would pull over at the next petrol station. Somewhere outside the town of Phitsanulok he found what he was looking for and drew into the forecourt.

'I've got to go to the bathroom,' Sitha said stubbornly.

'Cross your legs. I know you tarts aren't used to that, but try it.'

'Don't be stupid. You're the ones who'll suffer when I wet myself.'

'Let her go,' one of the guards drawled. 'Where's the bitch going to run?'

'Can you untie my hands?' Sitha asked.

'Do you think we're stupid?'

In reply she gazed at the man sweetly.

'Do it,' the first guard ordered.

After untying the rope that bound Sitha's wrists, the two guards in the back hoisted her out of the car and walked with her towards the ladies' toilet.

'Are you guys going to come in with me?'

They looked at each other, and one said: 'We'll be out here. If you're not out in three minutes we're coming in to get you.'

The moment the door closed behind her Sitha sank against the wall, fighting to keep control of her nerves. This could well be her last chance of finding an escape before Chiang Mai, where Eddy Passenta's men were to rendezvous with them and take them to the drug baron's ranch in the nearby hills.

Checking that all of the cubicles were empty, she found a single skylight which had rusted shut. By shoving it hard with her shoulder, she managed to open it a little and a further push produced a gap that she felt she just might be able to squeeze through. She stood on tiptoe, balanced precariously on one of the toilet seats, and wiggled her shoulders into the opening, pushing herself up until her waist was on the sill and she could tip her body forward and squeeze through the gap. Almost out, she lost her balance and fell the last few feet to the ground, landing heavily and cutting her knees and forearms. Even so, she forced herself to listen in case her fall had been heard.

She had emerged at the back of the building into an unlit gravel yard, and after a quick scan of the area she limped away and scrambled down a high grassy bank. Losing her footing halfway down she rolled right to the bottom, then, dazed, cut and bruised, crawled into some trees. The petrol station was now out of sight beyond the bank above her but she knew that it would only be seconds before the guards went in to look for her. Her trail wouldn't be difficult to follow, so she had to put as much distance between herself and the garage as possible.

She had barely gone a few paces when she stopped. If the guards traced her down here they would catch up with her easily. Somehow she had to throw them off the scent. Retracing her steps to the bottom of the bank, she tore a strip of cloth from the sleeve of her blouse and threw it in the direction that she had first started to run. Then, having laid the false trail, she skirted the perimeter of the land behind the petrol station, keeping to the foot of the bank.

No sooner had she reached the far end of the plot than she heard raised voices and the sound of running feet, crashing down the steep slope down which she had rolled minutes earlier. She had done it! They had been as stupid as they looked and taken the bait.

As she continued her circuit of the compound, Sitha waited until she could barely make out the voices, lost in the depths of the trees and going ever farther away from the garage and her. The two men seemed to be calling to one another and in the treetops overhead she caught the passing beam of a powerful torch.

'Good hunting, boys,' she muttered.

Turning away from the perimeter fence, she hobbled off through the undergrowth. It was pitch-dark by now and once in the bushes she could barely see her hand in front of her face. So she never saw the figure of a man looming in front of her until she bumped right into him. Screaming, she lashed out with her fists but he caught her hands in his and held her fast.

'Well, well, well. If it isn't our passenger. And where do you think you're going?'

In the dark Sitha recognized the voice of the first guard.

'What a stroke of luck the men's toilet was out of order. But then I always did prefer going behind a bush.'

13

Darkness was falling by the time the train crawled out of Bangkok's northern suburbs and steadily built up speed at the start of its long haul across the sweeping plains of central Thailand. Running parallel to the River Chaophraya, it carved a straight line through an endless terrain of rice paddies and farmland, clumps of palm and banana trees punctuating the landscape.

Sy's contact had done them proud, providing not just seats but four double cabins in one of the first-class sleeping cars.

'This is a bit of all right.'

Admiring the snug little compartment, Terry hoisted his holdall on to the top bunk.

'I take it I'm down here?' Suki said.

'I need the height, love. Good all-round fields of fire,' Terry joked, sitting on the edge of his bunk and swinging his legs.

Later, gathering with the others in the dining car, he ran through the plan of action that they would follow on arrival in Chiang Mai the following morning. In between mouthfuls of curry and Singha beer he emphasized the need for them to appear like any other group of tourists.

'Even if Fat Eddy's not expecting trouble, he's bound to have a number of people keeping an eye out. You can bet that anything suspicious or out of the ordinary will be reported to him, so from the moment we arrive we're on holiday, right?'

Racking his brain for every scrap of detail, Sy described the layout of Eddy Passenta's ranch. As far as he could remember there was no perimeter wire or fence, as the drug baron relied on the rule of terror to keep snoopers at bay. More serious rivals had long since been eradicated in his area and he enjoyed the complete domination of the district.

'What about patrols, sentries and watch-towers?' asked Tommy.

'I don't remember any watch-towers or patrols, but he did have sentries out. Quite a few, if I'm correct. He used a system of sentries reinforced as necessary by a quick-reaction force which is held centrally under the command of one of his lieutenants.'

'Weaponry?'

'Well, in those days they mostly used old M16s stolen from the military, but I've heard that he's re-equipped his men with Kalashnikovs.'

'AK47s or the later '74?' Tommy pressed.

Sy flushed. 'I'm sorry. I wouldn't know the difference if I saw the two side by side.'

'That's OK,' Terry consoled him. 'They both kill you. The AK47 just leaves a bigger hole, that's all. What about dogs?'

'Guard dogs?'

'Any dogs? They all yap at strangers.'

'There were a few stray mongrels from one of the nearby farmsteads. Eddy told the guys to feed them scraps. I never knew why he encouraged them.'

'It wasn't from the goodness of his heart, I'll bet,' Craig said.

'Tommy, can I leave those to you?' Terry asked.

'You got it, boss.'

When the meal had been finished and the plates cleared away, Terry ordered another round of beers.

'One for the road and then we'd better turn in for an early night. We might not get much kip tomorrow night if all goes according to plan.'

'We'll get even less if it doesn't,' Craig added.

Back in the sleeper, Terry had just turned off the light and clambered on to his bunk, when Suki pulled herself up and pushed her way in beside him.

'I hope this is strong enough to take the two of us,' she said softly as she rolled herself in Terry's arms and peered out of the window at the passing landscape bathed in a ghostly silver moonlight.

'I wish we were on holiday,' she said. 'It seems criminal to be in such a beautiful country as this and yet wondering if we're going to be alive this time tomorrow.'

'That's a question you can ask wherever you are. You can get knocked over by a bus or . . .'

'You know what I mean, smart-arse.'

Terry ran his fingers through her jet-black hair, trailing it across the white sheets. 'Yes. I do. But so long as we've got to play this bloody game we'd better make the most of every moment.'

Reaching up to him, Suki brushed his mouth with her lips, her hand seeking him under the sheets.

'I'm glad you said that.'

In the pale reflected glow from the cabin walls Terry could see her smiling. He couldn't remember when he had last felt this way about anyone. It seemed that all the years of war and fighting had left him drained to the point where his spirit had all but died. Yet here in this remote corner of the planet he had come across water, and his spirit, recognizing perhaps a last chance for revival, was drinking deeply, quenching its thirst without thought of the future and the pain it might hold.

Shifting his weight to one side, he ran his hand the length of Suki's body, settling on her thigh as he kissed her. Feeling her shudder, edging beneath him, he supported his weight on his fists until Suki drew him down on to her, encircling him with her legs on the narrow bunk, gently raising her hips until finding him.

He felt her mouth against his, then on his cheeks, eyes and ears. She gasped as she felt him and pushed for greater closeness as if she would absorb him in her very being. Speeding towards the northern hills, the night express enfolded them, its own pounding heartbeat matching the pulse of their locked entwined bodies, rhythm speaking to rhythm in a passionate communion of souls.

By dawn the train had entered the hill country and was winding its way through an altogether different landscape. Peering blearily out of the windows, Terry found himself looking on to hillsides richly forested in teak. After stopping at the bustling town of Lampang the train pressed on, weaving through one last series of valley passes before entering the mountain-ringed plain at whose heart Chiang Mai waited, its old buildings clustered on the banks of the River Ping. By the time they drew into the main station Terry and the others had breakfasted, packed and were ready to disembark. Craig joked that Tommy had strip-cleaned and reassembled his Glock so many times that it could probably fire itself. Terry had also carefully checked the Colt Commando that Craig had procured for him. His favourite assault weapon, it fitted snugly into his holdall, the outside pouches of which were stuffed with fully charged magazines.

Craig and Manny had settled for M16s, preferring the longer-range accuracy over the Colt Commando's close-quarter fire-power. All except Tommy carried Browning 9mm pistols as backup, reinforced with pocketfuls of grenades, both HE and white-phosphorus. In addition to his Glock, Tommy carried a satchel containing two single-shot M72 rocket launchers, neatly telescoped into their short dispos-able containers, which were wrapped inoffensively in his spare shirts.

But despite their modest arsenal, well concealed in stylish holdalls, it was just another group of visiting tourists who stepped down on to the platform of Chiang Mai station at just after eight o'clock that morning. Suki was bright and enthusiastic, making a great show of wanting to see something of the town; Lalin draped herself over Sy's arm, her gaudy make-up toned down for the sake of anonymity; while Craig, Tommy and Manny melted easily into the scores of tourists arriving in Chiang Mai for the sights and the temples.

'What's it to be, elephants or minibus?'

Emerging from the tourist information office, Sy waved a leaflet at Terry. 'Don't worry. I told them we'd settle for the minibus. We can pick it up right away.'

'How far is it to the ranch?'

Sy studied his map. 'I'd say a good four hours.'

'You're sure you know the way?'

'It's all coming back to me. I haven't been here for

ages, but nothing's changed. Just a few more tourists, that's all.'

Stowing their holdalls in the back of the hired dark-blue Honda, they clambered in while Sy took the wheel, heading north out of town along the main road along the Ping valley towards Mae Rim. Racing through villages, trailing a cloud of dust, Sy pushed the little minibus up to full speed, a cool breeze from the higher altitude gusting through the open windows. After two hours he swung off the main road on to an unmade track, and an hour later pulled up on the edge of a plantation.

'If you continue along this track you come to Eddy Passenta's front door. We'll take another route that approaches from the side. There's plenty of cover to hide the bus and we can travel the final couple of miles on foot – just to be sure they don't see any dust trail.'

Veering off through the trees, Sy wound his way along a barely perceptible track. In the back, Lalin complained that she was feeling sick but rather than waste time by stopping, Craig pushed her head out of the back window.

'There we are, gorgeous. Better out than in.'

Afterwards she wiped her mouth miserably, smearing her lipstick across her cheek. Craig took out his handkerchief, spat on it and scrubbed her face.

'Dearie me, what a sight. Whatever will the General think when he sees his former lover?'

After thirty minutes of difficult cross-country driving, Sy pulled out on to a narrow track that wound steeply upwards in a series of hairpin bends through ever-thickening forest. Trees and undergrowth crowded in on the track, threatening to swamp it with branches that whiplashed against the sides of the van, their stripped leaves floating into the cabin. When at last the track suddenly disappeared altogether, Sy stepped on the brake and the vehicle came to a shuddering halt, fully immersed in the heart of the forest without even room to turn round.

'I hope to fuck this is it, because I'd hate to have to back out of all this shit,' Terry said.

Sy was beaming all over his face. 'This is an excellent sign. When I last used this track it was clearer than this and went much closer to the ranch. If they're not using it any more we're unlikely to meet anyone on the way.'

'OK, guys,' Terry said. 'Time to change.'

Stripping off their T-shirts and jeans, the men changed into combat gear while the two women dressed in dark green. Discarding his crumpled white suit with reluctance, Sy put on a khaki safari suit.

'Blimey,' Terry said. 'Get a load of Robert shagging Redford.'

'Smart, eh?' Sy grinned.

'Do you know how to use this?' Craig asked, handing him a Browning.

'I've used a Colt 45 before.'

'Same principle. Point it and fire away.'

When everyone was ready Terry detailed an order of march and with Sy in the lead, they set off into the dense undergrowth. Terry was careful to note the compass bearings, jotting down beside each of them the number of paces travelled along it, and recording the new bearing whenever Sy switched direction. By working out the back-bearings and matching them to each distance covered, they would be able to retrace their steps back along the various legs of the journey and locate the minibus when the time came.

Close behind Sy, Terry and Manny, Suki and Lalin moved through the unfamiliar environment, trying to watch their footfall on the cluttered jungle floor as Terry had warned them. Bringing up the rear, Tommy and Craig paused every hundred yards, listening to the jungle noises for any change in the bird calls which would signal that there were other people about. For over an hour the little column moved silently through the jungle, undisturbed until Sy stopped and Terry hand-signalled a halt.

'This is it,' Sy whispered, sinking to his knees. 'The ranch is over the next rise. There's a small outcrop of rock which gives a good view of the airstrip.'

'Nice work. I'll check it out for a lie-up position.'

Moving stealthily forward, Terry located the place that Sy had indicated and crawled out on to the exposed rock on his stomach. Peering carefully over the top, he found himself looking down on a thin strip of reddish-brown earth, not much of a landing field but capable of taking a transport plane. To one side and perched on a low, round-topped hill, Fat Eddy's ranch was the image of luxury. The blue shimmer of a swimming pool glinted between whitewashed buildings whose red-tiled roofs were more like those of a Mexican hacienda than a Thai drug baron's stronghold. Surrounding the main cluster of buildings, well-manicured gardens fell away in steps to the bottom of the hill. Ornamental pools and bright, multicoloured groupings of shrubs and bushes gave the whole place the feel of an oasis in the middle of a green desert.

'Nice place you've got there, Eddy,' Terry muttered to himself. 'Let's hope you've got room to accommodate a few unexpected guests.'

For the meal that evening Fat Eddy had ordered his cook to prepare his favourite dishes. First on the menu was *larb luad* soup, made from a mixture of fresh blood and herbs. He relished the thought of Lon San being forced to eat it, obliged for the sake of good manners to ignore the pungent taste and odour. Next came the main course, *kow soy* noodles in a particularly fierce curry sauce, accompanied by the local Chiang Mai speciality of fried frog skin, all washed down with plenty of fiery Mekong whisky. For the survivors, Fat Eddy had ordered a particularly old durian as dessert, the fruit's soft, cream-coloured flesh oozing a smell capable of turning the strongest of stomachs. Even he had almost retched at the first whiff of it.

Sure enough, the meal had hardly begun when he noted with delight the expression of severe discomfort on Lon San's face. Having seated himself at the head of the table, the drug baron had a clear view of all his guests, ensuring that none of them would be able to skip any of the dishes without being seen.

'Comrade, have some more,' he barked, directing the cook to ladle an extra helping of soup into Lon San's bowl. The table had been placed on the large paved terrace but even in the open air the smell was overpowering. A ring of small electric bulbs was strung from the overhanging trees, and to one side the swimming pool was illuminated with underwater lights. The night sky was clear and the stars glistened as sharp as crystal.

'I must congratulate you on your *larb luad*,' General Sarit Chamonon said, smiling. 'I don't know why, but it's never as good as this in Bangkok.'

'It's the way the blood's matured,' Fat Eddy enthused, grinning at the General, who had also noticed Lon San's expression. 'I like to let it stand for a good while. Adds to the flavour.'

In an effort to direct the conversation on to a new tack, Lon San asked the General to confirm the time of Colonel Kon's expected arrival.

'He should be here shortly after daybreak tomorrow,' the General replied. 'Don't worry, my friend. This time I promise you'll get your arms shipment.'

'And once they're safely unloaded,' Fat Eddy cut in, 'I'll arrange the onward transit to Paksaket for you.'

Lon San smiled bitterly, fully aware that trading with one such as Eddy Passenta was an occupation fraught with danger. Still, if the fat, drug-addled idiot tried to swindle him he would find himself with a blood feud on his hands, and the Khmer Rouge would be a very different opponent from some petty rival baron. Eddy Passenta would regret any breach of their agreement.

'I will be in your debt.'

'No you won't,' Fat Eddy guffawed. 'Payment on delivery, that's my policy.'

'Of course,' Lon San said, revolted. 'It's always good to know exactly where one stands.'

When the meal was finally over and Lon San had forced down the last mouthful of durian, clenching his stomach muscles to hold the food inside, he excused himself and went to his room, leaving Fat Eddy and the General to enjoy a fresh bottle of whisky on the terrace. In a room adjoining his own, Lon San had quartered his two-man escort. After confirming that one of them would remain awake at all times throughout the night, he told them to keep their Kalashnikovs handy.

The following day would be long, he thought, but with luck by evening the arms would be his. Then, once they were complete at Paksaket, he could begin the offensive that he had long been planning. Soon the renegade government in Phnom Penh would be on the run and the Khmer Rouge installed in their rightful place in Cambodia. As a result of his own central part in their return to power, Lon San was sure that he could expect gratitude from Pol Pot. Recognition of his services would undoubtedly bring a top appointment in the new government.

After that there would be a lot of reckoning and settling of scores. They had done the job badly the first time twenty years ago: too many of the old hierarchy had got away. In the new Killing Fields they would ensure that no one escaped. The last of the Trons in particular, Lon San reflected gleefully. He would get even with Manny Tron one day, however long it took. But for now he would have to make do with the man's sister and he had something special planned for her, although that would have to wait until tomorrow.

Side by side on the outcrop of bare rock, Terry, Craig and Manny watched the distant banquet through binoculars.

'So, that's Lon San,' said Terry.

'Yes,' Manny said evenly, containing his hatred with difficulty. 'The butcher of the Killing Fields.'

'And the fat bugger's Placenta Passenta,' Craig chuckled.

'I'm going to have fun sticking that pig.'

'And we all remember our good friend Sarit Chamonon,' Terry said, adjusting his binoculars to bring the General into focus. '*Bon appétit*, lads. Enjoy the last supper.'

Back at the harbour where Tommy and Sy had been looking after the women, Terry outlined his plan for the following day.

'We'll wait until Kon's plane arrives. That should give us a ready-made diversion. Once everyone's concentrating on the unloading down on the airstrip, we'll sneak in the back door, locate Sitha and bug out.'

'What about the arms?' Manny asked. 'We can't just leave them for Lon San.'

'That's not the immediate problem. Our first priority's to get Sitha away. Once that's done, we can plan what to do about the shipment. If they're going to be transported down to Paksaket we'll have time to make another plan. Perhaps we can fly in some reinforcements, but for now there's no question of trying to take on the whole lot of them. We'd never get away with it.'

'He's right, Manny,' Tommy said. 'Sitha's the priority. This is personal now.'

'What do you want us to do?' Suki asked.

'I'm going to move you and Lalin to a fire support position a bit closer. If anything goes wrong you can blaze away in the general direction of the airstrip with the M16s. I don't want either of you anywhere near the fighting, but if you have to you can keep folks pinned down in the open while we get away.'

When Terry was happy that everyone understood their part in the morning's operation, he, Tommy and

Craig sat down to check the weapons, taping their fully charged magazines together in pairs for rapid reloading.

'If they spot us we'll make sure we give a good account of ourselves,' Terry said, unpacking and arming the M72 rockets.

General Chamonon was up early the next morning. After dressing in combats, he oiled his hair into position in front of the mirror before venturing down to the breakfast table where Fat Eddy was already coming to the end of a substantial meal. Greeting the General with a full mouth, Fat Eddy poured him some coffee and waved for the cook to bring more food. A little later Lon San appeared to be greeted in the same manner.

'Thank you, but I'll skip breakfast this morning,' Lon San replied.

'Feeling a bit off?'

'Not at all,' Lon San said brightly. 'In fact I feel in excellent shape.'

'Of course he does,' General Chamonon remarked when Lon San was out of earshot, strolling down through the gardens towards the airstrip. 'Today he gets his new toys to play with.'

On cue, the drone of an aircraft became audible in the distance, growing ever louder until out of the north-east the outline of the Chinese transport plane appeared, dropping steadily on its approach towards the airstrip. Cursing his lost breakfast and the early arrival of Colonel Kon, the General, with Fat Eddy beside him, followed Lon San down through the gardens. From the surrounding buildings, guards and workmen ran towards the dirt strip where the drug baron's marshallers were already preparing to receive the aircraft and guide it in.

After sinking past the final treetops, brushing the highest branches with its undercarriage, the heavily laden plane dropped neatly on to the airstrip, roared to a halt in an enormous cloud of red earth, turned and taxied back to the waiting crowd of men. Having brushed the dust from his uniform, the General strode across to the door that was flung open as soon as the plane had come to rest. Colonel Kon jumped to the ground, stretched his limbs and waved at his friends.

'Here we are. Just as we promised,' he said.

Lon San was the first to reach him. 'This is a great day,' he said, his voice breaking with emotion as the aircraft's engines died. 'A great day.'

The Chinese Colonel smiled and shook the offered hand. 'Whatever you say. It's good to do business with you.'

'You've got everything?'

'Of course. Exactly as agreed.'

As Fat Eddy waddled up with the General, he was surprised to see Lon San chuckling with delight and clapping Kon on the back in an uncharacteristic display of camaraderie.

'Shall we start at once?' Lon San asked eagerly.

'I thought we could take some refreshment first,' Fat Eddy replied with a leer. 'Comrade Lon San has provided us with a particularly charming Cambodian companion.'

'That sounds interesting,' Kon said.

Lon San laughed. 'Of course. I'd forgotten.'

'Well, I hadn't,' Fat Eddy said. 'We've been

keeping her on ice for you, Leonard. Something special to slake your thirst.'

As he crawled through the undergrowth towards the edge of Fat Eddy's grounds, Terry suddenly froze. Barely twelve inches to one side of him three fine wires protruded from the earth, each no more than two inches long.

'Mines!' he hissed.

Behind him Craig blanched. 'No wonder the fucker doesn't need a fence.'

Terry reached for his jungle knife and edged carefully forward, feeling in the earth in front of him with the tip of the blade, tense for the slightest resistance, which might indicate another mine. It was hard to be sure, but from the look of the wires he judged them to be anti-personnel mines of Chinese or Soviet design. It was impossible to guess how deep the minefield was, but they were probably lucky to have got this far without triggering one. Whoever had laid them was an amateur, for had the wires been properly concealed with scrub, Terry would have blundered straight into a booby-trap.

A little further on he encountered another mine. Better sited than the first, it had been planted in the middle of an inoffensive-looking clump of flowers. After marking it with a strip torn from his handkerchief, Terry skirted around it and pressed on. Six more mines, which he likewise flagged, slowed his progress still further until he became concerned that they might not have time to penetrate the ranch complex before the men returned from the airstrip. However, after covering the final yards to the garden and finding them free of mines, he crawled on to the lush watered grass and stood up in the shelter of thick bushes.

'If we come back this way, last man through picks up the bits of handkerchief,' he said when the others were grouped around him. 'If anyone pursues us they might run into one themselves.'

Working in pairs, Terry and Craig covered each other forward through the gardens in a series of bounds, Tommy and Manny doing the same, with Sy attached to them for his own protection. As he covered Craig over the next stretch, approaching the pool, Terry was glad to see that they had managed to achieve complete surprise. Fat Eddy was obviously not expecting any interference and all of the guards had been diverted to the airstrip to help unload the plane. Yet it was unlikely that he would have stripped the entire ranch of men, especially if he was holding Sitha there.

Sure enough, Craig had just gone firm behind a low wall ringing one of the ornamental ponds when Terry rounded a corner and ran straight into a guard. For a split second the two men stared at each other, but Terry's reactions were the faster. Even as the man was levelling his Kalashnikov at the Welshman's chest, the finger tightening on the trigger, Terry's booted foot was swinging up, the toecap smashing into the side of the man's jaw where it met his ear. Shattering the bone and stunning the nerves underneath, the *mawashi geri* kick knocked the guard unconscious and as he collapsed to the ground Terry caught him, letting him down lightly to minimize the noise.

'One down, about fifty to go,' he whispered to Craig as he jogged over to his side.

As Terry and Craig stood ready to provide covering

fire if necessary, Tommy, Manny and Sy darted across the next stretch of ground towards the first building, a large wooden barn. The huge doors were ajar and Tommy slipped inside, with Manny and Sy behind him, to see in the half light a sleek new Range Rover parked next to two battered jeeps and a Nissan land-cruiser.

'Nice stuff. The drugs business is obviously paying well,' Tommy murmured.

They moved quietly to the door on the far side and Tommy was just reaching for the handle when it swung open and he found himself staring into the astonished face of one of the drivers. The man opened his mouth like a fish on a river bank but before he could utter the scream that was forming in his throat, Tommy's foot shot up, the instep driving into the man's testicles. With eyes bulging from his head, the driver doubled forward, but Tommy brought his knee savagely up into his face, dropping him into the earth floor of the garage.

'This run of luck can't last much longer,' Tommy whispered. 'All hell's going to blow in a minute and then God help us.'

By the time Fat Eddy had reached the paved terrace again the sweat was pouring off him as if someone had turned on a tap. In fact, the last thing he wanted was a romp on top of some scrawny Cambodian slut that Lon San and the General had procured. Still, he was keen that the Chinese Colonel should get a good impression of his hospitality on his first visit to the ranch. He could be a useful business partner in the future. Fat Eddy was aware of the opportunities opening up in the new China, and as one of the most powerful drug barons in north-eastern Thailand, he fully intended to be in on the action. With the world's biggest market a relatively short hop over the mountains, he could see himself becoming in the future a major supplier of drugs to the expanding cities, and Colonel Kon would be the ideal conduit.

After ushering his guests into the cool shade of the hall, Fat Eddy led the way up a flight of stone steps and along a broad corridor that opened into a large upper room where a tray of drinks had been prepared. Two guards stepped forward to help the new arrivals with the refreshments and a moment later, the door of an adjoining room opened and a third guard came in, Sitha struggling in his firm grasp.

'Ah! There you are,' General Chamonon said pleasantly. 'I'm glad you arrived safely, my dear.'

Fat Eddy giggled as he told the story of how she had tried to give the General's men the slip at the petrol station on the journey to the ranch.

'I'm glad you failed,' Colonel Kon said, his eyes alive and roaming freely over her. 'I understand now, Comrade Lon San, why you are so keen to recapture the land of your birth. If it holds such enchanting creatures as this it is worth a hundred plane-loads of arms.'

Sickened to the core, Sitha had eyes for only one man in the room. Glaring bitterly at Lon San, she spat out her words with all the venom she could muster.

'You! Don't think for one minute that you'll get away with this!'

Lon San smiled pleasantly. 'But I already have. When we've finished with you here you can come and help us unload the arms. I'm only sorry your brother's not here to watch you entertain us.'

He was just about to tell Colonel Kon about how he had plucked Sitha from the centre of Phnom Penh, when a burst of automatic fire shattered the peace of the gardens outside. For a full three seconds, Lon San, Fat Eddy, Colonel Kon and General Chamonon stared stupidly at each other in stunned surprise.

'Find out what that was!' Fat Eddy barked furiously at one of the guards, who was already halfway down the corridor. But the sound of firing had now erupted on the airstrip as well, and as Lon San dashed to the window to check on the arms plane, Sitha threw back her head and laughed.

'You've got your wish, Comrade! Prepare to be entertained!'

14

From her vantage point on the hillock Suki had seen the contact coming but had been powerless to stop it. Manny, having separated from Tommy and Sy, was rounding the corner of an outbuilding when a door opened behind him and one of Fat Eddy's men stepped out into the courtyard. Finding himself staring at an intruder, the man dropped the rice bowl he was carrying and fumbled to draw a pistol from his jacket pocket. Too far away to tackle the man silently, Manny had no choice but to open fire. With a single burst from his M16 he sent him spinning backwards into the dirt.

Looking down at the airfield, Suki watched in horror as the drug baron's men caught the first sound of the gunshots and then started to run back towards the foot of the hill leading to the ranch. Jamming the butt of the M16 into her shoulder and cheek, she aimed as Terry had taught her and squeezed off a series of short bursts, noting the impact of the bullets in the dirt far away and adjusting her aim to bring her fire more accurately on to the running men.

'Let me help,' Lalin said, hurrying up beside her.

'You?'

'In my village I used to go hunting with my father when I was a child,' Lalin snapped. 'Is there another rifle?'

'In the holdall.'

Lalin lay down beside Suki with the other M16 and began to fire off single rounds at the scurrying figures below them.

'Not bad,' Suki said admiringly as one of the guards toppled over, struck in the centre of his chest by Lalin's fire.

Lalin grinned. 'This is better than hunting forest monkeys. I have waited a long time for this.'

'OK, boyos, get stuck in!'

With the element of surprise gone, Terry realized that their only hope of success lay in a cocktail of daring, bluff, speed and fire-power. Rushing for the steps to the terrace, he felt the air snap at his ears and seeing a kneeling guard firing at him from behind the stone balustrade, fired back as he ran with a long burst from the hip. His Colt Commando raked the stonework and the guard dropped out of sight, but as the man came up again to return Terry's fire he made the fatal mistake of using the same firing position. Popping his head and rifle above the balustrade to look for his attacker, he found himself instead staring down the barrel of Terry's assault rifle, the last thing he ever saw as a narrow tongue of flame erupted from the muzzle.

'Let's hope Suki can hold them on the airfield long enough for us to find Sitha and bug out,' Craig shouted, dropping into position beside Terry.

'She's a good girl. She'll keep their heads down all right.'

Glancing across to the other side of the pool, Terry saw Manny, Sy and Tommy approaching the main ranch building from the back. Having caught their attention by waving, he signalled for them to infiltrate through the rear kitchens while he and Craig went for the main front entrance, working through the dining-room and hall. When Tommy had acknowledged the instruction and the three men had disappeared from sight, Terry burst from cover, with Craig standing ready to provide supporting fire. Bounding up the steps, he emerged on to the terrace as two men ran out of the building. Dressed in Khmer Rouge uniforms and both armed with Kalashnikovs, they dived for cover at the sight of the foreign mercenary. Caught in the middle of the open terrace, Terry sprinted straight at them, his rifle blazing as he ran, screaming with all the considerable power of his lungs.

When he was almost on top of them, the first one opened fire, sending bullets ripping through Terry's shirt and trousers. Smarting at the burning sensation that told him he was hit, Terry pushed himself on as his own bullets hit their target in the centre of his opponent's chest and throat. Switching his attention to the other guerrilla, he was surprised to find the man gone.

'Where the fuck are you?' he gasped, dropping behind a brick barbecue stand, hunting for the wound in his leg. But while he had been focusing on one man, the other had pulled back, wriggling on his belly back into the hall.

'You OK?' Craig said, running towards Terry.

'Watch out!' Terry screamed. 'There's one left!'

But even as the impact of his words was registering on Craig's face, his legs starting to react with a sideways swerve, a burst of Kalashnikov fire raked across his chest, stopping him in his tracks.

Bent double, Terry burst over to Craig and when, in great pain himself, he had dragged his wounded friend into the scant cover, he frantically ripped open a field dressing, fumbling to fasten it over the gaping bullet wounds to stem the bleeding. But the blood was coming in spurts, light and frothy, signalling to Terry that Craig had suffered a sucking chest wound and was done for.

'Fuck it,' Craig murmured. 'Bit of a bummer, eh?'

'Hang in there, boyo.'

'Look out for yourself, Dojo.'

'Craig!' Terry shouted, forcing his words to penetrate the fog gathering in the American's mind. 'Hold on! That's a fucking order!'

Craig smiled weakly. 'I'm going to have to pass on that one. Catch you later.'

Craig's eyes stared fearlessly past Terry as if casting beyond him in search of the next objective, somewhere out over the endless green spread of jungle where the blue sky dipped down to brush the distant hills.

After laying Craig's head gently back on the paving stones, Terry reached for a white-phosphorus grenade, pulled the pin and lobbed it into the large hall, waiting for it to explode with a blazing orange intensity as fierce and consuming as his anger. Rising from behind the brickwork, he watched as the Khmer Rouge guerrilla staggered into view, his clothes alight, fragments of phosphorus searing into his flesh.

'You don't deserve this,' Terry said, putting the man out of his agony with a three-round burst to the heart.

But the phosphorus had also set light to the furnishings, and as the fire took hold Terry knew that speed was now of the essence. Rushing into the blazing hall, he almost opened fire on Manny, who dived through the door from the kitchen.

'Craig's dead,' Terry shouted. 'You all OK?'

Manny nodded his head. 'Tommy dealt with two guys but that's all.'

'Sitha must be upstairs. I'll take point. You give me backup. Tell Tommy and Sy to go round the back in case there's another exit from this place.'

'Got it.'

As they worked cautiously through the extensive kitchen and food storage area, Tommy reckoned that he'd rather be alone than have Sy toting a Browning behind him. The guy clearly had little idea how to use a handgun and Tommy felt his back tingle at the thought of a rogue 9mm bullet loosed off in error by his team-mate.

'Just keep that thing pointed away, right? Leave the killing to me.'

'Whatever you say,' Sy replied. He liked Tommy and it was clear that the ex-Hong Kong detective and Triad soldier was in love with his sister. It wasn't much of a match but then who was he to complain? His own life had been one long catalogue of betrayals and mistakes. Only over the last few days had he felt some return of his former spirit, the same that had burned so brightly in him all those years ago. It seemed that even in the direst circumstances there was always the hope of salvation, even for a wretch like Sy Tron, traitor and drug addict.

They had left the kitchen by a back door and were making for a fire escape, when a woman's voice called out to them in warning.

'Sitha!' Tommy cried, spinning on his heel to find

himself facing the vast bulk of Eddy Passenta. Holding the hostage in front of him, Fat Eddy was awkwardly descending the fire escape.

'Back off, Cantonese arsehole!' the drug baron shouted, the barrel of his Walther pistol rammed under Sitha's chin. 'This what you want, is it? You came all the way for this tart?'

Tommy sought for an angle, his Glock tight in a combat grip. There was plenty of the drug baron to shoot at as Sitha was hardly big enough to cover even half of his expansive girth, but Fat Eddy's gun was cocked and the slightest pressure on the trigger would set it off.

'OK,' Tommy shouted. 'You've got a clear road, Passenta. But let the girl go.'

'Sure, sure. What the fuck do you take me for?'

Fat Eddy backed away towards the garden, waiting until he was at the top of the steps leading down the hill to the airfield before swinging his aim on to Tommy.

'Bye bye, Chinaman.'

'No!'

Struggling for all she was worth, Sitha started to break free from Fat Eddy's vice-like grip. But just as the drug baron fired, Sy stepped calmly in front of the intended target, and there the Walther's rounds found him, his eyes fast on Sitha, seeing in his sister's shocked return gaze the forgiveness he had sought but never hoped to find.

As the wasted body of the Cambodian crumpled back against Tommy, Fat Eddy tried to regain his hold on the girl but she had torn free of him and was running towards her dead brother. Instead, Fat Eddy looked up to find himself facing the Glock 17, the eyes of the Chinaman narrowed at him down the barrel.

'Bye bye, fat man.'

One by one, Tommy pumped his rounds into Fat Eddy's quivering flesh. Staggering back over the top step, the drug baron felt each impacting bullet like a sledgehammer blow. His pistol flew from his chubby fist and his hands fumbled at the multiplying wounds as if trying to stop up the holes in a leaking saucepan. But Tommy had reloaded with a fresh magazine before the encounter and directed each bullet precisely, working his way methodically through all seventeen rounds until Eddy Passenta had rolled down the hill and lay dead at the bottom.

At the very beginning of the battle, Colonel Kon had taken one look at the scene in the courtyard and bolted for the steps. By the time Terry and the others were starting to fight their way through the main building, he had reached the edge of the airstrip. Ignoring the fire of the two M16s coming from the nearby hill, he sprinted towards the plane, screaming at the pilot to start the engines. Close behind him, General Chamonon panted and wheezed, never having run so fast since the time, many years ago now, before he opened his first brothel and gambling den in Bangkok; thereafter he had never bothered with fitness as there had been a plentiful supply of henchmen to do the physical jobs for him. But now, as he started across the open dirt strip, he felt as if he was caught in one of those dreams where he was bogged down in a slow-motion quagmire of deep mud, his legs powerless to speed his escape.

Only Lon San had bided his time. He had encountered these same mercenaries before and he knew that the time of reckoning had come. Let the spineless Thai General and the corrupt Chinese arms dealer run away if they chose. He would fight and die as a true Khmer.

Waiting until Fat Eddy had left by the fire escape with the girl, Lon San ran to his room and picked up a Kalashnikov AK74 assault rifle and some grenades. He could hear the noise of the westerners fighting through the ground floor. Smoke from the downstairs blaze wafted along the corridor and it was only a matter of time before the entire building was engulfed in flames. From the back of the house he had heard Fat Eddy's shouted challenge to an unseen opponent and as still more voices sounded from the main stairs of the hall, he realized that his only avenue of escape lay along the outside balcony that ran the length of the upper floor. If he could make it to the far end of the building he might be able to lower himself over the side. There would be a sheer drop but it was his only chance.

After checking that the balcony was clear, Lon San padded silently along the cool tiles. Between the clouds of smoke he caught a glimpse of the airstrip, where men were scrambling to cram themselves into the transport plane. Several bodies lay where they had been shot but at least a score of guards were fighting, pushing and punching their way on board. At the head of the throng, Colonel Kon and General Chamonon disappeared inside the aircraft, and Lon San cursed as he heard the engines cough into life. Not a single rifle had been unloaded and once again his attempt to secure the arms had

266

failed. Somehow the western interferers would pay dearly for it.

He was almost at the end of the balcony when a door burst open in front of him and a man in combat kit staggered into the fresh air, coughing and spluttering. He had been blinded by the smoke and his face was covered with soot but through the dirt and grime Lon San recognized him as one of the mercenaries. Reacting instantly, he swung the butt of his Kalashnikov savagely into the man's face, screaming as he did so. It was as if the gods that he had long denied had presented him with a sacrificial offering.

Collapsing to his knees, Terry lashed out in a defensive block, his Colt Commando skidding across the tiles and tipping over the edge into the courtyard below. But now that he was blinded by smoke and his own blood, and stunned by the unexpected blow, his arms met only thin air. The next blow crashed down on the back of his head and in a blur of lights, the world disappeared.

Standing over him in triumph, Lon San cocked his rifle and placed the muzzle against Terry's temple. But the next moment, Lon San himself was flying across the balcony, his head ringing from a glancing blow. Struggling to sit up, he leaned back against the balcony railings and stared in surprise at the small figure of a man before him.

'You! I know you,' he said, half question, half statement.

The man looked down at Lon San, unimpressed with the fallen leader of the Khmer Rouge.

'What's your name?' Lon San asked, as he caught sight of his assault rifle but decided it was too far to make a snatch at it.

'Than Promarik,' the man replied.

A mist cleared from Lon San's brain. 'Of course. I've watched you fight.'

'Don't try for the gun,' Than warned him. He opened his hands. 'They don't look like much but I'm still quicker than you.'

Lon San sat back and appraised the fighter. His face was bruised. 'Looks like you took a beating. Who was the lucky guy?'

Than nodded at Terry, unconscious on the floor.

'Him?' Lon San said, thunderstruck. 'Then why the fuck did you stop me?'

'You wouldn't understand.' Than knelt down and examined Terry's wound. Tearing a strip off his own shirt, he dabbed at the blood and then secured the cloth like a bandage around the Welshman's forehead.

'Well, now I've seen everything. Brothers in arms!' Lon San said contemptuously.

'Something like that,' Than replied. 'He is a Sensei. A Master. You do not butcher his kind like some pig.'

'I'll butcher him any way you like,' Lon San chuckled grimly. 'Just give me my gun back.'

'I have been a stupid, ignorant man,' Than went on, ignoring the Khmer Rouge leader. 'It took a beating from a man like this to make me see what I had become.'

'That's all very charming, I'm sure, but can I get up now?' Lon San asked, his hand sliding under his jacket while Than busied himself with Terry.

'No.'

'I'm sorry you said that,' Lon San replied, producing a pistol. 'I could have used a man like you.'

'Everyone's used me. All my life.'

'How tragic. Look, I'm crying.'

The blast of the first round shocked even Lon San. Fired at such close quarters it flung the slender frame of the Thai boxer against the far wall. By the time the fourth bullet slammed into the crumpled body, Than Promarik was dead.

'Grenade!'

Lon San whirled at the cry from the end of the balcony to see another figure and, in between, the cylindrical canister of a white-phosphorus grenade rattling towards him along the floor. Diving through a doorway, he rolled away, cursing his luck for being unable to finish off the westerner. Obviously, to be using WP the man's comrade had assumed he was already dead, but then as Lon San scuttled for cover in the seconds before the grenade's detonation, he consoled himself that this new opponent had unwittingly become the killer of his own friend.

The smile of satisfaction died on his face as the grenade burst into a belching cloud of bright green smoke, harmless but effective. Fumbling for one of his own grenades, Lon San ripped out the pin and screamed as he hurled it into the heart of the cloud. But he had thrown too hard, his aim spoiled by the rage inside him, and his grenade clattered over the balcony, exploding a moment later on the terrace below. As he sought for a new escape route, Lon San was troubled by some dim sense of foreboding, for in the split second that he had locked eyes with his new assailant he had recognized something familiar in the man.

'Lon San.'

Lon San froze, and slowly started to turn.

'That'll do,' the other man commanded from behind. 'Drop the pistol first.'

Lon San obeyed.

'And the other grenades in your pocket, unless I'm mistaken and they're your bollocks, in which case I'll cut them off later.'

After placing the two grenades gingerly on the floor beside him, Lon San turned to face the man.

'Yes. Who'd have guessed?' Manny said, seeing recognition dawn on Lon San's face.

Lon San shrugged. 'OK, get on with it. This is what you've been waiting for.'

Manny walked slowly towards his sworn enemy. As he did so, he unbuckled his cartridge belt, dropped it to the floor and kicked it aside. Then, two steps from Lon San, he flung away his rifle. At one step he swung, his balled fist crashing into Lon San's mouth. Recovering his balance, Lon San threw himself on his attacker and the two men staggered against the wall of the spacious room, the smoke and heat from the rapidly spreading fire starting to lap at the outer reaches. Fighting with a savagery born of years of bitter rivalry, the two Cambodians each carried with them the clash and struggle of their beliefs. Pounding at each other, they rocked and crashed from one end of the room to the other, neither giving quarter nor asking any. Ripped and bloodied, their clothes in tatters, they grabbed and tore as if each would pull his opponent limb from limb.

But to Manny's hatred was added the drive for revenge. Blind to the pain of Lon San's blows, all he could see were the faces of those he had loved, now so many scattered bones littering the Killing Fields of the Khmer Rouge. All he could think of was the cool detachment with which this despised man and his fellows had conducted their genocide, packaging their murderous barbarism in a tissue of ideological jargon and lies. With every punch Manny pounded out his message. It was a barbarism that must never be allowed to happen again.

At last, his arms hanging useless at his sides, Lon San tottered backwards into the smoke. On all sides the walls, ceiling and overhead beams rimmed the two men with fire. Slender orange flames lapped at Lon San's shredded clothing, catching and framing him, as he waved and shrieked, in an oval film of bright yellow fire, until at last, his life consumed like spent oil, he fell and burned in silence.

Covering his mouth and nose, Manny fought his way through the smoke and found Terry propping himself up on his hands and knees.

'This way,' Manny shouted above the noise of crashing timbers, pulling his friend to his feet and half guiding, half dragging him down the fire escape. In the garden below they found Sitha and Tommy. Kneeling beside her dead brother, Sitha looked up at Manny, her cheeks wet with tears.

'He stepped in front of the bullets. He gave himself for us, Manny.'

Manny bent down beside her and stared into Sy's face. It was peaceful. In the moment of death it seemed to have taken on a quality that Manny could recognize, something of the boy that he had known when they had played together in the streets and markets of Phnom Penh. But that had been a thousand years ago. Since then, a whole world had fallen, and now, in the smoke and fire of battle, another was being created. Death and life. War and peace. By his sacrifice, Sy Tron had played his small part in the building of the bridge that linked the two, enabling his brother and sister to make the crossing and to live in the new world that would be fashioned to replace the old.

From the airstrip at the bottom of the hill came the surging roar of engines. Terry set off unsteadily down the steps, lumbering down them three at a time.

'Don't be stupid, Dojo,' Tommy shouted. 'Let them go.'

'No fucking way!'

Seeing the house in flames and hearing the noise of the battle, the guards who had been unable to fight their way on to the transport plane had disappeared into the jungle. Daunted by the ferocity of the engagements on the hill above them and by the weight of supporting fire from the hillock where Suki and Lalin were concealed, they had believed themselves to be under attack by a vastly superior force and had concluded that escape was their only remaining option. So when Terry emerged on to the airstrip he found it deserted except for the aeroplane lumbering to the far end in preparation for take-off.

Unarmed except for his 9mm Browning, he desperately hunted around for a weapon.

'Terry! Over here!'

Turning at the sound of Suki's voice, Terry saw the two girls running towards him.

'How did we do?'

'Fantastic.'

'God, you look a mess.'

'I'll tell you about it later,' Terry said, grabbing at

the bag slung over Suki's shoulder. 'Quick, give it to me.'

He dropped the bulky holdall on the ground, ripped open the zipper and rummaged inside.

'Well, well, well. What have we here?'

In the cockpit of the transport plane, Colonel Kon and General Chamonon clung to their seats behind the two pilots. In the body of the aircraft behind them, a score of Fat Eddy's men squatted alongside the crates of arms and ammunition.

'Get this fucker off the ground,' the General growled. 'Once we're at Paksaket I'll be back here with my whole division if necesaary. How dare they attack me in my own country!'

Colonel Kon glared at him. 'Who said anything about Paksaket? This plane's going straight back to Kunming. You can hitch a ride home from there.'

'Don't be stupid. Tell them to fly to Paksaket!' the General ordered, reaching for his pistol. But Kon got to his first. Feeling the gun-metal cold under his fleshy chin, the General tittered nervously. 'OK, OK. Kunming it is.'

In front of them the pilot shrieked. In the middle of the runway three hundred yards distant, a tiny figure was kneeling, a slim khaki tube over his shoulder.

'Rocket attack!'

Watching in fascinated horror as the tube erupted in flame, General Chamonon and Colonel Kon clung to their seats as the pilot swung the aircraft viciously over. A second later the missile streaked along the side of the fuselage, narrowly missing the tail fin and exploding harmlessly in the jungle behind.

'Ha! The idiot!' the General snorted.

Bringing the aircraft back to the centre of the runway, the pilot opened the throttle and the powerful engines roared to full pitch. Screaming past the tiny figure of the foreign mercenary as he flung himself out of the way, the plane slowly lifted off the ground and with a final lurch became airborne.

'We've done it! We've fucking done it!' the General shouted in delight, hugging Colonel Kon, their enmity of a moment ago completely forgotten in the blissful relief of escape.

'The incompetent moron's only got short-range anti-tank rockets. We're free!'

Throwing away the empty missile casing, Terry rolled out of the way of the aircraft wheels and dashed for the holdall. Taking out the second and last M72 rocket, he held it in an overhand grip and snapped it open, popping the sight eyepiece into place. As he traced the retreating aircraft rapidly accelerating out of range, he knew that he had barely seconds to act. Intended for use against static bunker targets or slow-moving tanks, the 66mm M72 rocket had a nominal effective range of only 200 metres. However, fired at a forty-five-degree angle, it was capable of reaching 350 metres before burning out and dropping to earth with the warhead. Realizing that it was too late to fire the rocket directly at the rear of the plane, now already at the 200-metre mark, Terry steadied himself in the middle of the runway with feet planted shoulder-width apart. Sighting on the plane to get the correct line of fire, he gauged the distance and then raised his aim to a point in the open sky above the body of the aircraft.

'Steady, lad,' he murmured to himself. 'Become one with the target.'

He squeezed the firing button, bracing himself as the rocket motor exploded into life and the deafening roar of the backblast scorched the ground behind him for a full forty metres.

'This is it, Dojo,' he whispered, tossing aside the spent empty casing. 'If you've fucked up now, they go free.'

Arching lazily through the sky, the missile trailed a thin plume of smoke. Rising level with the ascending plane, it continued on until the rocket motors burned out, sputtered and died. With agonizing slowness, the tiny dark cone of the warhead angled down and fell, gathering speed as it dropped, whistling through the last metres of empty space and finally crashing on to the centre spine of the aircraft's broad back. As the tip of the missile's nose encountered the resilient outer skin of the fuselage, it crumpled in on itself, detonating the shaped explosive charge lodged at its core. Powering down into the packed heart of the transport, the rocket found the crates of high explosive, the thousands of rounds of ammunition, the boxes of anti-personnel and land-mines, and the jovial figures of General Chamonon and Colonel Kon, celebrating their escape to freedom with the complete shipment of Khmer Rouge weaponry.

The blast from the orange fireball that erupted over the jungle flung Terry, Suki and Lalin to the ground like discarded toys. The heat from the explosion shot outwards so that even beside the blazing ranch house, Manny, Tommy and Sitha had to shield their faces, squinting sideways at the awesome spectacle. But at the livid heart of the exploding plane itself the

incinerated remains of all those on board shot through
the scalding air, firing outwards, mingling, cooling,
and finally floating through the jungle's high canopy
of leaves with the patter of monsoon rain.

Epilogue

'I'm just afraid you're going to regret it,' Sitha said, swinging her hand in Tommy's as the two of them walked slowly through the darkened streets of Phnom Penh. 'I mean, it'll be such a change for you.'

'A change from what?' Tommy asked. 'From being chased by the Triads and the police? That's the sort of change I can handle. And besides,' he continued, smiling at her, 'when I thought I'd lost you I realized that if I got you back it would be for keeps.'

Sitha laughed. 'Nothing's for keeps.'

'Leave that to Glock and me,' Tommy said, patting his jacket pocket.

The night sky was crisp and clear and all around them the trees were alive with fireflies, the delicate floating spots of light glowing for a moment and then dying, to be replaced a second later by others, starting on their own brief passage between dark and dark.

'You know, I believe that Lalin has found a new home,' Sitha said out of the blue, her voice alive with mischief. 'Did you see the way she was giving Yon Rin the eye at dinner?'

Tommy laughed. 'The old buzzard wasn't doing so badly himself. There's a fair bit of spark in those embers yet. Especially with a little stoking from the right woman!'

It had been a strange evening, Tommy thought,

as they walked on, working their way back to the villa in a large, ambling circle. The dinner had been relaxed and happy, but to some extent everyone had been preoccupied with private memories. The voices of Colin and Craig still seemed to echo on the veranda, and Manny had been locked in his own regret for the years of missed reconciliation with his brother, now lost for ever through Sy's final selfless act of courage.

But the obvious happiness of Tommy and Sitha had pulled everyone together in the end. Manny had made a speech welcoming Tommy into the family and Minister Yon Rin, in between fighting off Lalin's advances, had offered him a key training post in the country's new Special Branch. With his experience, the Minister had said, they could winkle out the Khmer Rouge sleepers hiding in the capital and continue the fight for freedom in Cambodia.

Turning into the last street before the villa, Tommy checked his watch and hugged Sitha to him.

'Where are they now?' she asked.

'Somewhere over Vietnam.'

As soon as dinner had ended, they had taken Terry and Suki to the airport for their flight. Lalin had cried profusely until sufficiently comforted by Yon Rin, and Manny had made yet another speech, this time wishing Terry and Suki a happy holiday in Okinawa.

'Will it work out between them?' asked Sitha.

'I know it will,' said Tommy quietly.

Shifting in his seat to get comfortable, Terry was careful not to wake Suki, whose head was resting on his shoulder where it had lain since take-off, when the drone of the engines had lulled her to sleep. He felt tired himself but his mind was racing and he knew there would be no rest for him until he had worked through the problems.

What the hell was he thinking of, he wondered? Suki Yamato was an intelligent young woman with a bright future in the United Nations. What could he ever offer someone like her? Sure, she was happy enough to be with him for now, but it could only end in tears. What kind of a life had he ever been able to fashion for himself, let alone for someone else? He was unreliable, unemployed, and to cap it all, a sodding mercenary! It was hardly a stable career. Apart from that, his only other asset was his karate dojo in Swansea. Swansea, of all places! That would go down like a lead balloon with Suki the moment she saw it. If she ever did.

The more Terry thought about it, the more convinced he became that the whole business was a huge mistake. Yes, he loved her. He loved her desperately. But a holiday in Okinawa visiting Master Nishime Higashi was one thing. A long-term relationship was quite another. He would have to end it, breaking it to her gently at the first opportunity.

Feeling the need for a stiff drink, he reached down to the holdall at his feet in which Manny had packed him a bottle of Mekong whisky as a souvenir. He unzipped the bag and fumbled around inside until his fingers met the familiar shape of the bottle. Checking that he hadn't disturbed Suki, he gently pulled it out, smiling to see a small note attached. He unfolded it and read the bold, deliberate script.

Terry,
Here's a little present that I found among Lon

San's possessions when we were searching the ruins of Passenta's place afterwards. There was a whole case of the stuff. I gave it all to Yon Rin, but he insisted you have at least one bottle. Who'd have thought that Lon San was a secret drinker! Be careful you don't get hooked on the stuff yourself. Good luck. Remember me when you and Suki need a godfather for your first-born.

Manny

Terry had pulled off the wrapper, unscrewed the cap and got the bottle halfway to his lips before he realized that something was wrong.

'What the . . .?'

Hearing his voice, Suki stirred in her sleep.

'It's all right, love,' Terry reassured her. 'Go back to sleep.'

Holding the bottle up to the light, he stared in wonder at the kaleidoscope of colours jammed behind the glass, the myriad collection of priceless gems jostling into new patterns of brilliance at every tilt of the bottle.

Perhaps everything would be all right after all. If he could only get it through customs.

OTHER TITLES IN SERIES FROM 22 BOOKS

Available now at newsagents and booksellers
or use the order form opposite

All at £4.99 net

22 Books offers an exciting list of titles in these series. All the books are available from:

Little, Brown and Company (UK) Limited,
PO Box 11,
Falmouth,
Cornwall TR10 9EN.

Alternatively you may fax your order to the above address.
Fax number: 0326 376423.

Payments can be made by cheque or postal order (payable to Little, Brown and Company) or by credit card (Visa/Access). Do not send cash or currency. UK customers and BFPO please allow £1.00 for postage and packing for the first book, plus 50p for the second book, plus 30p for each additional book up to a maximum charge of £3.00 (seven books or more). Overseas customers, including customers in Ireland, please allow £2.00 for the first book, plus £1.00 for the second book, plus 50p for each additional book.

NAME (BLOCK LETTERS PLEASE) ....

....

ADDRESS ....

....

....

☐ I enclose my remittance for £_____

☐ I wish to pay by Access/Visa

Card number

☐☐☐☐☐ ☐☐☐☐☐ ☐☐☐☐☐ ☐☐☐☐☐

Card expiry date

☐☐ ☐☐

077123 83950

0208
Wk   562 3592
Mob 07932
       361872